## *"I Think You Could Persuade Me to Do Anything,"*

Noah said. His finger trailed down her throat to rest against her collar. Her heart fluttered.

She stepped away and eyed him suspiciously. "What would it take for you to listen to my side of the story?"

He shrugged. "Not much."

*"How* much?"

Noah's eyes gleamed devilishly. "Why don't we start with dinner?"

"All right, Noah. Why not?" Sheila countered. "But I insist we keep the conversation on business."

"Just come with me," he suggested wickedly. "The conversation—and the night—will take care of themselves."

---

**LISA JACKSON**

was raised in Molalla, Oregon, and now lives with her husband, Mark, and her two sons in a suburb of Portland. Lisa and her sister, Natalie Bishop, who is also a Silhouette author, live within earshot of each other and do all of their work in Natalie's basement.

Dear Reader:

Romance readers have been enthusiastic about Silhouette Special Editions for years. And that's not by accident: Special Editions were the first of their kind and continue to feature realistic stories with heightened romantic tension.

The longer stories, sophisticated style, greater sensual detail and variety that made Special Editions popular are the same elements that will make you want to read book after book.

We hope that you enjoy this Special Edition today, and will enjoy many more.

The Editors at Silhouette Books

# LISA JACKSON
# Tears of Pride

*Silhouette Special Edition*
Published by Silhouette Books New York
America's Publisher of Contemporary Romance

**Silhouette Books by Lisa Jackson**

*A Twist of Fate* (SE #118)
*Dark Side of the Moon* (IM #39)
*The Shadow of Time* (SE #180)
*Tears of Pride* (SE #194)

SILHOUETTE BOOKS, a Division of Simon & Schuster, Inc.
1230 Avenue of the Americas, New York, N.Y. 10020

Copyright © 1984 by Lisa Jackson
Cover artwork copyright © 1984 Herb Tauss

Distributed by Pocket Books

ISBN: 0-671-53694-X

First Silhouette Books printing October, 1984

10 9 8 7 6 5 4 3 2 1

Map by Ray Lundgren

America's Publisher of Contemporary Romance

Printed in the U.S.A.

To Mary Clare, my editor,
with love and affection.

# Tears of Pride

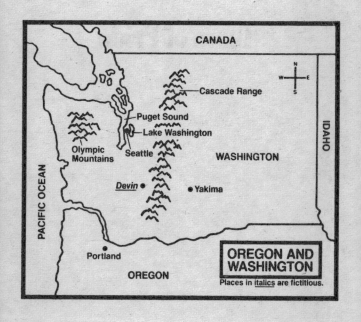

CANADA

N
W   E
S

Cascade Range

Puget Sound
Lake Washington
Seattle

Olympic
Mountains

WASHINGTON

IDAHO

PACIFIC OCEAN

*Devin* •

• Yakima

Portland •

OREGON

**OREGON AND
WASHINGTON**

Places in *italics* are fictitious.

# Chapter One

He stood alone, and his vibrant blue eyes scanned the horizon, as if he were looking for something . . . or someone. The cold morning fog on the gray waters of Elliott Bay hampered his view, but the lonely, broad-shouldered man didn't seem to notice. Haggard lines were etched across his forehead and an errant lock of dark brown hair was caught in the Pacific breeze. Noah Wilder didn't care. Though dressed only in a business suit, the icy wind blowing across Puget Sound couldn't cool the anger and frustration burning within him.

Realizing that he had wasted too much time staring at the endlessly lapping water, he began to walk along the waterfront, back to a job he could barely stomach. He gritted his teeth in determination as he continued southward and tried to quiet the anger and fear that were tearing him apart. Just half an hour earlier he had been notified that his son was missing from school. It had happened before. Noah closed his mind to the terrifying thoughts. By now, he was used to the fact that his rebellious son hated school—especially the school into which he had been transferred just two months before. Noah hoped that Sean wasn't in any real trouble or danger.

He paused only once as he walked back to the office and that was to buy a newspaper. Knowing it was a mistake, he opened the paper to the financial section. Although this time the article was buried, Noah managed to find it on the fourth page. After all this time, he had hoped that the interest in the scandal would have faded. He was wrong. "Damn," he muttered to himself as he quickly scanned the story.

It had been four weeks since the fire, but that had been time enough for Noah Wilder to have the opportunity to curse his father too many times to count. Today was no exception. Actually the fire and the scandal surrounding it were only a couple of problems on a long list that seemed to grow daily. The fire and the suspected arson complicated matters for Noah, and until the entire business was resolved, he knew that he would suffer many more long hours in the office and endure countless sleepless nights. It was just his luck that the blaze had started while his father was out of the country. At the thought of Ben Wilder, Noah's frown deepened.

The early morning was still thick with fog, the air thick with the smell of the sea. A few shafts of sunlight pierced the gray clouds and reflected on the water collected on the concrete sidewalk, but Noah was too preoccupied with his own black thoughts to notice the promise of spring in the brisk air.

An angry horn blared, and a passing motorist shouted indignantly at Noah as he stepped onto the street against the traffic. He ignored the oath and continued, without breaking stride, toward the massive concrete and steel structure that housed Wilder Investments, his father's prosperous holding company. Damn his father! This was one helluva time for Ben to be recuperating in Mexico, leaving Noah to clean up all of the problems at the company. If it weren't for his father's recent heart attack, Noah would be back in Portland where he belonged, and perhaps Sean wouldn't be missing from school again. At the thought of his rebellious son, Noah's stomach tightened with concern. The lines deepened on his forehead, and his thoughtful scowl gave him a ragged, anxious appearance. Unfortunately, Noah could blame no one but himself for his son's attitude.

Noah should never have let Ben talk him into taking control of Wilder Investments, not even for a short period of time. It had been a mistake, and Sean was the person who was paying for it. Noah shouldn't have let his emotions dictate the decision to move to Seattle, and Ben's heart attack shouldn't have made any difference in that decision. Noah uttered an oath under his breath and slapped the rolled newspaper against his thigh in frustration. It had been difficult enough trying to raise a son alone in Portland. But now, in Seattle, along with the problems of managing Wilder Investments, it was nearly impossible for Noah to find enough time for his son.

Noah pushed open the wide glass doors of the Wilder Building and strode angrily to the elevator. It was early in the day, and the lobby was nearly empty. Silently the elevator doors parted and Noah stepped inside, grateful that he was alone. This morning he had no use for small talk with the employees of his father's multimillion dollar corporation. Anyone or anything that reminded him of Ben Wilder only served to deepen Noah's simmering anger.

After pushing the button for the thirtieth floor, he glared at the headlines of the financial section of the paper and reread the beginning of the article that had ruined his morning. His stomach knotted as the headline jumped up at him. "BURNED" WILDER INVESTMENTS SUSPECTED OF IN-SURANCE FRAUD. Noah gritted his teeth and tried to control his anger. The first paragraph was worse than the condemn-ing headline: *Noah Wilder, acting president of Wilder Investments, was unavailable for comment against the rumor that Wilder Investments might have intentionally started the blaze at Cascade Valley Winery. The fire, which started in the west wing of the main building, took the life of one man. Oliver Lindstrom, the deceased, was in partnership with Wilder Investments at the time of the blaze . . .*

The elevator stopped, and Noah drew his eyes away from the infuriating article. He'd already read it, and it only served to make him more frustrated with his father and his decision to prolong his stay in Mexico. To top things off, Sean had taken off from school this morning and couldn't be found. Where the hell could Sean have gone? Noah bit at his lip as his eyes glinted in determination. Regardless of anything else, Noah promised himself that he would find a way to force Ben to return to Seattle to resume control of Wilder Investments. This time Sean came first. There was just no other alternative.

Noah stepped from the elevator and headed for his father's auspicious office. He paused only slightly at Mag-gie's desk to order a terse directive. "See if you can get Ben on the phone immediately." He forced a smile that he didn't feel and entered the spacious, window-lined office where all of the decisions for Wilder Investments were made. Pitching the bothersome newspaper onto the contem-porary oak desk, Noah shrugged out of his suit jacket and tossed it unceremoniously over the back of a well-oiled leather couch.

The bank of windows behind the desk overlooked Pioneer Square, one of Seattle's oldest and most prestigious areas. Brick buildings, set on the sides of the rolling hills overlooking the sound, boasted turn of the century architecture contrasting sharply to the neighboring modern skyscrapers. The area was packed with an interesting array of antique shops, boutiques and restaurants.

Beyond Pioneer Square were the soothing gray waters of Puget Sound, and in the distance were the proud Olympic Mountains. On a clear day, they stood as a snow-laden barrier to the Pacific Ocean. Today they were merely ghostly shadows hiding in the slate-colored fog.

Noah cast a glance at the calm view over the rooftops of the city before sitting stiffly down in his father's leather chair. It groaned against his weight as he leaned back and ran an impatient hand through his thick, coarse hair. Closing his eyes, he attempted to clear his mind. Where was Sean?

He shook his head and opened his eyes to see the newspaper lying flat on the desk. The picture of the charred winery met his gaze. The last thing he wanted to think about this morning was the fire. One man was dead, arson was suspected and the Northwest's most prominent winery, Cascade Valley, was inoperable, caught in a lawsuit contesting the payment of the insurance proceeds. How in the world had he been so unlucky as to get trapped in the middle of this mess? The intercom buzzed, interrupting his thoughts.

"I've got your mother on line two," Maggie's voice called to him.

"I wanted to speak with Ben, not my mother," was Noah's clipped, impatient reply.

"I wasn't able to reach him. It was hard enough getting through to Katharine. I swear there must be only one telephone in that God-forsaken village."

"It's all right, Maggie," Noah conceded. "I shouldn't have snapped. Of course I'll talk to Katharine." Noah waited, his temper barely in check. Although he was furious with himself and his father, there was no reason to take it out on Maggie. He told himself to calm down and tried to brace himself against the wall of excuses his mother would build for his father. After pushing the correct button on the telephone, he attempted to sound casual and polite— two emotions he didn't feel at the moment. "Hello, Mother. How are you?"

"Fine, Noah," was the cool automatic response. "But your father isn't feeling well at all." Beneath Katharine's soft, feminine voice was a will of iron.

Noah's jaw tightened involuntarily, but he managed to keep his voice pleasant and calm. "I'd like to speak to him."

"I'm sorry, Noah. That's out of the question. He's resting right now." His mother's voice continued to drone in low, unemotional tones, giving Noah an updated prognosis of his father's condition. As he listened, Noah rolled up the sleeves of his shirt and began to pace angrily in front of the desk. He rubbed the back of his neck with his free hand while he clutched the other in a death grip around the telephone receiver. His knuckles whitened in annoyance as Katharine continued to speak tonelessly to him from somewhere in northern Mexico. Noah cast a dark glance out of the window into the rising fog and hoped for a break in the one-sided conversation.

It was obvious that Katharine Wilder was protecting her husband from the demands of his son. Noah could envision the tight, uncompromising line of his mother's small mouth

and the coldness in her distant blue eyes as she spoke to him
from some three thousand miles distance.

"So you can see, Noah, it looks as if we have no other
choice but to stay in Guaymas for at least another two
months . . . possibly three."

"I can't wait that long!"

There was a long, unyielding sigh from his mother. Her
voice sounded a little more faint. The frail telephone
connection to Mexico seemed to be failing. "I don't see that
you have much of a choice, Noah. The doctors all agree that
your father is much too ill to make the exhaustive trip back
to Seattle. There's no way he could hope to run the
company. You'll just have to hang on a little longer."

"And what about Sean?" Noah demanded hotly. There
was no response. Noah's voice quieted slightly. "Just let
me talk to Ben."

"You can't be serious! Haven't you heard a word I've
said? Your father is resting now—he can't possibly come to
the phone!"

"I need to talk to him. This wasn't part of the bargain,"
Noah warned, not bothering to hide his exasperation.

"Perhaps later . . ."

*"Now!"* Noah's voice had risen as his impatience began
to get the better of him.

"I'm sorry, Noah. I'll talk to you later."

"Don't hang up—"

A click from a small town in Mexico severed the
connection.

"Damn!" Noah slammed the receiver down and smashed
one fist into an open palm. He uttered a stream of invectives
partially aimed at his father, but mainly at himself. How
could he have been so gullible as to have agreed to run the
investment firm while Ben was recuperating? It had been an
emotional decision and a bad one at that. Noah wasn't prone

to sentimental decisions, not since the last one he had made, nearly sixteen years before. But this time, because of his father's delicate condition, Noah had let his emotions dictate to him. He shook his head at his own folly. He was a damned fool! "Son of a . . ."

"Pardon me?" Maggie asked as she breezed into the office in her usual efficient manner. Nearly sixty, with flaming red hair and sporting a brightly colored print dress, she was the picture of unflappable competency.

"Nothing," Noah grumbled, but the fire in his bright blue eyes refused to die. He slumped into his father's desk chair and attempted to cool his smoldering rage.

"Good!" Maggie returned with an understanding smile. She placed a stack of correspondence on the corner of the desk.

Noah regarded the letters with a frown. "What are those?"

"Oh, just the usual—except for the letter on the top of the pile. It's from the insurance company. I think you should read it." Maggie's friendly smile began to fade.

Noah slid a disgusted glance at the document in question and then mentally dismissed it as he looked back at the secretary. She noticed his dismissive gesture, and a perturbed expression puckered her lips.

"Would you put in a call to Betty Averill in the Portland office? Tell her I won't be back as soon as I had planned. Have her send anything she or Jack can't handle up here. If she has any questions, she can call me."

Maggie's intense gaze sharpened. "Isn't your father coming back on the first?" she asked. Maggie normally didn't pry, but this time she couldn't help herself. Noah hadn't been himself lately, and Maggie laid most of the blame on his strong-willed son. The kid was sixteen and hell-on-wheels.

"Apparently not," Noah muttered in response.

"Then you'll be staying for a few more months?"

Noah narrowed his eyes. "It's beginning to look that way, isn't it?"

Maggie tried to ignore the rage in Noah's eyes. She tapped a brightly tipped finger on the correspondence. "If you're staying on as head of Wilder Investments—"

"Only temporarily!"

Maggie shrugged. "It doesn't matter, but perhaps you should read this insurance inquiry."

"Is it that important?" Noah asked dubiously.

Maggie frowned as she thought. "It could be. That's your decision."

"All right . . . all right, I'll take a look," Noah reluctantly agreed. Before Maggie could back out of the office, he called to her. "Oh, Maggie, would you do me a favor?" She nodded. "Please keep calling the house, every half an hour if you have to. And *if* you do happen to get hold of my son, let me know immediately. I want to talk to him!"

Maggie's smile was faintly sad. "Will do." She closed the door softly behind her.

When Maggie was gone, Noah reached for the document that she had indicated. "What the hell is this?" he muttered as his dark brows pulled together in concentration. He scanned the letter from the insurance company quickly and several phrases caught his attention: *non-payment of benefits . . . conflict of interest . . . lawsuit contesting the beneficiary . . . Cascade Valley Winery.*

"Damn!" Noah wadded the letter into a tight ball and tossed it furiously into the wastebasket. He pushed down the button on the intercom and waited for Maggie's voice to answer. "Get me the president of Pac-West Insurance Company on the phone, *now!*" he barked without waiting for her response.

The last thing he needed was more problems with the insurance proceeds for the winery located in the foothills of the Cascade Mountains. He had hoped that by now the insurance company would have straightened everything out, even with the suspected arson complicating matters. Apparently he had been wrong, very wrong. Maggie's efficient voice interrupted his conjecture.

"Joseph Gallager, president of Pac-West Insurance, is on line one," she announced briskly.

"Good." He raised his hand to connect with Gallager, but paused. Instead he spoke to the secretary. "Do you have the name of the private investigator that my father uses?"

"Mr. Simmons," Maggie supplied.

"That's the one. As soon as I'm off the line with Gallager, I might want to talk to Simmons." An uneasy feeling settled over him at the mention of the wily detective. "Oh, Maggie . . . did you call the house?"

"Yes, sir. No one answered."

Noah's blue eyes darkened. "Thanks; keep trying," he commanded through tightly clenched teeth. Where was Sean? Noah turned his dark thoughts away from his defiant son and back to the problems in the office. Hopefully, the president of Pac-West Insurance could answer a few questions about the fire at the winery and why the insurance benefits hadn't been paid to Wilder Investments. If not, Noah would be forced to contact Anthony Simmons. Noah's lip curled into an uncompromising frown as he thought about the slick private investigator that Ben insisted upon keeping on the company payroll. Though he hated to rely on the likes of Simmons, Noah didn't have much of a choice. If the insurance company refused to pay because of the suspected arson, maybe Simmons could come up with a culprit for the crime and get rid of any lingering suspicion that Wilder Investments had had something to do with the blaze. Unless, of course, Ben Wilder knew something he wasn't telling his son.

The law offices of Fielding & Son were sedately conservative. Located on the third floor of a ninteenth-century marble bank building, they were expensively decorated without seeming garish. Thick rust-colored carpet covered the floors, and the walls gleamed with finely polished cherrywood. Verdant Boston ferns and lush philodendron overflowed the intricately woven baskets suspended from the ceiling. Leather-bound editions of law texts adorned shelves, and polished brass lamps added a warmth to the general atmosphere.

Despite all of the comfortable furnishings, Sheila was tense. She could feel the dampness of her palms, though they were folded on her lap.

Jonas Fielding mopped the sweat from his receding hairline with a silk handkerchief. Although it was only late May, the weather in the valley was unseasonably warm, and the small, delicately framed woman sitting opposite him added to his discomfort. Her large gray eyes were shadowed in pain from the recent loss of her father. There was an innocence about her, though she was dressed in a tailored business suit. Jonas couldn't help but remember Sheila Lindstrom as a little girl.

Jonas had practiced law for nearly forty years. Though he could have retired years ago, he hadn't, and it was times like this that he wished he had left the firm to his younger associates. Looking at Sheila, he felt very old, and the burden of his seventy years seemed great.

He should have become accustomed to grieving relatives long ago, but he hadn't, especially when the deceased had been one of his friends. Working with family members for the estate was a dismal part of his job, one that he would rather sluff off on a young associate. However, in this case it was impossible. Oliver Lindstrom had been a personal friend of Jonas Fielding. Hence, he had known Oliver's daughter, Sheila, all of her thirty-one years.

Jonas cleared his throat and wondered why the devil the air conditioning in the building wasn't working properly. The offices seemed uncomfortably confining this afternoon. Perhaps it was his imagination. Perhaps dealing with Sheila was the cause of his irritability. He detested this part of his job. To give himself a little space, he stood up and walked over to the window before addressing her.

"I understand that all of this business about your father's will and the complication with the insurance proceeds is a bit much for you now, because of your father's death." Sheila's small face whitened and she pinched her lower lip between her teeth. "But you have to face facts . . ."

"What facts?" she asked shakily. Her voice was dry with emotions that wouldn't leave her. "Are you trying to tell me something I already know—that everyone in this valley, and for that matter the entire Pacific Northwest, thinks my father committed suicide?" Sheila's hands were shaking. It was difficult but she held onto her poise, holding back the tears that were burning in her throat. "Well, I don't believe it, not one word of it! I won't!" Nervously she ran her fingers through the thick, chestnut strands of her hair. "You were a friend of my dad. You don't think that he actually took his own life, do you?" Round, gray eyes challenged the attorney.

The question Jonas had been avoiding made him squirm against the window ledge. He rubbed his hands on the knees of his suit pants, stalling for time to compose a suitable answer. He wanted to be kind. "I don't know, Sheila. It seems unlikely. . . . Oliver had such zest for life. . . . But, sometimes, when his back is up against the wall, a man will do just about anything to preserve what he has worked for all of his life.''

Sheila closed her eyes. ''Then you do believe it,'' she whispered, feeling suddenly small and very much alone. ''Just like the police and the press. They all think that Dad started the fire himself and got caught in it by mistake . . . or that he took his own life.''

''No one suggested—''

''No one had to! Just look at the front page of the paper! It's been four weeks, and the newspapers are still having a field day!''

''Cascade Valley employed a lot of people from around here. Since it's been closed, unemployment in the valley has doubled. There's no two ways about it, Sheila; Cascade Valley is news. *Big news.*'' Jonas's voice was meant to be soothing, but Sheila refused to be comforted.

''I guess I don't see why everyone seems to think that my father killed himself. Why would he do that—for the money?''

''Who knows?'' Jonas shrugged his aging shoulders as he made his way to the desk. ''All of the talk—it's only speculation.''

*''It's slander!''* Sheila accused, lifting her regal chin upward defiantly. ''My father was a decent, law-abiding citizen, and nothing will change that. He would never . . .'' Her voice cracked with the strain of the past month as she remembered the gentle man who had raised her. Since her mother's death five years before, Sheila had become closer to her father. The last time she had seen him alive, just last spring vacation, he had been so robust and healthy that Sheila still found it impossible to believe he was gone. When she had visited him, he had been remote and preoccupied, but Sheila had chalked it up to the

problems that the winery was experiencing at the time. Although her father had seemed distant, Sheila was sure that no problem at Cascade Valley had been serious enough to cause him to take his life. He had been stronger than that.

Sheila managed to compose herself. There was too much pride in her slender body to allow Jonas Fielding to witness the extent of her grief. "Is there any way I can get the winery operating again?"

Jonas shook his balding head. "I doubt it. The insurance company is balking at paying the settlement because of the possibility of arson."

Sheila sighed wearily, and her shoulders sagged. Jonas hesitated before continuing. "There's more to it than that," he admitted.

Sheila's head snapped up. "What do you mean?"

"The papers that were in your father's safety deposit box—did you read them?"

"No . . . I was too upset at the time. I brought everything here."

"I didn't think so."

"Why?"

"I found the partnership papers among the rest. Did you know that Oliver didn't own the business alone?"

"Yes."

The elderly attorney seemed to relax a little. "Have you ever met his business partner?"

"Years ago—when I was very young. But what does Ben Wilder have to do with anything?" she asked, confused by the twist in the conversation and Jonas's inability to meet her gaze.

"As I understand it, when the business was purchased nearly eighteen years ago, Ben and Oliver were equal partners." Sheila nodded, remembering the day when her father had made the ecstatic announcement that he had purchased the rustic old winery nestled deep in the eastern foothills of the Cascades. "However, during the course of the last few years, Oliver was forced to borrow money from Wilder Investments . . . to cover expenses. He put up his share of the business as collateral."

A tight, uneasy feeling gripped Sheila's stomach. "You didn't know about that?"

Jonas shook his head. "All the legal work was done by Ben Wilder's attorneys. I would have advised Oliver against it."

Sheila suddenly felt guilty as she remembered the course of events over the past five years. "Why exactly did Dad borrow the money?"

Jonas was evasive. He rubbed his palms together. "Several reasons . . . the economy had been rotten . . . and then there was a problem with the tampered bottles in Montana. From what I can see in the ledgers, sales have been down for several years."

"But there's more to it than that, isn't there?" Sheila whispered. Her throat became dry as she began to understand the reasons for her father's debt to Ben Wilder. *It was her fault!* Guilt, in an overpowering rush, settled in her heart.

Jonas dreaded what he had to say. "Your father took out the loan four years ago."

Sheila blanched. Her suspicions were confirmed.

Hesitating only slightly, the old attorney continued. "As I remember, there were several reasons for the loan. The most important thing at the time was that Oliver wanted to help you recover from your divorce from Jeff. Your father thought you should go back to school for your master's degree. He didn't want for you or Emily to be denied anything you might need, just because your marriage had failed."

"Oh, God, *no!*" Sheila sighed. She closed her eyes against the truth and sank lower into the chair. At the time of the divorce she hadn't wanted to take her father's money, but he hadn't given her much of a choice. She was a single mother without a job or the skill for decent employment. Her father had insisted that she attend a private school in California where the tuition along with the living expenses for herself and Emily were outrageous. Oliver had forced the money upon her, telling her that the California sun would help her forget about Jeff and the unhappy marriage. Begrudgingly she had accepted her father's help, assuring herself that she would pay him back with interest.

That had been over four years ago, and so far, Sheila hadn't managed to pay him a penny in return. *Now her father was dead.* He had never once mentioned that Cascade Valley was in financial trouble. Then again, Sheila had never asked. Guilt took a strangle hold of her throat.

Jonas handed her the partnership papers. She glanced through them and saw that the attorney's assessment of the situation was correct. After perusing the documents, Sheila raised her head and handed the papers back to her father's elderly friend.

"If only your father had come to me," Jonas offered. "I could have avoided this mess."

"Why didn't he?"

"Pride, I'd guess. It's all water under the bridge now."

"There's a letter demanding repayment of the loan to Wilder Investments," Sheila thought aloud.

"I know."

"But it wasn't written by Ben Wilder. The signature is . . ." Sheila's voice failed her, and her brows drew together as she recognized the name.

"Noah Wilder. Ben's son."

Sheila became pensive. She didn't know much about the man; Noah Wilder had always been a mystery to her. Despite her grief for her father, she was intrigued. "Is he in charge now?"

"Only temporarily, until Ben returns from Mexico."

"Have you talked to either Ben or his son and asked them if they might consider extending the loan?" Sheila asked, her tired mind finally taking hold of the situation. Without help from Wilder Investments Cascade Valley Winery was out of business.

"I've had trouble getting through to Noah," Jonas admitted. "He hasn't returned any of my calls. I'm still working on the insurance company."

"Would you like me to call Wilder Investments?" Sheila asked impulsively. Why did she think she could get through to Noah Wilder when Jonas had failed?

"It wouldn't hurt, I suppose. Do you know anything about Wilder Investments or its reputation?"

"I know that it's not the best, if that's what you mean. Dad never mentioned it, but from what I've read, I'd say that the reputation of Wilder Investments is more than slightly tarnished."

"That's right. For the past ten years Wilder Investments has been walking a thin line with the S.E.C.; however, any violations charged against the firm were never proven. And, of course, the Wilder name has been a continued source of news for the scandal sheets."

Sheila's dark eyebrows lifted. "I know."

Jonas tapped his fingers on the desk. "Then you realize that Wilder Investments and the family itself is rather . . ."

"Shady?"

Jonas smiled in spite of himself. "I wouldn't say that, but then I wouldn't trust Ben Wilder as far as I could throw him." His voice became stern. "And neither should you. As sole beneficiary to your father's estate, you could be easy prey for the likes of Ben Wilder."

"I guess I don't understand what you're suggesting."

"Don't you realize how many marginal businesses have fallen victim to Wilder Investments this year alone? There was a shipping firm in Seattle, a theater group in Spokane and a salmon cannery in British Columbia."

"Do you really believe that the Wilder family wants Cascade Valley?" Sheila asked, unable to hide her skepticism.

"Why not? Sure, in the last few years Cascade has had its trouble, but it's still the largest and most prestigious winery in the Northwest. No one, even with the power and money of Ben Wilder, could find a better location for a vineyard." Jonas rubbed his upper lip and pushed aside the moisture that had accumulated on it. "Your father might not have been much of a businessman, Sheila, but he did know how to bottle and ferment the best wine in the state."

Sheila leveled her gaze at Jonas's worried face. "Are you implying that Wilder Investments might be responsible for the fire?"

"Of course not . . . at least I don't think so. But regardless of who started the blaze, the fact stands that Wilder Investments is the only party who gained from it. Ben Wilder won't pass up a golden opportunity when it's offered him."

"And you think the winery is that opportunity."

"You'd better believe it."

"What do you think he'll do?"

Jonas thought for a moment. "Approach you, unless I miss my guess." He rubbed his chin. "I'd venture to say that Ben will want to buy out what little equity you have left. You have to realize that between the first and second mortgages on the property, along with the note to Wilder Investments, you own very little of the winery.''

"And you don't think I should sell out?''

"I didn't say that. Just be careful; make sure you talk to me first. I'd hate to see you fleeced by Ben Wilder, or his son.''

Sheila's face became a mask of grim determination. "Don't worry, Jonas. I intend to face Ben Wilder, or his son, and I plan to hang on to Cascade Valley. It's all Emily and I have left.''

# Chapter Two

$\mathcal{T}$he door to Ben's office swung open, and although Noah didn't look up, his frown deepened. He tried to hide his annoyance and pulled his gaze from the thick pile of correspondence he had been studying. It was from a recently acquired shipping firm, and some of the most important documents were missing. "Yes," he called out sharply when he felt, rather than saw, his father's secretary enter the room. He looked up, softening the severity of his gaze with a smile that didn't quite reach his eyes.

"I'm sorry to disturb you, Noah, but there's a call for you on line one," Maggie said. Over the past few months she'd become accustomed to Noah's foul moods, provoked by his father's business decisions.

"I'm busy right now, Maggie. Couldn't you take a message?" He turned his attention back to the stack of paperwork cluttering the desk. Maggie remained in the room.

"I know you're busy," she assured him, "but Miss Lindstrom is the woman waiting to speak with you."

"Lindstrom?" Noah repeated, tossing the vaguely familiar name over in his mind. "Is she supposed to mean something to me?"

"She's Oliver Lindstrom's daughter. He died in that fire a few weeks ago."

The lines of concentration furrowing Noah's brow deepened. He rubbed his hands through the thick, dark brown hair that curled above his ears. "She's the woman who keeps insisting I release some insurance money to her, isn't she?"

Maggie nodded curtly. "The same."

All of Noah's attention was turned to the secretary, and his deep blue eyes narrowed suspiciously. "Lindstrom died in the fire, and according to the reports, arson is suspected. Do you suppose that Lindstrom set the fire and inadvertently got trapped in it?" Without waiting for a response from Maggie, Noah reached for the insurance report on the fire. His eyes skimmed it while he posed another question to the secretary. "Didn't I write to this Lindstrom woman and explain our position?"

"You did."

"And what did I say? Wasn't it a phony excuse to buy time until the insurance investigation is complete?" He rubbed his temple as he concentrated. "Now I remember . . . I told her that everything had to wait until Ben returned."

"That's right." Maggie pursed her lips in impatience. She knew that Noah had complete power over any business decision at Wilder Investments, at least until Ben returned from Mexico.

"Then why is she calling me again?" Noah asked crossly. That fire had already cost him several long nights at the office, and the thought of spending more time on it frustrated him. Until the insurance report was complete, there wasn't much he could do.

Maggie's voice was tiredly patient. She had become familiar with Noah's vehement expressions of disgust with his father's business. The insurance problem at the winery seemed to be of particular irritation to him. "I don't know why she's calling you, Noah, but you might speak to her. This is the fifth time she's called this afternoon."

Guiltily Noah observed the tidy pile of telephone messages sitting neglected on the corner of his desk. Until this moment he had ignored them, hoping that the tiny pink slips of paper might somehow disappear.

"All right, Maggie," he conceded reluctantly. "You win. I'll talk to—"

"Miss Lindstrom," the retreating secretary provided.

In a voice that disguised all of his irritation, he answered the phone. "This is Noah Wilder. Is there something I can do for you?"

Sheila had been waiting on the phone for over five minutes. She was just about to hang up when Ben Wilder's son finally decided to give her a little portion of his precious time. Repressing the urge to slam the receiver down, she held her temper in tight rein and countered his smooth question with only a hint of sarcasm. "I certainly hope so—if it's not too much to ask. I'd like to make an appointment with you, but your secretary has informed me you're much too busy to see me. Is that correct?"

There was something in the seething agitation crackling through the wires that interested Noah. Since assuming his father's duties temporarily last month, no one had even hinted at disagreeing with him. Not that Noah hadn't had his share of problems with Wilder Investments, but he hadn't clashed with anyone. It was almost as if the power

Ben had wielded so mightily had passed to Noah and none of Ben's business associates had breathed a word of opposition to Ben's son. Until now. Noah sensed that Miss Lindstrom was about to change all of that.

"On the contrary, Miss Lindstrom. I'd be glad to meet with you, but we'll have to make it sometime after next week. Unfortunately, Maggie's right. I'm booked solid for the next week and a half."

"I can't wait that long!" Sheila cried, her thin patience snapping.

Her response surprised Noah. "What exactly is the problem? Didn't you get the letter I sent?"

"That's precisely why I'm calling. I really do have to see you. It's important!"

"You're hoping that I'll reverse my decision, I suppose?" Noah guessed, wondering at the woman's tenacity. He thumbed through his phone messages. Maggie was right. Sheila Lindstrom had called every hour on the hour for the past five.

"You've got to! If we hope to rebuild the winery and have it ready for this season's harvest, we've got to get started as soon as possible. Even then, we might not make it. . . ."

Noah interrupted. "I understand your problem." There was a hint of desperation in her voice that bothered him. "But, there's really nothing I can do. You understand that my father is out of the country and—"

"I don't care if your father is on the moon!" Sheila cut in. "If you're in charge of Wilder Investments, you're the man I have to deal with. Surely you can't be so much of a puppet that you can't make a simple business decision until your father returns."

"You don't understand," Noah began hotly in an attempt to explain, and then mentally cursed himself for letting this unknown woman force him into a defensive position. It really was none of her business.

"You're right, Mr. Wilder. I *don't* understand. I'm a businesswoman, and it seems utterly illogical to me that you would let a growing concern such as Cascade Valley sit in disrepair, when it could be productive."

Noah attempted to keep his voice level, even though he knew that the woman was purposely goading him. "As I understand it, Miss Lindstrom, Cascade Valley has been running at a loss for nearly four years."

There was a pause on the other end of the line, as if Sheila Lindstrom were studying the weight of his words. Her voice, decidedly less angry, commanded his attention. "I think it's evident from this discussion that you and I have a lot to talk over," Sheila suggested. Though she sounded calm, a knot of tension was twisting her stomach. "If it isn't possible for you to meet with me today, perhaps you could come to the winery this weekend and get a first-hand impression of our mutual problem."

For a moment the soft, coaxing tone of her voice captivated Noah, and he was tempted to take her up on her offer. He would love to leave the problems at Wilder Investments, if only for a weekend, but he couldn't. There were situations in Seattle that he couldn't ignore. It wasn't just the business; there was Sean to consider. A note of genuine regret filled his voice. "I'm sorry, Miss Lindstrom," he apologized, "it's out of the question. Now, if you would like to make an appointment, how about the week after next—say, June eighth?"

"No, thank you," was the curt reply. She was furious when she slammed the receiver back into the cradle of the pay telephone. The city of Seattle, usually a welcome sight to her, held no fascination today. She had come prepared to push her pleas on Noah Wilder, hoping to make him understand her desperate plight. She had failed. After being put off by his secretary, placed on hold forever, and making five fruitless telephone calls, Sheila wondered if it was possible to reason with the man. He was obviously just a figurehead for his father, a temporary replacement who held no authority whatsoever.

Sheila was lost in thought as she walked down the rain-washed sidewalk before wandering into a quiet bistro that had a view of Puget Sound. The cozy interior of the brightly lit café didn't warm her spirits, nor did the picturesque view of the shadowy sound. Her eyes followed the flight of graceful sea gulls arcing over the water, but her thoughts were distant.

Absently, she stirred a bit of honey into her tea. Though it was past the dinner hour, she wasn't hungry. Thoughts of the winery sitting charred and idle filled her mind. It just didn't make sense, she reasoned with herself. Why would Ben Wilder leave town and let his obviously incapable son run a multi-million dollar investment business? Pensively sipping the tea, Sheila tried to remember what she could about her father's business partner. Tiny, fragmented thoughts clouded her mind. Though her father had been partners with Ben Wilder for over seventeen years, the two men had had little personal contact. Ben's son, Noah, was a mystery. He was the only heir to the Wilder fortune and had been a rebel in his youth.

Sheila ran her fingers through the thick strands of her shoulder-length hair as she tried to remember what it was about Noah Wilder that kept haunting her? Slowly, vague memories surfaced.

Although she hadn't been meant to hear the whispered conversation between her father and mother some sixteen years in the past, Sheila had listened at the closed kitchen door with all the impish secrecy of a normal fifteen-year-old. From what she pieced together, Sheila understood that her father's business partner's son had gotten some girl in trouble. The family disapproved. At the time Sheila had been puzzled by the conversation and then had quickly forgotten it. Although she had always been interested in Noah Wilder, she didn't know him and had dismissed her parents' secretive conversation.

The recent problems of the Wilder family were just as cloudy in her mind. Her father had mentioned that some of the bottles of Cascade Valley Cabernet Sauvignon had been tampered with and discovered in Montana, and Sheila remembered reading about the supposed S.E.C. violations in one of Wilder Investment's takeover bids. However, she had ignored the gossip and scandals concerning her father's business partner. At the time Sheila had not been interested in anything other than the fact that her marriage was breaking apart and that she would have to find some way to support her young daughter. Her father's business concerns hadn't touched her. She had been too wrapped up in her own problems.

Sheila set down her teacup and thoughtfully ran her fingertips around its rim. If only she had known what her father was going through. If only she had taken the time to help him, as he had helped her. As it was, his name was now smeared by the speculation and gossip surrounding the fire.

Thinking about her daughter's welfare and her father's reputation spurred Sheila into action. She pushed her empty teacup aside. Despite the warnings of Jonas Fielding against it, Sheila knew it was imperative that she talk with Ben Wilder. He had been a friend of her father as well as his business partner, and if anyone could see the logic in her solution to the problem at the winery, it would be Ben.

She opened her purse and withdrew a packet of old

correspondence she had discovered in her father's private
office. Fortunately the papers in the fireproof cabinet hadn't
burned, and on an old envelope she found Ben Wilder's
personal address. The envelope had yellowed with age, and
Sheila realized that her plan was a long shot. Ben Wilder
could have moved a dozen times since he had mailed the
letter. But how else would she find him? He was a man who
prized his privacy.

Despite the odds against locating him, Sheila knew she
had to find someone who might be able to get in touch with
him. A phone number was all she needed. If she could
convince him that it was in his best interest to reopen the
winery, Ben would be able to order the reconstruction of
Cascade Valley. *Wouldn't his arrogant son be burned!*
Sheila smiled to herself and felt a grim sort of pleasure
imagining Noah's reaction when he found out about her
plans. He would be furious! Sheila grabbed her purse,
quickly paid the check and nearly ran out of the restaurant.

When Noah hung up the telephone, he had a disturbing
feeling that he hadn't heard the last from Sheila Lindstrom.
The authoritative ring in her voice had forced him to reach
for the file on the fire. After glancing over the letters from
Sheila a second time and thinking seriously about the
situation at the winery, Noah felt a twinge of conscience.
Perhaps he'd been too harsh with her.

In all fairness, the woman did have an acute problem, and
she deserved more than a polite brush-off. Or did she?
Anthony Simmons, Ben's private detective, hadn't yet filed
his report on the arson. Could Oliver Lindstrom really have
been involved? What about Lindstrom's daughter, sole
beneficiary to the old man's estate? Noah shifted restlessly
in his chair. Perhaps he should have been more straightfor-
ward with her and told Sheila about Simmons's investiga-

tion into the cause of the fire. Was he getting to be like his father, preferring deceit to the truth?

Noah's jaw tightened. He felt the same restless feeling steal over him that had seized him countless times in the past. There was something about the way his father did business that soured his stomach. It wasn't anything tangible, but there was just something wrong. If only he could put his finger on it. Wilder Investments put him on edge, just as it had in the past. That was one reason Noah had quit working for his father seven years before. The quarrel between Ben and Noah had been bitter and explosive. If it hadn't been for his father's recent heart attack and the one, large favor Ben still kept hanging over Noah, he would never have agreed to return, not even temporarily. Noah's face darkened with firm resolve. At least now he was even with his father, out of the old man's debt. They were finally square after sixteen unforgiving years.

Maggie knocked on the door before entering the office. "You wanted me to remind you of the probation meeting," she announced with a stiff smile. This was the part of her job she liked least, dealing with her boss on personal matters. In this case it was like rubbing salt into an open wound.

"Is it three o'clock already?" Noah asked, grimacing as his wristwatch confirmed the efficient secretary's time schedule. "I've got to run. If there are any more calls, or people who need to see me, stall them until tomorrow . . . or better yet, till sometime next week. Unless, of course, you hear from Anthony Simmons. I want to speak to him right away. He owes me a report on that fire at Cascade Valley."

Maggie's eyebrows lifted slightly. "Yes, sir," she replied before stepping back into the hallway.

Noah threw his coat over his shoulder and snapped his

briefcase closed. He half-ran out of the office and down the hallway before stopping. On impulse he turned to accost his father's secretary once again. "Oh, Maggie?"

The plump redhead was a few paces behind him. "Yes?"

"There is one other thing. If Sheila Lindstrom should call again, tell her I'll get back to her as soon as possible. Get a number where she can be reached. I'll check back with you later."

The smug smile on Maggie's round face only served to irritate Noah further. Why did he feel a sudden urge to amend his position with the intriguing woman who had called him earlier in the day? For all he knew, Sheila Lindstrom might be involved with the arson. He didn't know anything about her. It was crazy, but he felt almost compelled to speak to her again. Perhaps it was the mood of the letters she had sent him, or maybe it was her quick temper that had sparked his interest in her. Whatever the reason, Noah knew that it was very important that he talk with her soon. She was the first one of his father's business associates who had shown any ounce of spunk. Or was it more than that?

He shrugged off the unanswered question as he slid behind the wheel of his silver Volvo sedan and headed for the meeting with Sean's probation office. Noah had been dreading this meeting for the better part of the week. Sean was in trouble. Again. When the school administrator had called last week and reported that Sean hadn't shown up for any of his midmorning classes, Noah had been worried. Then, when he finally found out that his son had cut classes with a group of friends and later had been picked up by the police for possession of alcohol, Noah had become unglued. He was angry and disgusted, both at himself and his son.

If Sean was in trouble, Noah had himself to blame.

Sixteen years ago he had begged for the privilege and responsibility of caring for his infant son, and he was the one who had insisted on raising the child alone. Unfortunately, he had made a mess of it. If Sean didn't straighten out soon, it could spell disaster.

Although it wasn't quite three thirty, the Friday afternoon traffic heading out of the city was thick, and driving was held to a snail's pace. Even Seattle's intricate freeway system couldn't effectively handle the uneven flow of motorists as they moved away from the business district of the Northern Pacific city.

The high school that Sean attended was near Ben's home, and in the twenty minutes it took to get to the school, Noah found himself hoping that the probation officer would give Sean another chance. Noah knew that he had to find a way to get through to his son.

Noah's car crested a final hill, and he stopped the car in front of a two-story brick building. At the sound of the afternoon bell, he turned all of his attention to the main entrance of the school. Within minutes a swarm of noisy teenagers burst through the doors of the building and began to spill down the steps. Some held books over their heads, others used umbrellas; still others ignored the afternoon drizzle altogether.

Noah's eyes scanned the crowd of teenagers as it dispersed over the school yard. Nowhere did he see his blond, athletic son. The thought that Sean might have stood him up crossed Noah's mind, but he pushed it quickly aside. Surely the kid wouldn't be that stupid! Sean knew the importance of today's meeting with the juvenile officer. He wouldn't blow it. *He couldn't!*

Noah continued to wait. His hands gripped the steering wheel more tightly with each passing minute. There was no sign of his son. The teenagers on the steps thinned as they dashed across the lawn, heads bent against the wind and rain. The roar of car engines and rattling school buses filled the air. Still no Sean. Noah's impatience was beginning to surface, and he raked his fingers through the thick, coarse strands of his near-black hair. *Where the devil was that kid?* The appointment with the juvenile officer was in less than thirty minutes, and Sean was nowhere in sight.

Angrily Noah opened the car door, pulled himself to his full height, slammed the door and pushed his hands deep into his pockets. He leaned against the car, oblivious to the rain that ran down his back. His eyes skimmed the empty school yard. No sign of his son. He checked his watch once, uttered a low oath and continued to lean against the car.

# Chapter Three

$\mathcal{I}$t was dusk when Sheila found the address listed on the torn envelope, and even though twilight dimmed her vision, she could tell that the house Ben Wilder called home was immense. The three-story structure stood high on a cliff overlooking the banks of Lake Washington, and the grounds surrounding the manor encompassed several acres. The stately stone house was surrounded by a natural growth of sword ferns and ivy. To Sheila, the building seemed strangely cold and uninviting. Even the sweeping branches of the fir trees and the scarlet blossoms of the late-blooming rhododendron didn't soften the hard, straight lines of the manor.

An uneasy feeling that she was intruding where she didn't belong nagged at Sheila's mind, and she considered retreating into the oncoming night. She chided herself for her case of nerves. What would it hurt to knock on the door and inquire as to the whereabouts of Ben Wilder? Nothing ventured; nothing gained. Wasn't that the phrase?

It was obvious that someone was home. Not only was there smoke rising from one of the chimneys, but also, several windows in the stone mansion glowed brightly from interior lights. Even the porch lanterns were lit. It was almost as if her presence were expected. A cold chill of apprehension skittered up her spine.

Ignoring her mounting misgivings, Sheila parked her car behind the silver Volvo sitting in the long, circular drive. Before she could think twice about the consequences of what she was about to do, she slid out of her car, gathered a deep breath of damp air and walked to the door. A quiet rain had begun to settle over the city, and droplets of moisture clung to Sheila's hair. After hiking the collar of her raincoat more tightly around her throat, she knocked softly on one of the twin double doors. As she nervously waited, she wondered who would answer her knock and what his reaction would be to her inquiry. Would she really be able to procure information as to the whereabouts of Ben Wilder or was this just one more leg in the wild goose chase she had been participating in all afternoon?

The door opened suddenly. Sheila wasn't prepared to meet the forceful man standing in the doorway. In a house the size of a Tudor, she had expected a servant to greet her, but she had been mistaken. The tall, well-built man standing in the light from the hallway presented himself with an arrogance that spoke of power rather than servility. His face was handsome, though not in a classical sense. His features were even, but severe. The angle of his jaw was strong, and dark, ebony brows hooded deepset delft-blue eyes. The lines of worry on his face intensified his masculinity and the power of his gaze. His eyes sparked with interest as he looked down on Sheila. Involuntarily her pulse quickened and fluttered in the hollow of her throat. Surely he could sense her unease.

"Is there something I can do for you?" he asked with practiced boredom. Sheila instantly recognized his voice. It belonged to Noah Wilder. Of course! Why hadn't she expected him . . . *or had she?* Had her subconscious sought him out? She swallowed with difficulty while her heart clamored in her chest.

"I was looking for Ben Wilder," was her inadequate response.

"Ben?" He cocked a wary black eyebrow before crossing his arms over his chest and leaning on the doorjamb. The light fabric of his shirt strained over his shoulder muscles. A lazy smile softened the severe planes of his face. "You want to see Ben? Who are you?"

There was something disturbing in Noah's deep blue eyes, something that took hold of Sheila and wouldn't let go. With difficulty she drew her eyes away from the alluring depths of his gaze. She drew in a steadying breath and ignored both her racing pulse and the strong desire to run back into the safety of the night. "My name is Sheila Lindstrom. I believe I spoke with you earlier this afternoon."

He didn't seem surprised by her announcement. His smile broadened to show the hint of a dimple. He was interested but cautious. "You're the lady with the urgent problems at Cascade Valley, right?"

"Yes." At least he remembered her. Was he amused? Why the crooked, knowing grin?

"You called the office and Maggie told you where you could reach me?" he guessed, rubbing his chin while his eyes inched slowly up her body. What was it about her that he found so attractive?

Before she could answer his question, his eyes left her face. A car engine whined on a nearby road, and Noah's head snapped upward. His eyes followed the sound, and every muscle in his body tensed as he looked past her toward the sound.

The car drove past the main gates and turned into another driveway. "No," Sheila said, responding to his question of a few moments before.

"No?" Noah's interest was once again on the conversation. His eyes searched hers.

"I told you I'm looking for your father."

"And I told you he was out of the country." Something in his gaze seemed to harden.

"I was hoping that someone here might be able to give me an address or a telephone number where he might be reached," she admitted, pressing onward despite the chill in Noah's gaze.

His lips tightened into a scowl, and his voice became still colder. "Come in, Miss Lindstrom, and get out of the rain. You were right. Earlier today you indicated that we have a few things to iron out, and I agree with you. Let's get on with it." He moved out of the doorway as if he expected her to enter.

Sheila hesitated for a moment as her resolve faltered. When his eyes had darkened in disdain, she felt her poise crumbling. She was the intruder. "I think it would be better if I talked to your father. If you could just give me the number. . . ."

"I asked you to come inside! I think it's an excellent suggestion, as it's getting dark and the wind is beginning to pick up. I'm not about to stand here and get wet while I argue with you. The choice is yours; either you can come into the house and talk to me or you can stand out on this porch alone. I'm not going to stand out here much longer.

You were the one who was so desperate to talk to me this afternoon. Now you have the opportunity. Take it!''

*It was a mistake to enter this man's home*. Sheila could feel it, but she was cornered. With what little dignity she could piece together, she reluctantly accepted Noah's invitation and quietly strode into the formal entry hall. Antiques and portraits adorned the walls of the expansive foyer. A large crystal chandelier warmed the entrance in a bath of filtered light, which reflected against the polished wood floor and the carved walnut staircase. Expensive Persian carpets, rich in hues of burgundy and navy, seemed to run endlessly along several of the corridors that branched from the central reception area.

Noah closed the door behind her and indicated the direction she should follow. Sheila tried to hide the awe that was flooding through her at the ostentatious display of Wilder wealth. Although the Wilder name was familiar throughout the Northwest, never had Sheila guessed her father's business partner to be so affluent. The size and elegance of the gracious old house overwhelmed her, and she had to remind herself of Ben Wilder's infamous reputation for gaining his wealth. Nothing stood in his way when he wanted something; no amount of money was an obstacle that couldn't be overcome. She slid a glance toward the tall man walking silently at her side. Was he the same as his father?

Without breaking stride Noah touched Sheila's elbow, nudging her into a room near the back of the house. A dying fire and a few table lamps illuminated the room, which appeared to be a library. Hard-cover editions rested on an English reading table, and other books were stored behind the leaded glass of the built-in cabinets. A leather recliner sitting near the fireplace was partially extended, and a

half-finished drink rested on a side table, indicating that
Noah had been in this room just moments before, waiting.
But for whom? Certainly not Sheila. He had no idea that she
would grace his doorstep this evening. Once again the
overwhelming sensation that she was intruding upon him
cut her to the bone. Noah Wilder was just as mysterious as
she had imagined.

"Sit down, Miss Lindstrom," Noah suggested as he
stood near a bar. "May I get you a drink?"

"No . . . thank-you." She sat on the edge of a wing-
backed chair and prayed that she looked calmer than she
felt.

"Coffee, perhaps?"

She looked up at him and shook her head. She could feel
his eyes on her face; they were the bluest eyes she had ever
seen, erotic eyes that mystified her. "No . . . nothing,
thanks."

Noah shrugged, pulled at his tie and dropped into the
oxblood red recliner facing her. In the warm glow from the
smoldering embers he studied her face. His stare was so
intense that after a moment of returning his direct gaze, she
let her eyes fall and pretended interest in the dying fire. But
the blackened logs and the quiet flames reminded her of her
father and the inferno that had taken his life. Unconsciously
she bit at her lower lip and tried to concentrate on anything
but the nightmare of the last month.

Noah was disgusted with himself when he realized how
fascinated he was becoming with the beguiling woman he
had found on his doorstep. Earlier today he had known that
she interested him, but never had he expected to become so
utterly captivated by her beauty and unconscious vulnerability. Lines of worry etched across her otherwise flawless-
ly complected forehead, and a deep sadness lingered in her

eyes. Still, she was beautiful. The combination of her thick chestnut-colored hair, her delicately structured oval face and her large, nearly luminous gray eyes bewitched him. Noah didn't fall easy prey to beautiful women; most of them bored him to death. But this intriguing woman with her sharp tongue and gorgeous eyes captivated him. It was difficult for him to disguise his interest in her.

Sheila was nervous, though she proudly attempted to shield herself with a thin veil of defiant poise. Her cheeks were flushed from the cold, and tiny droplets of moisture clung to her dark hair, making it shine to the color of burnished copper.

Noah took a swallow from his drink. What bothered him most was the shadow of despair in her eyes. It puzzled and nagged at him, and he wondered if he had inadvertently contributed to that pain. An odd sensation swept over him. *He wanted to protect her*. He felt the urge to reach out and soothe her . . . comfort her . . . make love to her until she forgot everything else in her life other than him.

His final thought struck him savagely. What was he doing, fantasizing over a woman he had barely met, a virtual stranger? He reined in his emotions and blamed his traitorous thoughts on the long, tense day and the worry that was eating at him. What did he know of Sheila Lindstrom? He tried to convince himself that she was just another woman. One that, for all he knew, wanted nothing more from him than a piece of his father's fortune. He drained his drink.

"All right, Miss Lindstrom," Noah said, breaking the heavy silence. "You have my undivided attention. What is it that you want from me?" He folded his hands and leaned back in the recliner.

"I told you that I want to get in touch with your father."

"And I told you that your request was impossible. My

father is in Mexico, recuperating from a recent illness. You'll have to deal with me.''

"I've tried that," she pointed out.

"You're right. You did try, and I wasn't very accommodating. I apologize for that. . . . I had other things on my mind at the time. But right now I'm prepared to listen. I assume that you want to talk about the insurance claim for Cascade Valley Winery?''

Sheila nodded, a little of her confidence returning. "You see, Ben was a personal friend of my father's. I thought that if I could reason with him, I could convince him of the importance of rebuilding the winery before the fall harvest.''

"Why do you think Wilder Investments would want to continue operating Cascade Valley?''

Sheila eyed Noah dubiously. "To make money, obviously.''

"But the winery wasn't profitable.''

"Only in the last few years," she countered. Was he testing her? "It's true that we've had a run of bad luck, but now—''

*"We?''* he interrupted abruptly. "Do *you* manage the operation?''

"No," Sheila admitted honestly. Her face clouded in thought. "No . . . I don't. Dad took care of that. . . .'' Her voice faded when she thought of her father.

Noah's question was gentle. "Your father was the man who was killed in the fire?''

"Yes.''

"And you think that you can take over where he left off?''

Sheila squared her shoulders and smiled sadly. "I know I could," she whispered.

"You worked in the winery?''

"No . . . yes . . . only in the summers." Why couldn't she think straight? It wasn't like her to be tongue-tied, but then Noah Wilder was more intimidating than any man she had ever met. "I helped Dad in the summers, when I was free from school and college. I'm a counselor at a community college." Sheila purposely omitted the five years she had been married to Jeff Coleridge. That was a part of her life she would rather forget. Her daughter, Emily, was the only satisfying result of the sour marriage.

Noah regarded her thoughtfully. He pinched his lower lip with his fingers as he turned her story over in his mind. His eyes never left the soft contours of her face and the determination he saw in her gaze. "So what, exactly, qualifies you to manage the operation—a few summers on the farm?"

She recognized his ploy and smile. "That along with a Master's degree in business."

"I see." He sounded as if he didn't.

Noah frowned as he stood and poured himself another drink. The woman was getting to him. Maybe it was all of the worries over his son, or the anxiety that plagued him at the office. It had been a long, hard day, and Sheila Lindstrom was getting under his skin. He found himself wanting to help her, for God's sake. Without asking her preference, he poured a second drink and set it on the table near her chair. After taking a long swallow of his brandy he sat on the edge of the recliner and leaned on his elbows. "What about the vineyards? It takes more than a college education to oversee the harvest and the fermentation."

Sheila knew that he was goading her, and although she was provoked at the thought, she replied in a calm voice that overshadowed his impertinent questions. "The winery employs a viticulturist for the vineyards. Dave Jansen is a respected viticulturist who grew up in the valley. His research has helped develop a stronger variety of grape, hardier for the cold weather. As for the actual fermentation and bottling, we employ an enologist who is more than capable—"

"Then what about the losses?" he demanded impatiently as he frowned into his drink. Why did he care? "Assuming that your father knew what he was doing, he made one helluva mess of it, according to the latest annual report."

Sheila's throat was hoarse and dry. The pent-up emotions she had kept hidden within her for the last month were about to explode, and she knew that if prodded any further, her restrained temper would be unleashed. She had expected a rough business meeting with a member of the Wilder family, but she was unprepared for this brutal inquisition from Noah and the way his overpowering masculinity was affecting her. She found it impossible to drag her eyes away from his face. "As I stated before . . . we've had a run of bad luck."

*"Bad luck?* Is that what you call it?" Noah asked. He wondered why his words sounded so brittle in the warm den. "The tampered bottles found in Montana, and the expensive recall? The damaged crops last year because of the early snowfall? The ash and debris from the Mount St. Helen's eruption? And now the fire? From what I understand, the fire was set intentionally. Do you call that bad luck?" His eyes had darkened to the color of midnight as he calculated her reaction.

"What would you call it?" she challenged.

"Mismanagement!"

"Natural disasters!"

"Not the fire."

For a moment there was a restless silence; Sheila felt the

muscles in her jaw tightening. She made a vain effort to cool her rising temper. It was impossible. "What are you inferring?" she demanded.

"That your father wasn't exactly the businessman he should have been," Noah snapped. He was angry at himself, at Ben and at Oliver Lindstrom. "I'm not just talking about the fire," he amended when he noticed that the color had drained from her face. "That loan to him from Wilder Investments. What was it used for—improvements in the winery? I doubt it!"

Sheila felt the back of her neck become hot. How much did Noah know about her? Would she have to explain that most of the money her father had borrowed was given to her?

Noah's tirade continued. "I don't see how you can possibly expect to turn the business around, considering your lack of experience." His fingers tightened around his glass.

Sheila's thin patience snapped, and she rose, intending to leave. "Oh, I see," she replied, sarcastically. "Cascade Valley doesn't quite hold up to the sanctimonious standards of Wilder Investments. Is that what you mean?"

His eyes darkened before softening. Despite his foul mood a grim smile tugged at the corners of Noah's mouth. "Touché, Miss Lindstrom," he whispered.

Sheila was still prepared for verbal battle and was perplexed by the change in Noah's attitude. His uncompromising gaze had yielded. When he smiled to display straight, white teeth and the hint of a dimple, the tension in the air disintegrated. Sheila became conscious of the softly pelting rain against the windowpanes and the heady scent of burning pitch. She felt her heart beating wildly in her chest, and she had the disturbing sensation that the enigmatic man watching her wistfully could read her mind. He wanted to touch her . . . breathe the scent of her hair . . . make her forget any other man in her life. He said nothing, but she read it in the power of his gaze. Was she as transparent as he?

Sheila felt an urgency to leave and a compulsion to stay. Why? And why did the needs of Cascade Valley seem so distant and vague? The closeness of the cozy room and the unspoken conversation began to possess her, and though she didn't understand it, she knew that she had to leave. Noah Wilder was too powerful. When he took hold of her with his eyes, Sheila wanted never to be released. She reached for her purse. When she found her voice, it was ragged, torn with emotions she didn't dare name. "Is . . . is it possible to meet with you next week?"

Noah's eyes flicked to her purse, the pulse jumping in the hollow of her throat and finally to her face. "What's wrong with right now?"

"I . . . have to get back . . . *really.*" Who was she trying to convince? "My daughter is waiting for me." She started to turn toward the door in order to break the seductive power of his gaze.

"You have a daughter?" The smile left his face, and his dark brows blunted. "But I thought . . ." He left the sentence unfinished as he got out of the chair.

Sheila managed a thin smile. "You thought I wasn't married? I'm not. The divorce was final over four years ago. I prefer to use my maiden name," she explained stiffly. It was still difficult to talk about the divorce. Though she didn't love Jeff, the divorce still bothered her.

"I didn't mean to pry." His sincerity moved her.

"I know. It's all right."

"I'm sorry if I brought up a sore subject."

"Don't worry about it. It was over long ago."

The sound of tires screaming against wet pavement as a car came to a sudden halt cut off the rest of her explanation. Sheila was grateful for the intrusion; Noah was getting too close to her. The engine continued to grind for a moment and then faded into the distance. Noah was instantly alert. "Excuse me," he muttered as he strode out of the room.

Sheila waited for just a minute and then followed the sound of Noah's footsteps. She had to get out of the house; away from the magnetism of Noah Wilder. As she walked down the hallway, she heard the sound of the front door creaking open.

"Where the hell have you been?" Noah demanded. The worry in his voice thundered through the hallways. At the sound Sheila stopped dead in her tracks. Whoever he had been waiting for had finally arrived. *If only she had managed to leave earlier*. Why hadn't she listened to her common sense and left Noah Wilder the moment she had met him? The last thing she wanted was to be caught up in a family argument.

There was a muted reply to Noah's demand. Sheila couldn't hear the words over the pounding of her heartbeat. She was trapped. She couldn't intrude into a very personal confrontation. She had to find a way to escape.

Noah's voice again echoed through the house. "I don't want to hear any more of your pitiful excuses! Go upstairs and try to sleep it off. I'll talk to you in the morning, and believe you me, there are going to be some changes in your behavior! This is the last time you stumble into this house drunk on your can, Sean!"

Sheila let out a sigh of relief. It was Noah's son who had come home, not his wife. Why did she feel some consolation in that knowledge? Sheila retreated to the library, but

Noah's harsh words continued to ring in her ears. Why was Noah so angry with his son, and why did it matter to her? It was better not to know anything more about Noah Wilder and his family. It was too dangerous.

Once back in the den, Sheila fidgeted. She knew that Noah was returning, and the knowledge made her anxious. She didn't want to see him again, not here in this room. It was too cozy and seemed seductively inviting. She needed to meet with him another time, in another place . . . somewhere *safe*.

She rushed through the room and paused at the French doors. She pushed down on the brass handle and escaped into the night. A sharp twinge of guilt told her she should make some excuse for leaving to Noah, but she didn't know what she would say. It was easier to leave undetected. She couldn't afford to get involved with Noah Wilder or any of his personal problems. Right now she was a business partner of Wilder Investments, nothing more.

Sheila shuddered as a blast of cold air greeted her. She had to squint in the darkness. Soft raindrops fell from the sky to run down her face as she attempted to get her bearings in the moonless night. "Damn," she muttered under her breath when she realized that she hadn't walked out of a back entrance to the house as she had hoped but was standing on a spacious flagstone veranda overlooking the black waters of Lake Washington. She leaned over the railing to view the jagged cliff and saw that there was no way she could hope to scale its rocky surface. She couldn't escape.

"Sheila!" Noah's voice boomed in the night. It startled her, and she slipped on the wet flagstones. To regain her balance, she tightened her grip on the railing. "What the devil do you think you're doing?" In three swift strides he was beside her. He grabbed her shoulders and yanked her away from the edge of the veranda.

Sheila froze in her embarrassment. How stupid she must look, trying to flee into the night. It seemed that her poise and common sense had left her when she had met Noah.

"I asked you a question—what were you doing out here?" Noah gave her shoulders a hard shake. His eyes were dark with rage and something else. Was it fear?

Sheila managed to find her voice, though most of her attention remained on the pressure of Noah's fingers against her upper arms. "I was trying to leave," she admitted.

"Why?"

"I didn't want to hear your argument with your son."

The grip on her shoulders relaxed, but his fingers lingered against her arms. "You would have had to have been deaf not to hear that argument. I'm just glad that you weren't considering jumping from the deck."

"What? Of course not. It must be over fifty feet straight down."

"At least."

"And you thought I might jump?" She was incredulous.

"I didn't know what to think," he conceded. "I don't know you and I don't really understand why you came out here or why you were leaning over the railing." He seemed honestly perplexed.

"There's nothing mysterious about it, I just wanted to leave. I was looking for a back exit."

"Why were you in such a hurry?" He examined her more closely. It was hard to tell in the darkness, but he was sure that she was blushing. Why?

"I don't feel comfortable here," she admitted.

"Why not?"

*Because of you. You're not what I expected at all. I'm attracted to you and I can't be!* "I've invaded your privacy and I apologize for that. It was rude of me to come to your home uninvited.''

"But you didn't know it was my home."

"That doesn't matter. I think it would be best if I were to leave. We can meet another time . . . in your office . . . or at the winery, if you prefer." He was close to her. She could see the interest in his cool blue eyes, smell his heady male scent, *feel* an unspoken question hanging dangerously between them.

"I don't know when I'll have the time," he hedged.

"Surely you can find an hour somewhere," she coaxed. The tight feeling in her chest was returning.

"What's wrong with now?"

"I told you . . . I don't want to interfere in your private life."

"I think it might be too late for that."

Sheila swallowed, but the dryness in her throat remained. Noah looked into the farthest reaches of her eyes, as if he were searching for her soul. She felt strangely vulnerable and naked to his knowing gaze, but she didn't shrink away from him. Instead she returned his unwavering stare. His fingers once again found her arms. She didn't pull away, nor did she sway against him. Though she was drawn to his raw masculinity, she forced her body to remain rigid and aloof as his hands slid up her arms to rest at the base of her throat.

Raindrops moistened her cheeks as she lifted her face to meet his. She knew that he was going to kiss her and involuntarily her lips parted. His head lowered, and the pressure of his fingers against her throat moved in slow, seductive circles as his lips touched hers in a bittersweet kiss that asked questions she couldn't hope to answer. She wasn't conscious of accepting what he offered until she felt her arms circle his waist. It had been so long since she had wanted a man. Not since Jeff had she let a man close to her. Never had she felt so unguarded and passionate. Until now, when she stood in the early summer rain, kissing a man she couldn't really trust. She felt a warm, traitorous glow begin to burn within her.

His hands shifted to the small of her back and pulled her against his hard, lean frame. She felt the rigid contours of his body, and the ache in hers began to spread. Lazily he brushed his lips over hers, and softly his tongue probed the warm recess of her mouth. All of her senses began to awaken and come alive. Feelings she had thought dead reappeared.

When he pulled away from her to look into her eyes, her rational thought came thundering back to her. She saw a smoldering passion in the smoky blue depths of his eyes, and she knew that her own eyes were inflamed with a desire that had no bounds.

"I'm sorry," she swiftly apologized, trying to take a step backward. The hands on her waist held her firmly against him.

"For what?"

"Everything, I guess. I didn't mean for things to get so out of hand."

He cocked his head to one side in a pose of disbelief. "You must enjoy running out on me. Is that it? Are you just a tease?" Was he kidding? Couldn't he feel her response?

"I meant that I hadn't planned to become involved with you."

"I know that."

"Do you?"

"Of course. Neither of us planned any of this, but we can't deny that we're attracted to each other. We both felt it earlier in the study, and we're feeling it now." One of his fingers touched her swollen lips, challenging her to contradict him.

Her knees became weak as his head once again lowered and his lips, deliciously warm and sensitive, touched hers. She was drawn to him, but she fought the attraction. She pulled away. Her own lips were trembling and for an unguarded instant, fear lighted her eyes.

Noah was wary. "Is something wrong?"

She wanted to laugh at the absurdity of the situation. "Is anything wrong?" she echoed. "Are you kidding? How about everything? The winery is in a shambles, so I came to Seattle hoping that you would help me. Instead, I end up here looking for your father because I couldn't get through to you. On top of that I stumble onto your argument with your son, and finally, I fall neatly into your arms."

Noah put a finger to her lips to silence her. "Shhh. All right, so we've got a few problems."

"*A few?*"

"What I'm trying to tell you is that sometimes it's best to get away and escape from those problems. It gives one a better perspective."

"You're sure?"

"What I'm sure of is that I find you incredibly attractive." Noah's voice was soothing, and Sheila felt her body lean more closely to his.

"This won't work, you know," she whispered breathlessly.

"Don't worry about tomorrow."

"Someone has to." Reluctantly she wrenched herself free of his arms and straightened her coat. "I came here to find your father because you refused to see me."

"My mistake," he conceded wryly.

She ignored his insinuation. "That's the only reason I'm

here. I didn't intend to overhear your argument with your
son, nor did I expect to get this close to you. I hope you
understand.''

The smile that slid across his face was seductively
charming. ''I understand perfectly,'' he responded gently,
and Sheila felt herself becoming mesmerized all over again.
He was powerful and yet kind, bold without being brash,
strong but not unyielding—the kind of man Sheila had
thought didn't exist. Her attraction to him was compelling,
but her feelings were precarious.

''I have to go.''

''Stay.''

''I can't.''

''Because of your daughter?''

''She's one reason,'' Sheila lied. ''There are others.''

His smile broadened, and she saw the fla﹖ of his white
teeth. ''Come on, let's go inside. You're getting soaked.''

''At least I'm wearing a coat,'' she taunted, noticing the
way his wet shirt was molding to the muscular contours of
his shoulders and chest.

''I didn't expect you to run out into the rain.''

''It was a stupid thing to do,'' she admitted. ''It's just
that I didn't want to intrude. I didn't think you—''

''Have problems of my own?''

Embarrassment crept up her throat. ''I'm sorry.''

''Don't worry about it. I should have been a little more
discreet when Sean came home. I lost control when I saw
him drunk again.'' Noah wiped the rain from his forehead
as if he were erasing an unpleasant thought. He touched her
lightly on the elbow and guided her back into the house.

It was difficult for Noah to ignore any part of her; he
couldn't help but notice the quiet dignity with which she
carried herself, the curve of her calf as she walked, or the

shimmer of her chestnut hair, which had darkened into unruly curls in the rain.

"Thank you for seeing me," she said softly. "I don't suppose you would consider telling me how to reach your father?"

"I don't think that would be wise."

Sheila smiled sadly to herself. "Then I'll be going. Thank you for your time."

"You're not really planning to drive back to the valley tonight?" he asked, studying the tired lines of her face. How far could he trust her? She seemed so open with him, and yet he felt as if she were hiding something, a secret she was afraid to share.

"No. I'll drive back in the morning."

He stood with his back to the fire, warming his palms on the rough stones. "But your daughter. I thought she was expecting you."

"Not tonight. She's probably having the time of her life. That grandmother of hers spoils her rotten."

Noah rubbed his chin and his dark brows raised. "I didn't realize your mother was still alive."

A pensive expression clouded Sheila's even features. "She's not. Emily is staying with my ex-husband's mother. . . . We're still close."

"What about your ex-husband? Are you still close to him, too?" Noah asked, brittlely. Why the devil did he even care? He watched a play of silent emotions darken Sheila's eyes, and without knowing why, Noah Wilder immediately despised the man who had caused Sheila so much pain. He could feel the muscles in his jaw begin to tighten.

"Jeff and I are civil," Sheila replied, hoping to close the unwelcome subject.

"Then you still see him?" Noah persisted.

"It can't be avoided . . . because of Emily."

"Is he good with your daughter?"

"Yes . . . I suppose so. Does it matter?" Sheila asked, experiencing a hot flash of indignation. She didn't like discussing her feelings about Jeff with anyone, especially not a man she was beginning to admire.

"Doesn't it . . . matter, I mean?"

"To me, yes. But why do you care?"

His voice lowered at the bitterness in her words. "I didn't mean to bring up a sore subject."

Sheila stiffened, but pushed back the hot retort forming in her throat. It was none of Noah's business. Her divorce from Jeff had been a painful experience, one she would rather not think about or discuss.

"I think I had better leave," she stated evenly. She reached into the front pocket of her purse and fished for her keys. The conversation was getting far too personal.

"You mean you want to run away, don't you?"

"What?"

"Isn't that what you were doing when I found you out on the veranda, leaning over the rail? Weren't you attempting to avoid a confrontation with me?"

"You were arguing with your son! I was only trying to give you some privacy."

His eyes darkened. "There's more to it than that, isn't there?"

"I don't know what you're suggesting."

"Sure you do." He moved from the fireplace to stand only inches from her. "Any time the conversation turns a little too personal, you try to avoid me," he accused. A dangerous glint of blue fire flashed in his eyes.

Sheila stood her ground. "I came here to talk about business. There was nothing personal about it."

"Save that for someone gullible enough to believe it."

She glared at him defiantly but held onto her poise. "Quit beating around the bush and just say what it is that's bothering you."

"You came over here with the intention of contacting Ben. You were sidestepping me. Don't take me for such a fool. I know that you were deliberately trying to avoid me."

"Only because you were being completely unreasonable!" she snapped. He was impossible! When she looked into his intense cobalt eyes, she felt as if she wanted to float dreamily in his gaze forever. The smell of burning logs mingled with the earthy scent of Noah's wet body. Raindrops still ran down the length of his tanned neck.

"I'm not an unreasonable man," he stated calmly. His hand reached up to touch her chin, and Sheila felt a shiver skitter down her spine. His eyes studied her face, noting in detail the regal curve of her jaw, the blush on her creamy skin and the seductive pout on her full lips. "Please stay," he implored.

"Why?" She longed for an excuse, *any* excuse to spend some more precious time with him.

"We could start by talking about the winery and your plans for it."

"Would you change your position on the insurance settlement?"

The corners of his mouth quirked. "I think you could persuade me to do anything." His finger trailed down her chin and throat to rest against the collar of her coat. Her heart fluttered.

She stepped away from him and crossed her arms over her chest. Eyeing him suspiciously, she asked, "What would it take?"

"For what?"

"For you to listen to my side of the story."

He shrugged. "Not much."

"*How* much?"

Noah's smile spread slowly over his face and his eyes gleamed devilishly. "Why don't we start with dinner? I can't think of anything I'd rather do than listen to you over a glass of Cascade Valley's finest."

He was mocking her again, but there was enough of a dare in his words to tempt Sheila. "All right, Noah. Why not?" she countered impulsively. "But let's set out the ground rules first. I insist that we keep the conversation on business."

"Just come with me," he suggested wickedly. "The conversation . . . and the night will take care of themselves."

*Chapter Four*

$\mathcal{T}$he restaurant Noah selected was located on one of the steep hills near the heart of the city. It was unique, in that the originally Victorian structure had been built by one of Seattle's founding fathers. The old apartment building had been remodeled to accommodate patrons of *L'Epicure*, but the structure retained its authentic nineteenth-century charm. White clapboard siding, French gray shutters and an elegant touch of gingerbread adorned the entrance. Flickering sconces invited Sheila inside.

A formally dressed waiter led them up a narrow flight of stairs to a private room in the second story of the gracious old apartment house. An antique table sat in an alcove of leaded glass, giving the patrons a commanding panorama of the city lights. Raindrops lingered and ran on the windowpanes, softly blurring the view and creating an intimate atmosphere in the private room.

"Very nice," Sheila murmured to herself as she ran her fingers along the windowsill and looked into the night.

Noah helped her into her chair before seating himself on the other side of the small table. Though he attempted to appear calm, Sheila could sense that he was still on edge. The quiet, comfortable silence they had shared in the car had been broken in the shadowy confines of the intimate restaurant.

Before the waiter left, Noah ordered the specialty of the house along with a bottle of Chardonnay by Cascade Valley. Sheila lifted her brows at Noah's request, but the waiter acted as if nothing were out of the ordinary.

"Why would a European restaurant carry a local wine?" she inquired after the waiter had disappeared from the room.

Noah's smile twisted wryly. "Because my father insists upon it."

The waiter returned with the wine and solemnly poured the wine first into Noah's glass, and upon approval, into Sheila's. After he had left once again, Sheila persisted with her questions.

"*L'Epicure* keeps wine for your father?"

"That's one way of putting it. *L'Epicure* is a subsidiary of Wilder Investments," he explained tonelessly.

Sheila's lips tightened. "I see. Just like Cascade Valley."

Noah nodded. "Although the restaurant carries a full cellar of European wines, Ben insists that Cascade Valley be fully represented."

"And your father is used to getting what he wants?"

Noah's blue eyes turned stone cold. "You could say that." Any further comment he would have made was repressed by the appearance of the waiter bearing a tray overloaded with steaming dishes of poached halibut in mushroom sauce, wild rice and steamed vegetables. Sheila waited until the food was served and the waiter had closed the door behind him before continuing the conversation.

"I take it you don't like working for your father?" she guessed as she started the meal.

Noah's dark eyebrows blunted, and the fork he had been holding was placed back on the table. He clasped his hands together and stared at her over his whitened knuckles. "I think we should get something straight: I do *not* work for Ben Wilder!"

"But I thought—"

"I said I do not work for Ben! Nor do I collect a salary from Wilder Investments!" His clipped words were succinct and effectively closed the subject. The angry edge of his words and the tensing of his jawline left little doubt that he preferred not to speak of his father or his business.

"I think you owe me an explanation." Sheila sighed, setting her uneaten food aside. Somehow she had to keep her temper in check. What sort of game was he playing with her? "Why am I sitting here wasting my time, when you just intimated that you have nothing to do with Wilder Investments?"

"Because you wanted to get to know me better."

Sheila found it difficult to deny the truth, and yet she couldn't help but feel betrayed. He had tricked her into coming with him, when all along he couldn't help her in her quest to save the winery and her father's reputation. Was it her fault for being so mystified by him? Ignoring his wish to avoid discussing Wilder Investments, Sheila continued to push her point home. "I'm listening," she said quietly. "I want to know why you led me on—or have you forgotten our ground rules?"

"I didn't lead you on."

"But you just said that you don't work for Wilder Investments."

"I said that I don't work for *my father*, and I'm not on the company payroll."

"That doesn't make a lot of sense," Sheila pointed out, her exasperation beginning to show. "What is it exactly that you do?"

Noah shrugged, as if resigned to a fate he abhorred. "I do owe you an explanation," he admitted thoughtfully. "I used to work for Ben. From the time I graduated from college I was groomed for the position Ben's only heir would rightfully assume: the presidency of Wilder Investments, whenever Ben decided to retire. I was never very comfortable with the situation as it was, but"—he hesitated, as if wondering how much of his private life he should divulge—"for personal reasons I needed the security my position at Wilder Investments provided."

"Because of your wife and son?" Sheila immediately regretted her thoughtless question.

Noah's eyes darkened. "I've never had a wife!" He bit out the statement savagely, as if the thought alone were repulsive to him.

Sheila flushed with color. "I'm sorry," she apologized hastily. "I didn't know. . . . You have a child . . ."

Noah's glare narrowed suspiciously. "You didn't know about Marilyn? If that's the truth, you must have been the only person in Seattle who didn't know the circumstances surrounding Sean's birth. The press couldn't leave it alone. All of Ben's money couldn't even shut them up!"

"I've never lived in Seattle," she explained hurriedly, still embarrassed. Surely he would believe her. "And—and I didn't pay any attention to what my father's business partner was doing, much less his son. . . . I was only a teenager and I didn't know anything about you."

Noah's anger subsided slightly as he noticed the stricken look on Sheila's near-perfect face. "Of course not—it happened years ago."

Sheila's hands were trembling as she reached for her wine glass and let the cool liquid slide down her parched throat. She avoided Noah's probing gaze and pushed the remains of her dinner around on her plate. Although the food was delicious, her hunger had disappeared.

Noah speared a forkful of fish and ate in the thick silence that hung over the table. It was a long moment before he began to speak again. When he did, his voice was calm and toneless, almost dead from the lack of emotion in his words. "There were many reasons why I quit working for my father . . . too many to hope to explain. I didn't like the idea of being treated as 'Ben Wilder's son' by the rest of the staff, and I had never gotten on well with my dad in the first place. Working with him only served to deepen the rift between us." His teeth clenched, and he tossed his napkin onto the table as he remembered the day that he had broken free of the cloying hands of Wilder Investments.

"I stayed on as long as I could, but when one of my father's investments went sour, he ordered me to investigate the reasons. A manufacturing firm in Spokane wasn't making it. Although it wasn't the manager's fault, Ben had the man fired." Noah took a drink of wine, as if to cast off the anger he felt each time he remembered the painful scene in his father's office, the office Noah now reluctantly filled. The image of a man near fifty, his shoulders bowed by the wrath and punishment of Ben Wilder, still haunted Noah. How many times had he pictured the tortured face of Sam Steele as the man realized Ben was really going to fire him for a mistake he hadn't made? Sam had looked to Noah for support, but even Noah's pleading was useless. Ben Wilder needed a scapegoat and Sam Steele presented the unlikely sacrificial lamb, an example to the rest of the employees of Wilder Investments. It didn't matter that Sam wouldn't be able to find another job at a comparable salary, nor that he had two daughters in college. What mattered to Ben Wilder was his company, his wealth, his *power*. Though it had all happened years ago, Noah felt an uncomfortable wrench in his gut each time he remembered Sam's weathered face after leaving Ben's office. "It doesn't matter, boy," Sam had said fondly to Noah. "You did what you could. I'll make out."

Sheila was staring at Noah expectantly, and he quickly brought his thoughts back to the present. "That incident," he stated hurriedly, "was the final straw. By the end of the afternoon I had quit my job, yanked my kid out of school and moved to Oregon. I told myself I would never come back."

Sheila sat in the encumbering silence for a minute, watching the lines of grief still evident on Noah's masculine face while he reflected upon a part of his life she knew nothing about. She longed to hear more, to understand more fully the enigmatic man sitting across the table from her. Yet she was afraid, unsure of growing any closer to him. Already she was inexplicably drawn to him, and intuitively she realized that what he was about to tell her would only endear him to her further. Those feelings of endearment would surely only cause her suffering. She couldn't trust him. Not yet.

"You don't have to talk about any of this," she finally managed to say. "It's obviously painful for you."

"Only because I was weak."

"I . . . don't understand," she whispered, gripping the

edge of the table for support as she lifted her eyes to meet the question in his. "And," she allowed ruefully, "I'm not sure that I want to understand you."

"You're the woman who insisted that I owed her an explanation," he reminded her.

"Not about *all* of your life."

"But I thought you wanted to get to know me."

"No . . . I just want to know how you're connected with Wilder Investments," she lied. She ignored the voice in her mind that was whispering, *Dear God, Noah, I don't understand it, but I want to know everything about you . . . touch your body and soul.* Instead she lowered her eyes. "You are in charge of the company, aren't you?"

"Temporarily, yes."

"And you do make all of the decisions for Wilder Investments."

"Unless the board disapproves. So far they haven't." The mindless members of the board wouldn't dare argue with Ben's son, Noah thought to himself.

Sheila held her breath as the truth hit her in a cold blast of logic. "Then you were lying to me when you said that you couldn't make a decision about the winery until your father got back into the country."

Noah's mouth twitched in amusement. "I prefer to think of it as stalling for time."

"We haven't got time!"

His smile broadened and his eyes lightened over the edge of his wineglass. "Lady, that's where you're wrong. We've got all the time in the world."

His gaze was warm. Though the table separated them, Sheila could feel the heat of his eyes caressing her, undressing her, bringing her body closer to his. Under the visual embrace she felt her skin begin to tremble, as if anticipating his touch. *Don't fall for him,* she warned herself. *Don't think for a minute that he cares for you. You're just a handy convenience that stumbled onto him tonight. Remember Jeff. Remember the promises. Remember the lies. Remember the pain. Don't let it happen again. Don't fall victim to the same mistake. Don't!*

Carefully she pieced together the poise that he could shatter so easily. "Perhaps we should go."

"Don't you even want to know why I'm back at Wilder Investments?" he invited.

"Do you want to tell me?"

"You deserve that much at the very least."

"And at the very most?"

"You deserve more—much more."

She waited, her nervous fingers twirling the stem of her glass. She cocked her head expectantly to one side, unconsciously displaying the curve of her throat. Why did he work for his father in a position he found so disagreeable? "I had assumed that you took command because of your father's heart attack."

"That's part of it," he conceded reluctantly. "But a very small part." She was quiet, and her silence prodded him on. "Actually, when Ben had the first attack and asked me to take over for a couple of weeks, I refused. I didn't need the headache, and I figured he would have half a dozen 'yes men' who could more than adequately fill his shoes while he was recuperating. So I refused."

Sheila's eyebrows drew together as she tried to understand. "What changed your mind?" she asked quietly.

"The second attack. The one that put Ben in the intensive care unit for a week." Noah's fingers drummed restlessly on the table as he thought for a moment. "My father hadn't trusted anyone to run the company other than himself. When I refused to help him, he ignored the advice of his doctor and picked up where he left off."

"That's crazy," she thought aloud.

Noah shook his head. "That's getting his way. The second attack almost took his life, and when my mother pleaded with me to help him out, I agreed, but only until a replacement could be found."

"And your father didn't bother to look for one," Sheila surmised.

"Why would he? He got what he wanted."

"But surely *you* could find someone—"

"I've looked. Anyone I've suggested has been turned down by the powers that be."

"Ben."

"Exactly."

Sheila was confused. When she thought of her family and all of the love they had shared, she found it hard to imagine the cold detachment between Ben Wilder and his only son. "Surely there must be some way of solving your problem. Can't you talk to your father?"

"It doesn't do any good. Besides, that's only part of the story. I owed my father a favor—a big favor.

The uneasy feeling that had been threatening to overtake Sheila all evening caused her to shudder involuntarily. "And you're repaying him now, aren't you?"

"In my opinion: yes. You see," he continued in a flat, emotionless voice, "when my son, Sean, was born, there were problems I wasn't able to handle alone. I was too young. I was forced to ask and rely upon my father for help. He complied, and the bastard has never let me forget it."

"But what about Sean's mother?" Sheila questioned. "Certainly she could have helped if there were a problem with the child. Sean was her responsibility as well as yours."

*"Marilyn?"* Noah's face contorted at the irony of the suggestion and the memory of a young girl he had once

thought he loved. "You don't seem to understand, Sheila. *Marilyn* was the problem, at least the most evident problem, and it took all of my father's money and power to deal with her effectively."

"I shouldn't have asked—it's none of my business," Sheila stammered, stunned by the look of bitterness and hatred on the angled planes of Noah's proud face.

"It doesn't matter anymore. Maybe it never did. Anyway, it's all a part of the past, dead and buried."

Sheila pushed herself onto unsteady legs as she rose from the table. "There's no reason for you to tell me all of this."

His hand reached out and captured her wrist, forcing her to stay near him. "You asked," he reminded her.

"I'm sorry. It was my mistake. Perhaps we should go."

"Before you see all of the skeletons in the Wilder closets?" he mocked.

She felt her spine become rigid. "Before I lose track of the reason I came here with you."

Her dark eyebrows lifted elegantly, and Noah thought her the most intriguingly beautiful woman he had ever met. "Am *I* coercing *you?*" she asked as her eyes dropped to her wrist, still shackled in his uncompromising grip.

"If you are, lady, it's only because I want you to," he rejoined, but the tension ebbed from his face and his hand moved slightly up her forearm, to rub the tender skin of her inner elbow. "Let's go," he suggested, helping her from the chair. His hand never left her arm as he escorted her down the stairs and into the night. He carried her coat and wrapped his arm over her shoulders to protect her from the damp breeze that still held the promise of rain.

The drive back to the Wilder estate was accomplished in silence as Noah and Sheila were individually wrapped in their own black cloaks of thought. Though separated from him in the car, Sheila felt mysteriously bound to the darkly handsome man with the knowing blue eyes. *What's he really like?* her mind teased. In the flash of an instant she had seen him ruthless and bitter, then suddenly gentle and sensitive. She sensed in him a deep, untouched private soul, and she longed to discover the most intimate reaches of his mind. What would it hurt? her taunting mind implored. What were the depths of his kindness, the limits of his nature? He'll hurt you, her bothersome consciousness objected. A man hurt you in the past, when you opened yourself up to him. Are you foolish enough to let it happen again? Just how far do you dare trust Noah Wilder, and how far can you trust yourself?

The Volvo slowed as Noah guided the car past the stone pillars at the entrance of the circular drive. The headlights splashed light on the trunks of the stately fir trees that guarded the mansion. As Ben Wilder's home came into view, Sheila pulled herself from her pensive thoughts and realized that she had accomplished nothing toward furthering her purpose. She had intended to find a way, any way, to get the insurance proceeds to rebuild the winery, and she had failed miserably. She didn't even know if Noah had the power or the desire to help her. Had the insurance company paid off Wilder Investments? The car ground to a halt as Sheila discovered her mistake. Caught in her fascination for a man she had been warned to mistrust, she had lost sight of her purpose for making the trip to Seattle.

"Would you like to come in for a drink?" Noah asked as he flicked off the engine and the silence of the night settled in the interior of the car.

"I don't think so," she whispered, trying to push aside her growing awareness of him.

"We have unfinished business."

"I know that. You've found a way to successfully dodge the subject of the winery all evening. Why?"

Noah smiled to himself. "I didn't realize that I was. Would you like to come inside and finish the discussion?"

Sheila caught her breath. "No."

"I thought you were anxious to get the insurance settlement," he replied, his eyes narrowing as he studied her in the darkness.

"I am. You know that, but I happen to know when I've been conned."

"Conned?" he repeated incredulously. "What are you talking about?"

"It was difficult to get you on the phone and when I finally did, you refused to see me with some ridiculous excuse that any decision about the winery had to be made by your father. Then you agreed to talk about it over dinner, but conveniently avoided the issue all night. Why would I think that anything's going to change? You haven't listened to me at all. . . ."

"That's where you're wrong. I've listened to everything you've said all evening," he interrupted in a low voice.

"Then what's your decision?"

"I'll tell you that, too, if you'll join me for a drink." His hand reached for hers in the car. "Come on, Sheila. We've got the rest of the night to talk about anything you want."

Again she felt herself falling under his spell, her eyes lost in his and her fingers beginning to melt in the soft, warm pressure of his hands. "All right," she whispered, wondering why this man, this *stranger,* seemed to know everything about her. And what he didn't know, she wanted to divulge to him. . . .

The fire in the den had grown cold, and only a few red embers remained to warm the room. Noah quickly poured them each a drink and took a long swallow of his brandy before kneeling at the fire and adding a wedge of cedar to the glowing coals. As he stood, he dusted the knees of his pants with his palms. Sheila sipped her drink and watched him, noticing the way his oxford cloth shirt stretched over his shoulders as he tended the fire and then straightened. In her mind she could picture the ripple of muscles in his back as he worked.

When Noah turned to face her, she couldn't hide the embarrassed burn of her cheeks, as if she expected him to read the wayward thoughts in her eyes.

"Can I get you anything else?" he asked, nodding toward the glass she held tightly in her hands.

"No . . . nothing . . . this is fine," she whispered.

"Good. Then why don't you sit down and tell me what you intend to do with the insurance settlement, should it be awarded you."

Sheila dropped gratefully into a wing-back chair near the fire and looked Noah squarely in the eyes. "I don't expect you to hand me a blank check for a quarter of a million dollars, you know."

"Good, because I have no intention of doing anything of the kind." Sheila felt butterflies in her stomach. Was he playing with her again? His face was unreadable in the firelight.

"What I do expect, however, is that you and I mutually decide how best to rebuild Cascade Valley, hire a contractor, put the funds in escrow and start work immediately." Her gray eyes challenged him to argue with her logic.

"That, of course, is assuming that the insurance company has paid the settlement to Wilder Investments."

"Hasn't that occurred?" Sheila asked, holding her breath. Certainly by now, over a month since the fire, payment had been made.

"There's a little bit of a hitch as far as Pac-West Insurance Company is concerned."

Sheila felt herself sinking into despair. "The arson?" she guessed.

Shadows of doubt crowded Noah's deep blue eyes. "That's right. Until a culprit is discovered, the insurance company is holding tightly onto its purse strings."

Sheila blanched as the truth struck her. "You think my father had something to do with the fire. . . . You think he deliberately started it, don't you?" she accused in a low voice that threatened to break.

"I didn't say that."

"You *implied* it!"

"Not at all. I'm only pointing out the insurance company's position . . . nothing else."

"Then I'll have to talk to someone at Pac-West," Sheila said. "One of those claims adjusters, or whatever they are."

"I don't think that will do any good."

"Why not?"

His smile didn't touch his eyes. "Because, for one thing, I've already tried that. The insurance company's position is clear."

"Then what can we do?" Sheila asked herself aloud.

Noah hedged for a moment. How much could he tell her? Was she involved in the arson? Had her father been? He rubbed his thumbnail pensively over his lower lip and stared at Sheila. Why did he feel compelled to trust this beguiling woman he didn't know? As he studied the innocent yet sophisticated curve of her cheek, the slender column of her throat and the copper sheen to her thick, chestnut hair, he decided to take a gamble and trust her . . . just a little. His intense eyes scrutinized her reaction, watching for a flicker of doubt or fear to cross her eyes.

"What we can do is investigate the cause of the fire ourselves," he explained thoughtfully.

Her eyebrows furrowed. "How?"

"Wilder Investments has a private investigator on retainer. I've already asked him to look into it."

"Do you think that's wise? Doesn't the insurance company have investigators on its staff?"

"Of course. But this way we can speed things up a little. Unless you're opposed to the idea."

If she heard a steely edge to his words, she ignored it and dug her fingernails into the soft flesh of her palm. "I'll do anything I can to clear my father's name and get the winery going again."

"It's that important to you?" he asked, slightly skeptical. "Why?"

"Cascade Valley was my father's life, his dream, and I'm not allowing anyone or anything to take away his good name or his dreams."

"You want to carry on the Lindstrom tradition, is that it? Follow in your father's footsteps?"

"It's a matter of pride . . . and tradition, I suppose."

"But your father bought his interest in the winery less than twenty years ago. It's not as if Cascade Valley has been a part of your family's history," he observed, testing her reaction. How much of what she was saying was the truth? All of it? Or was she acting out a well-rehearsed scene? If so, she was one helluva convincing actress.

Sheila was instantly wary. The doubts reflected in Noah's eyes lingered and pierced her soul. "What do you mean?"

He shrugged indifferently. "Running the day-to-day operation at the winery is a hard job. You'll have to be an accountant, manager, personnel director, quality control inspector . . . everything to each of your employees. Why would a woman with a small child want to take on all of that responsibility?"

"For the same reasons a man would, I suppose." Her eyes lighted with defiance.

His voice was deathly quiet as he baited her. "A man might be more practical," he suggested, inviting her question.

"How's that?"

"He might consider the alternatives."

"There are none."

"I wouldn't say that. What about the option of selling out your interest in the winery for enough money to support you and your daughter comfortably?"

Sheila tried to keep her voice steady. "I doubt that anyone would be interested in buying. The economy's slow, and as you so aptly pointed out earlier, Cascade Valley has had more than its share of problems."

Noah set his empty glass on the mantel. "Perhaps I can convince the board of directors at Wilder Investments to buy out your share of the winery."

Jonas Fielding's warning echoed in Sheila's ears. Noah was offering to buy out her interest in Cascade, just as the crafty lawyer had predicted. A small part of Sheila seemed to wither and die. In her heart she had expected and hoped for more from him. In the short time she had known him, she had learned to care for him and she didn't want to let the blossoming feelings inside her twist and blacken with deceit. She couldn't be manipulated, not by Ben Wilder, nor by his son. "No," she whispered nearly inaudibly as she lifted her eyes to meet his piercing gaze. "I won't sell."

Noah saw the painful determination in the rigid set of her jaw and the unmasked despair that shadowed her eyes as she silently accused him of a crime he couldn't possibly understand. She had tensed when he had mentioned the possibility of buying out the winery, but it had only seemed logical to him. What did she expect of him . . . more money? But, he hadn't even named a price. "I can assure you, Sheila, that Wilder Investments would be more than generous in the offer."

Her quiet eyes turned to gray ice. "I don't doubt that, but the point is, I'm not interested in selling."

"You haven't even heard the terms."

"It doesn't matter. I won't sell," she repeated coldly. How much like the father he so vehemently denounced was Noah Wilder?

Noah shrugged before draining his glass and approaching the chair in which she was seated. "It doesn't matter to me what you do with your precious winery," he stated evenly as he bent over the chair and placed his hands on each of the silvery velvet arms, imprisoning her against the soft fabric. "I only wanted you to be aware of your options."

His voice was gentle and concerned. Sheila felt as if she had known him all of her life rather than a few short hours, and she wanted to melt into his soft words. "I . . . understand my options," she assured him shakily.

"Do you?" His blue eyes probed deep into hers, further than any man had dared to see. "I wonder." His lips were soft as they pressed gently against her forehead, and Sheila sighed as she closed her eyelids and let her head fall backward into the soft cushions of the chair. A small, nagging voice in her mind argued that she shouldn't give into her passions; she shouldn't let the warmth that he was inviting begin to swell within her. But the sensuous feeling of his lips against her skin, the mysterious blue intensity of his eyes, the awareness in her body that she had presumed to have died in the ashes of her broken marriage, all argued with a twinge of conscience and slowly took over her mind as well as her body.

His hands were strong as they held her chin and tipped her lips to meet his. A sizzling tremor shook her body in response when the kiss began, and she sighed deeply, parting her lips and inviting him quietly to love her. When his passion caught hold of him and he tasted the honeyed warmth of her lips, he gently pushed his tongue against her teeth and entered the moist cavern of her mouth. Her moan of pleasure sent ripples of desire hotly through his blood. His hands slid down the length of her neck and touched the fluttering pulse that was jumping in the feminine hollow of her throat. His thumbs gently outlined the delicate bone structure in slow, swirling circles of sensitivity that gathered and stormed deep within her.

Sheila heard nothing over the resounding beat of her heart fluttering in her chest and thundering in her eardrums. She thought of nothing other than the cascading warmth and desire that were washing over her body in uneven passionate waves. Feelings of longing, yearning, desires that flamed heatedly, flowed through her as Noah kissed her. Involuntarily she reached up and wound her arms around his neck. The groan of satisfaction that rumbled in his throat gave her a deep, primeval pleasure, and when he pulled his lips from hers, she knew a deep disappointment.

He looked longingly into her eyes, asking her silent, unspoken questions that demanded answers she couldn't ignore. How much did he want from her? What could she give—what would he take?

"Sheila, dear Sheila," he murmured against her hair. It was whispered as a plea. She wanted him, ached for him, but remained silent.

His persuasive lips nuzzled against the column of her

throat to linger at the inviting feminine bone structure at its base. His tongue drew lazy circles around Sheila's erratic pulse, and Sheila felt as if her very soul were centered beneath his warm insistent touch. Her fingers entwined in the dark, coffee-colored strands of his hair, and she leaned backward, offering more of her neck . . . more of her being. When his wet tongue touched the center of her pulse, quick-silver flames darted through her veins, and she pushed herself more closely against his body.

His fingers found the buttons on her blouse, and cautiously he opened the top button. As he did so his head lowered, letting his lips caress the gaping space between the two pieces of silken cloth. Sheila moaned against him, asking for more of his gentle touch. He unbuttoned the next pearly fastener, and once more his lips dipped lower, touching her soft, warm flesh. Molten fire streamed through Sheila's veins at his expert touch and in anticipation of his next move. His hot lips seared her skin, and she was not disappointed when his fingers unhinged an even lower button, parting the soft, rose-colored fabric and exposing the gentle swell of her breasts straining achingly against the flimsy barrier of her bra. When his mouth touched the edge of her bra, outlining the lace with the moistness of his tongue, she thought the ache within her would explode. His breath fanned heatedly over her sensitive skin, and she felt her breath come in short gasps. There didn't seem to be enough air in the room to keep her senses from swimming in the whirlpool of passion moving her closer to this man she had barely met and yet known a lifetime. She was drowning in his velvet-soft caresses, losing her breath with each passing instant of his arduous lovemaking. *Take me,* a voice within her wanted to scream, but the words never passed her lips.

She felt the wispy fabric of her blouse as he eased it

gently past her shoulders, kissing her exposed neck and arms.

"Let me love you . . ." he moaned.

Her eyes, shining with a burning passion, yielded to his demands. But still the words froze in her throat.

Softly he pulled her out of the chair and gently eased her onto the carpet with the weight of his body. She felt the soft pile of the Persian rug against the bare skin of her back, and she knew that if she wanted to turn back, it would have to be soon, before all of the long-buried desire became alive again. His hands fitted warmly against her rib cage, outlining each individual bone with one of his strong, masculine fingers. A trembling sigh of submission broke from her lips.

He plunged his head between her breasts, softly imprinting his lips on the firm, white skin in the hollow. Her fingers traveled up his neck to hold his head protectively against her as one of his hands reached up to lovingly cup a breast. She took a quick intake of breath at the command of his touch. His fingers dipped seductively beneath the lace and her nipple tightened, expecting his touch.

"You're beautiful," he moaned before kissing the soft fabric of the bra and teasing the nipple bound within the gossamer confinement of lace and satin. Sheila felt her breast swell with desire and a flood of foreign, long-lost emotions raced through her blood.

Gently Noah lowered the strap over her shoulder, and her breasts spilled from their imprisonment. He groaned as he massaged first one, and then the other. Sheila thought she would melt into the carpet as he kissed his way over the hill of one of the shapely mounds before taking it firmly in his mouth and gently soothing all of the bittersweet torment from her body.

"Let me make love to you, beautiful lady," Noah

whispered, quietly asking her to give in to him. "Let me make you mine," he coaxed.

In response, Sheila felt her body arching upward to meet the weight of him. Whether it was wrong or right, she wanted him as desperately as he wanted her.

"Sheila." His voice was flooded with naked passion. "Come to bed with me." Her only response was to moan softly against him.

Slowly he raised his head to stare into the depths of her desirous gray eyes. The red embers from the fire darkened his masculine features, making them seem harsher, more defined and angular in the blood-red shadows of the dimly lit room. His eyes never left hers, and they smoldered with a blue flame of passion that he was boldly attempting to hold at bay.

"Tell me you want me," he persuaded in a raspy, breathless voice.

Her dark brows pulled together in frustration and confusion. Why was he pulling away from her? Of course she wanted him, needed him, longed to be a part of him. Couldn't he *feel* the desperate intensity of her yearning?

"Tell me!" he again demanded, this time more roughly than before. Her eyes were shadowed; was there a flicker of doubt, a seed of mistrust in their misty gray depths? He had to know.

"What do you want from me?" she asked, trying to control her ragged breathing and erratic heartbeat. Had she misread him? Suddenly she was painfully aware of her partially nude condition, and the fact that he was *asking* rather than *taking* from her.

"I want to know that you feel what I'm feeling!"

"I . . . I don't understand."

His fingers, once gentle, tightened against the soft flesh of her upper arms and held her prisoner against the carpet.

As he studied the elegant lines of her face, his eyes narrowed in suspicion. Never had he been so impulsive, so rash, when it came to a woman. Why did this woman bewitch him so? Why did she make him feel more alive than he had in years? Was it the provocative turn of her chin, the light that danced in her eyes, the fresh scent of her hair? Why was he taken in by her beauty, which was in the same instant innocent and seductive? For the last sixteen years of his life he had cautiously avoided any commitment that might recreate the scene that had scattered his life in chaos. He had been careful, never foolhardy enough to fall for a woman again. But now, as he stared into Sheila's wide, silver-colored eyes, he felt himself slipping into the same black abyss that had thrown his life into disorder long ago. Not since Marilyn had he allowed himself the luxury of becoming enraptured by a woman. And if he had been truthful, none he had met had deeply interested him. But tonight was different. Damn it, he was beginning to care for Sheila Lindstrom, though he knew little of her and couldn't begin to understand her motives. How far could he trust such a lovely, bewitching creature as the woman lying desirously in his arms?

Noah's death-grip on Sheila relaxed. "I want you," he said simply in a hoarse voice that admitted what he had felt from the first moment she had appeared on his doorstep.

"I know." She sighed. She crossed her arms over her breasts, as if to shield herself from the truth. But her eyes met Noah's unwaveringly. "I want you too," she conceded huskily.

The silence in the room was their only barrier, and yet Noah hesitated. "That's not enough," he admitted, wiping the sweat that had begun to bead on his upper lip. "There has to be more."

Sheila shook her head slowly in confusion, and the sweep

of her hair captured red-gold highlights from the flames. Try as she would, she couldn't understand him. What was he saying? Was he rejecting her? Why? What had she done?

Noah witnessed the apprehension and agony in Sheila's eyes and regretted that he was a part of her pain. He wanted to comfort her, to explain the reasons for his reservation, but was unable. How could he expect her to understand that he had loved a woman once in the past and that that love had been callously and bitterly sold to the highest bidder? Was it possible for Sheila to see what Marilyn had done to him when the bitch had put a price on her illegitimate son's head when Sean was born? Was it fair for Noah to burden Sheila with the guilt and agony he had suffered because of his love for his child? No! Though he wanted to trust her, he couldn't tell her about the part of his life he had shoved into a dark, locked corner of his mind. Instead, he took an easier, less painful avenue. "I get the feeling that you think I'm rushing things," he whispered as he pressed a soft kiss against her hair.

She smiled wistfully and blushed. "It's not your fault . . . I could have stopped you . . . I didn't want to."

"Don't blame yourself," he murmured quietly.

In the thickening silence, Sheila could sense Noah struggling with an inner battle, resisting the tide of passion that was pushing against him. She reached for her blouse, hoping to pull it back onto her body so she could leave this house . . . this man before he ignited the passions in her blood and she was once again filled with liquid fire. If possible she hoped to leave the quiet room and seductively intense man with whatever shreds of dignity she could muster.

"Wait!" he commanded as he realized she was preparing to leave. His broad hand grabbed her wrist, and the silken blouse once again fell to the floor.

Sheila felt her temper begin to flare, and the tears that had been threatening to spill burned in her throat. She was tired, and it had been a long, fruitless evening. She had accomplished nothing she had intended to do, and now she wasn't sure if she was capable of working with Ben Wilder or his son. Too many emotions had come and gone with the intimate evening, too many secrets divulged. And yet, despite the growing sense of intimacy she felt with Noah, she knew there were deep, abysmal misconceptions that she couldn't possibly bridge. "What, Noah?" she asked in a tense, raw whisper. "What do you want from me? All night long I've been on the receiving end of conflicting emotions." Her breath was coming in short, uneven gasps. Tears threatened to spill. "One minute you want me and the next . . . you don't. Just let me go home, for God's sake!"

"You're wrong!"

"I doubt that!" She pulled her hand free of the gentle manacle of his grip, scooted silently away from him, snatched up the blouse and quickly stretched her arms through the sleeves. Her fingers fumbled with the buttons, so intent was she on getting out of the house as rapidly as possible . . . away from the magnetism of his eyes . . . away from the charm of his dimpled, slightly off-center smile . . . away from the warm persuasion of his hands. . . .

Noah dragged himself into a sitting position before standing up and leaning against the warm stones of the fireplace. He let his forehead fall into the palm of his hand as he tried to think things out rationally. The entire scene was out of character for him. What the devil had he done, seducing this woman he had barely met? Why was she so responsive to his touch? He knew instinctively that she wasn't the type of woman who fell neatly into a stranger's arms at the drop of a hat, and yet she was here, in his home, warm, inviting, yielding to the gentle coaxing of his caresses. His mouth pulled into a grim frown. How did he let himself get mixed up with her . . . whoever she was? And what were her motives? "Don't go," he said unevenly, turning to face her.

She had managed to get dressed and was putting on her raincoat. She paused for only a second before hiking the coat over her shoulders and unsteadily tying the belt. "I think it would be best."

"I want you to stay, here, tonight, with me."

Sheila took in a long, steadying breath. "I can't."

"Why not?"

"I don't know you well enough."

"But if you don't stay, how will you ever . . . 'know me well enough'?" he countered. He stood away from her, not touching her. It was her mind he wanted, as well as her body.

"I need time. . . ." she whispered, beginning to waver. She had to get out, away from him. Soon, before it was too late.

He took a step toward her. "We're both adults. It's not as if this would be a first for either of us. You have a daughter and I have a son."

She paused, but only slightly. "That doesn't change things. Look, Noah, you know as well as I that I would like to fall into bed and sleep with you. But . . . I just can't. . . ." She blushed in her confusion. "I can't just hop into bed with any man I find attractive. . . . Oh, this is coming out all wrong." She took a deep breath and lifted her eyes to meet his. They were steady and strong, though tears had begun to pool in their gray-blue depths. "What I'm trying to say," she managed bravely, "is that I don't have casual affairs."

"I know that."

"You don't understand. I've never slept with any man, other . . . other than Jeff."

"Your ex-husband," Noah surmised with a tightening of his jaw.

Sheila nodded.

"It doesn't matter," Noah said with a shrug.

"Of course it does. Don't you see? I almost tumbled into bed with you . . . on the first night I'd met you. That's not like me, not at all. . . . I don't even know you."

His scowl lifted, and an amused light danced in his eyes. "I think you know me better than you're willing to admit."

"I'd like to," she conceded.

"But?"

It was her turn to smile. "I'm afraid, I guess."

"That I won't live up to your expectations?"

"Partially."

"What else?"

"That I won't live up to yours."

# Chapter Five

$\mathcal{N}$oah took a step toward her, leaving only inches to separate their bodies. "I doubt that you would ever disappoint me," he whispered. His fingers softly traced the line of her jaw and then continued on a downward path past her neck to rest at the top button of her coat. Easily it slipped through the buttonhole.

Sheila sucked in her breath as Noah took each button in turn. When he reached her belt, he worked on the knot with both of his hands. Sheila felt fires of expectation dance within her while his incredibly blue eyes held hers in a passionate embrace.

The coat parted. Noah's hands moved beneath it and found her breasts. A small sigh came unexpectedly from her lips, and Sheila knew that she wanted Noah more desperately than she had ever wanted any man. It had been so long since she had been held in a man's embrace. As Noah's thumbs began drawing delicious circles against the sheer fabric of her blouse, Sheila told herself that he was different from Jeff. He wouldn't hurt her. He *cared*.

The soft coaxing of Noah's fingertips made Sheila weak with longing. She leaned against him, tilted her head and parted her lips in silent invitation. Warm lips claimed hers and Noah's arms encircled her, crushing her against him. His tongue probed into her mouth to find its mate and touch her more intimately. Sheila wanted more of this mysterious man.

When he guided her to the floor, it was her hands that parted his shirt and touched the tense, hard muscles of his chest. It was her lips that kissed his eyes as he undressed her. She felt the warmth of his hands as each article of her clothing was silently removed.

It felt so good to touch him. Her fingers traced the outline of each of his muscles on his back and crept seductively down the length of his spine. When her fingertips touched the waistband of his pants, she hesitated. How much would he expect from her—how much did he want?

"Undress me," he persuaded, his eyes closing and his breath becoming shallow. "Please, Sheila, undress me."

She couldn't resist. He groaned as she unclasped the belt and gently pushed his pants over his hips. She stopped when she encountered his briefs.

"Take them off," he commanded, guiding her hand to the elastic band of his shorts. She paused, and he read the uncertainty in her eyes. He smiled wickedly to himself.

Slowly his hands moved over her breasts, massaging each white globe until the rosy tip hardened with desire. He teased her with the soft, whispering play of his fingers against her skin. "You're exquisite," he whispered as his head bent and his tongue touched the tip of her breast, leaving a moist droplet of dew on the nipple.

Sheila moaned in pleasure as the cold air touched the wet nipple, and she once again craved the sweet pressure of his mouth against her skin. As if to comply, he again lowered his head and ran his tongue over the soft hill of her breasts, lingering only long enough over her nipples to warm and then leave them.

Sheila felt a hot, molten coil begin to unwind within her and race like liquid fire through her veins. His kisses touched her breasts and then lowered to caress the soft skin of her abdomen. Lazily his tongue rimmed her navel, and Sheila felt her hips shift upward, pressing against his chest, demanding more from him.

"Please," she whispered hoarsely.

Noah was trying to control himself, to give as well as get pleasure. He was vainly fighting a losing battle with his passion. The last thing he wanted to do was come on like some horny college kid. Already, though he couldn't explain it, Sheila was important to him, and he wanted to please her. It had been difficult, but he had restrained himself to the point where he thought he would burst from the aching frustration in his loins.

Sheila's eyes reached for his, begging him to end her torture and take her. He could resist no longer. He slipped out of his shorts and lay beside her. The length of his body was pressed against hers, and his need for her was unhidden.

"I want to love you, Sheila," he whispered into her ear, while his hands cupped and stroked her breast.

"Yes."

"I want to make love to you and never stop. . . ."

She sighed her willingness. She could feel his breath on the back of her neck and the musky smell of brandy mingled with the scent of burning moss. Everything about the night seemed so right. She moved her legs and parted his. A strong, masculine hand pressed against her abdomen and forced her more intimately against him. Her body seemed to mold against his. It was as if she could feel each part of him, and she had to have more.

His hands moved leisurely up and down the length of her body, touching her breasts softly with his fingertips and then pressing a moist palm to her inner thighs with rough, demanding pressure. Involuntarily her legs parted, and she felt the heated moisture of his lips as he kissed each vertebra of her spine. Sharp, heated needles of desire pierced her when at last he gently rolled her onto her back and positioned himself above her.

Beads of sweat moistened his upper lip and forehead. His dark brow was furrowed, as if he were fighting an inner turmoil. The fireglow gave his skin a burnished tint and his blue eyes had deepened to inky black. In a ragged breath, with more control than he had thought possible, he whispered, ''Sheila, are you sure that this is what you want?'' He grimaced, as if in pain, against a possible rejection.

She wrapped her arms around his chest and pulled him down upon her. Her breasts flattened with the weight of his torso. ''I'm sure,'' she returned, caught up in the raw passion of the night.

With a growl of satisfaction he parted her legs with his knees and came to her to find that she was as ready as he. Never had he felt so desperate with need of a woman—not just any woman, but *this* woman with the mysterious gray eyes and the softly curving, voluptuous mouth. This woman with the vibrant chestnut hair that caught the reflection of the fireglow and framed an intelligent, evenly featured face. As he moved with her, attempting to withhold the violent burst of energy within him, he found himself falling more desperately under her bewitching spell. What was happening to him?

Sheila moaned beneath him, and the tension mounting steadily within him threatened to explode. He didn't care who she was, he had to have her. With a sudden rush of heat, he ignited into a flame that consumed the both of them. Sheila's answering shudder told him that she, too, had felt the ultimate consummation.

He lay upon her, continuing to kiss her cheeks while running his fingers through her hair. She looked at him through eyes still shining in afterglow. "Oh, Noah," she sighed contentedly.

"Shhh. . . ." He placed his finger to her lips to quiet her and reached behind him to pull a knitted afghan off the couch. Still holding her in his arms, he wrapped the soft blanket over their bodies. "Don't say anything," he whispered quietly.

Sheila wanted to stay with him. It was so warm and comfortable in the shelter of his arms. But as the afterglow faded and the reality of what she had done hit her, she was horrified. A deep crimson flush climbed steadily up her throat. What was she doing lying naked with a man she had only met a few hours earlier? What had happened to her common sense? It was true that Noah had surprised her with his commanding masculinity and seductive blue eyes, but that was no excuse for making love to him. It wasn't that she hadn't enjoyed it—quite the opposite. The passion that had risen in her was wilder than she had ever imagined, and even now she could feel her body stirring with traitorous longings at the nearness of this enigmatic man. She tried to loosen herself from the strength of his embrace.

"What are you doing?" he asked.

"I think I'd better leave."

"Why?"

"This is all wrong," she began, trying to slide away from him. His fingers clamped over her shoulders.

"This could *never* be *wrong*." The afghan slipped, exposing one swollen breast. He kissed the soft, ripe mound.

Sheila trembled at his touch. "Don't," she pleaded.

"Why not?" His rich voice had taken on a rough tone.

"I've got to go."

"Don't leave."

She pushed her palms against his chest. "Noah . . . please. . . ."

"Please what?"

"Please let me go."

"Later."

"Now!" Her voice quivered, and she felt tears of frustration burning in her throat. She longed to stay with him, feel his weight upon her, fall victim to his lovemaking. But she couldn't.

"We have the rest of the night."

"No . . . no, we don't," she said waveringly. Her gray eyes lifted to his and begged him to understand.

Slowly he released her and ran his fingers through his unruly hair. "What is this, some latent Victorian morality?"

"Of course not."

"Then I don't understand."

"Neither do I, not really." She pulled the afghan over the exposed breast, feeling a little less vulnerable under the soft covering.

"Sheila." His finger reached out and carefully raised her chin in so she could meet his confused gaze. "We're in the nineteen eighties."

"I know."

"But?"

"I just need time, that's all," she blurted out. How could she possibly explain her confused jumble of emotions. He was so close. She had only to stretch her hand and touch him to reignite the fires of desire. She shuddered and reached for her clothes.

"How much time?"

"I don't know . . . I don't understand any of this."

"Don't try."

Sheila closed her eyes and took a deep breath, hoping to clear her mind. "Look, Noah. I don't even know you, and I'm really not sure that I *want* to know you this well."

"Why not?" he persisted.

She struggled into her blouse. "You and I, whether we like it or not, are business partners."

"Don't give me any of that sanctimonious and over-used line about not mixing business and pleasure."

"I don't think of sex as pleasure!"

An interested black eyebrow cocked mockingly. "You're not going to try and convince me that you didn't enjoy yourself."

"No."

"Good, because I wouldn't believe you. Now, what's this all about?"

"When I said that I don't consider sex to be pleasurable, I meant *merely* pleasurable. Of course I enjoyed making love with you; I'd be a fool to try and deny it. The point is, I don't go in for 'casual sex' for the sake of pleasure . . . or any other reason."

"And you think that I do?"

"I don't know."

"Sure you do," he replied seductively. "I'm willing to bet that you know more about me than you're admitting."

"That's no excuse for hopping into bed with you."

"You don't need an excuse, Sheila. Just stay with me tonight. Do it because you want to."

"I can't." She had managed to pull on all of her clothes

and stand upright. Noah didn't move. He sat before the fire, his chin resting on his knees, but his eyes never let go of hers.

"Do whatever it is that you think you must," he whispered.

Sheila swallowed a lump that had been forming in her throat. She pulled on her raincoat and wondered if she was making the biggest mistake of her life. "Good-bye, Noah," she murmured. "I'll . . . I'll talk to you later. . . ." She ran out of the house before he could answer and before she could change her mind.

Noah waited and listened to the sounds of her leaving. The front door closed, and a car engine coughed before catching and fading into the night. When he realized that Sheila wasn't coming back, he straightened and pulled on his pants. He was more disturbed by his reaction to her than anything else. How could she have so easily gotten under his skin? Had all of the pressures of the office made him such an easy prey to a beautiful woman? There had to be more to it than met the eye. Why had she so easily responded to his touch? What the hell did she want from him—certainly more than a quick one-night stand. Or did she? He had thought that she had been hinting that she wanted out of the partnership with Wilder Investments. But when he had suggested buying her out, she had seemed indignant, as if she had already anticipated his offer and was more than ready to discard it before hearing the exact price.

Noah's clear blue eyes clouded with suspicion. Without thinking, he reached for the brandy bottle and poured himself a drink. He took a long swallow before swirling the amber liquor in the glass and staring into the glowing coals. What was Sheila Lindstrom's game?

Disregarding the fact that it was after two in the morning, Noah walked over to the desk and picked up the telephone.

He looked up a number and with only a second's hesitation dialed it. Several moments and nine rings later a groggy voice mumbled an indistinct greeting.

"Simmons?" Noah questioned curtly. "This is Noah Wilder."

There was a weighty pause on the other end of the line. Noah could imagine the look of astonishment crossing the detective's boyish face. "Something I can do for you?" Simmons asked cautiously. He hadn't dealt much with Ben Wilder's son, especially not in the middle of the night. Something was up.

"I want a report on the Cascade Valley Winery fire."

"I'm working on it."

Noah interrupted. "Then it's not complete?" he asked sternly.

"Not quite."

"Why not?"

The wheels in Simmons's mind began to turn. Wilder was agitated and angry. Why? "It's taken a little longer than expected."

"I need it now," Noah rejoined. His words were tainted with mistrust; Anthony Simmons could feel the suspicion that hung on the telephone line.

"I can have a preliminary report on your desk tomorrow afternoon," he suggested smoothly.

"And the final?"

"That will take a little longer."

"How much longer?"

"A week or two I'd guess," Simmons responded evasively.

"I can't wait that long! What's the hang-up?" Noah inquired. He waited for the slick excuses, but they didn't come.

"I'd like some time to check out the winery myself. You

know, look for a few skeletons hanging in some locked closets. . . ."

Noah debated. He didn't like the thought of Anthony Simmons being in such close proximity to Sheila. He had never completely trusted his father's private detective. However, he saw no other recourse; Noah needed information—and fast. Anthony Simmons could get it for him. "All right," Noah heard himself saying, "go to the winery and see what you can find out. Tell the manager, her name is Sheila Lindstrom, that you work for Wilder Investments and that you're trying to speed up the arson investigation in order to get the insurance money."

Simmons was hastily scratching notes on a small white pad on the nightstand. It had been some time since he had pocketed expense money from Wilder Investments and the thought of it warmed his blood. "Is there anything special you want on this Lindstrom woman?" he asked routinely. The moment of hesitation in Noah's response caught his attention. He had been trained to read people, be it in person, from a distance or over the phone. The slight hesitation in Noah's response triggered Simmons's suspicious instincts. There was more here than met the eye.

"Yes, of course," Noah said with more determination than he felt. "Anything you might find out about Miss Lindstrom or any of the employees could be useful."

"Right," Simmons agreed, making a special note to himself about the manager of the winery. He hadn't missed the interest in Noah's voice.

"Then I'll expect a full report in a week."

"You'll have it." With his final words Anthony Simmons disconnected the call and smiled wickedly to himself. For the first time in quite a few years he smelled money—lots of money.

When Noah hung up the telephone, he had an uneasy

feeling in the pit of his stomach. Simmons had been too accommodating, too confidently obliging; so unlike the Anthony Simmons Noah had dealt with in the past. His hand hesitated over the receiver as he thought fleetingly of redialing Simmons's number and pulling him off the case. Why did he feel that his final directive to Simmons was somehow dangerous?

Noah shook his head, walked away from the desk and finished his drink in one long swallow. He was beginning to get paranoid. Ever since he had laid eyes on Sheila Lindstrom, he had been acting irrationally. Whether she had intended it or not, Sheila Lindstrom was beginning to unbalance him. The corners of Noah's mouth tightened, and after forcing all thoughts of the intimate evening aside, he walked out of the den and began to mount the stairs. There wasn't much of the night left, but he had to try and get some rest; tomorrow promised to be another battle with his son. Also, Anthony Simmons had promised the preliminary report on the fire. For some reason that Noah couldn't quite name, he felt an impending sense of dread.

Sheila drove as if the devil himself were on her tail. She had checked out of the Seattle hotel without really understanding her motives. All she knew was that she had to get away from this city, the city Noah Wilder called home. The feelings he had stirred in her had blossomed so naturally in the warm embrace of his arms. But now, as she drove through the pelting rain, a cold despair began to settle over her. Why had she fallen such an easy victim to Noah's charm? Why did she still taste the lingering flavor of brandy on her lips where he had kissed her? Unconsciously her tongue rimmed her lips, and she could almost feel the power of his impassioned kiss.

Wrapped in her clouded thoughts, Sheila took the next

corner too quickly. The tires skidded on the wet pavement and the car swung into the oncoming lane. Severe head-lights bore down upon her, and she was forced to swerve back onto her side of the road. By the time the oncoming car had managed to get around her, Sheila's heart was hammer-ing in her ears. She had never been a careless driver, but tonight she couldn't seem to concentrate on the rain-washed highway winding through the dark mountains. "Dear God," she whispered in prayer as she clutched the steering wheel more tightly and realized that her palms were damp. Was it from the near collision—or the man who had played havoc with her senses?

Why did she feel as if she were walking a thin line with Noah? It was dangerous to become involved with anyone working for Wilder Investments. Jonas Fielding's fatherly voice echoed in her mind, reissuing the warning he had given Sheila in his office: "I wouldn't trust Ben Wilder as far as I could throw him. . . . *I'd hate to see you fleeced by him or that son of his.*" No, she argued with herself, Noah wouldn't cheat me . . . he couldn't! But hadn't he offered to buy out her portion of the winery, just as Jonas Fielding had warned?

The headache that had been threatening all day began to throb at the base of her skull. She attempted to concentrate on the thin white line in the center of the road, and managed to slow the pace of the car to a safer speed. It had been a long, strained day and Sheila was dog-tired by the time she crossed the Cascades.

Dawn was beginning to cast irregular purple shadows over the valley as Sheila drove down the final hills surrounding the small town of Devin. Located west of Yakima, it was hardly more than a fork in the road. Originally just a general store, the small hamlet had grown slowly and taken on the family name of the owners of the combined hardware, grocery and sporting goods store. That was years in the past, and by the 1980s, several shops lined the two streets that intersected near the original Devin store. Buildings, some eighty years old, complete with false wood facades, stood next to more recent post-war concrete structures. It wasn't a particularly beautiful town, but it was a friendly, comfortable place to live and a welcome sight to Sheila's weary eyes. She had only left Devin yesterday, but it seemed like a lifetime.

The outskirts of the town were beautifully tended farmlands. Softly rolling hills covered in sweet-smelling new hay gave the air a fresh, wholesome scent. Sheila rolled down the window of the car and let the wind stream past her face to revive her. Her dark hair billowed behind her, and despite the weariness of her bones, Sheila was forced to smile. With the rising sun, her problems seemed to shrink and fade.

The compact wagon rounded a final bend in the road before starting the slow, steady climb up the hill to the winery. From the gates the winery looked as proudly welcoming as ever. The main building was the most prominent, and could be seen from the drive. It had been designed with a distinctly European flair. French château architecture, two-storied and elegantly grand, was complete with stucco walls painted a light dove gray. Narrow-paned windows, graced with French blue shutters, were the full two stories in height, and the broad double doors gleamed in the early morning sunshine. With the stately, snow-laden Cascade Mountains as a backdrop, the parklike grounds of the winery gave the impression of wealth and sedate charm.

If only the truth were known, Sheila thought wryly to herself as she unlocked the rear door of the wagon and extricated her suitcase. It was fortunate, for appearance's sake, that the portion of the winery destroyed by the fire wasn't visible from the road. Sheila placed her luggage on the front porch and strolled lazily past the rose garden to the rear of the main buildings. She picked a single peach-colored blossom and held it to her nose. How long ago had her father planted this particular rose bush? One year? Fifteen? She couldn't remember. Each spring he had planted another variety to add to the abundance of the garden.

Sheila looked at the imposing buildings and meticulously tended grounds that supported the winery. All of the years Oliver Lindstrom had put into the operation of Cascade Valley seemed to slowly pass through her thoughts. He had worked so hard to make the Cascade Valley label nationally known and recognized. Sheila rubbed her palm over her forehead, and her shoulders slumped with a renewed sense of grief for her father. The guilt she bore took hold of her as she silently vowed to find a way for Cascade Valley once again to begin producing the finest wines in the Northwest. She couldn't hide from the fact that it was her fault her father had taken out the loans from Ben Wilder in the first place. If she hadn't needed money after her divorce from Jeff, maybe Oliver Lindstrom wouldn't have needed to borrow the money, maybe he wouldn't have felt so trapped, *maybe he would be alive today.*

Don't think that way, she chastised herself. She again smelled the brilliant peach-hued blossom and tried to shake her thoughts back to a viable solution to her problem. It was impossible; her thoughts were too dark and black, and for a fleeting moment she wondered if perhaps her father did start the fire.

She didn't answer the question and hurried to the back of the buildings. The charred west wing of the manor house, a black skeleton of sagging timbers, was still roped off. A garish sign with bold red letters was nailed to one of the surrounding pine trees. It stated, quite unequivocally, that there was no trespassing allowed, by order of the Sheriff's department for the county. *Suspected Crime Area* the sign pronounced boldly, and Sheila's heart cringed at the meaning of the words. The sign, an intruder on her father's personal life, increased the fires of determination burning within Sheila's heart. No one, including Noah Wilder, would take away her father's dream; not if she could help it.

At the thought of Noah, Sheila felt suddenly empty and hollow. As crazy as it sounded, she felt she had left part of herself in the warm den of the stone mansion high on the shores of Lake Washington. The vague thought that she might be falling in love with Noah Wilder flitted through her mind, but she resolutely pushed it away. What she felt for the man was sexual attraction, physical chemistry, that was all. Sheila was too much of a realist to consider falling in "love at first sight." The Cinderella story just never came true. The one love she had experienced had turned sour, and her marriage had become a dismal, humiliating sham. That feeling of love she had foolishly convinced herself she shared with Jeff Coleridge had taken months to grow. But, fortunately, not so long to die, she added ironically to herself.

She kicked a small stone on the flagstone path that led from the garden. There was no way she could be falling in love with Noah Wilder. It was ludicrous even to consider another side to the coin. She had met him only hours earlier in particularly seductive surroundings. She knew virtually nothing about him, except that he was perhaps the most magnetically powerful man she had ever laid eyes on. But what was it that made him tick? Yes, he was mysterious and alluring, but to try and call purely sexual attraction love was sheer folly; at least in Sheila's pragmatic estimation. Too many women fell into that vicious trap.

Sheila knew herself well enough to understand her guilt. Because of her uncharacteristic display of passion in the early hours of the morning, her subconscious was trying to soothe her by substituting love for lust. But Sheila wouldn't allow herself that leisure. To consider what had happened in the Wilder mansion an act of love was pure fantasy, and the easy way out—merely an appropriate, if false, excuse.

Sheila sighed to herself as she closed the garden gate. The problem was that there was no way she could avoid Noah Wilder or his enigmatic blue eyes. How could she hope to reopen the winery without his help? Unless his father came back to Seattle to take command of Wilder Investments, she was stuck with Noah. Just at the thought of seeing him again, her pulse began to race. Realistically she attempted to find an alternate solution to her problem, but found no way out of the inevitable conclusion: No one would lend her enough money to buy out Ben Wilder's interest in Cascade Valley. And even if she were lucky enough to get another mortgage on the property, Wilder Investments was unlikely to sell.

Before opening the back door to the undamaged portion of the château, she took one final look at the blackened west wing. "There's got to be a way to save it," she muttered to herself before hurrying inside the house and letting the screen door slam behind her.

# Chapter Six

The following Tuesday evening Sheila decided once again to attempt to assess the damage to the west wing of the manor building and try and come up with a temporary solution to the disrepair. She had spent the entire weekend and the last two evenings cleaning up that portion of the rubble that was not considered evidence in the ongoing police investigation. And yet, for all her efforts, the entire west wing was in shambles.

The late afternoon sun cast dark shadows on the charred walls of the château that had housed the commercial end of the winery. The living quarters, attached by a covered portico, hadn't been severly damaged. Sheila looked at the building apprehensively. What would it take to save it? Though parts of the grayish stucco walls had blackened, the elegance of the architecture remained. Several panes from the narrow windows had shattered from the intensity of the heat, and a couple of the cobalt-blue shutters hung at precarious angles from their original placement adorning the windows. But the walls of the building had remained intact, and even the gently sloping roof hadn't sustained too much damage.

Sheila sighed deeply to herself. Daylight was fading, she had final term papers to grade, and she had to get Emily into bed. Right now she couldn't spend any more time working on the winery.

"Emily," she called in the direction of the duck pond, "come on, let's get ready for bed."

Emily emerged from a stand of trees near the edge of the pond and reluctantly obeyed her mother. When she was within shouting distance, she began to voice her disapproval. "Already? It's not even nine o'clock."

"I didn't say you had to go to bed; I asked you to get ready," Sheila pointed out.

Emily's large green eyes brightened. "Then I can stay up?"

Sheila smiled. "For a little while. Right now, why don't you take a shower and I'll fix us some popcorn."

"Let's watch the movie," Emily suggested.

"I don't think so—not tonight. You still have school for another week."

"But next week, when school's out, I can stay up and watch the movie?"

"Why not?" Sheila agreed, fondly rumpling Emily's dark auburn curls.

"Great." Emily ran up the steps and flew through the front door leaving Sheila to wish that she had only half the energy of her eight-year-old daughter. From the exhausting work of the past few days, every muscle in Sheila's body rebelled. She hadn't realized what a soft job she had; teaching accounting to college students didn't entail much physical exercise.

Sounds of running water greeted her when she finally got inside the house. She and Emily were 'temporarily' camping out in the lower level of the house. It was the least damaged. Sheila wondered how long this temporary condition would continue. She had used some of her small savings to have the electricity reconnected and the plumbing repaired, but as to the rest of the house, she was still waiting for the insurance settlement. Fortunately she did have a few dollars left in the savings account, but she was steadfastly holding on to them. After paying the expenses of Oliver's funeral she had less than a thousand dollars in the bank and hoped to stretch it as far as possible. With the coming of summer, she was out of a job until school started in the fall.

The interior of the château had suffered from the fire. As Sheila walked through what had been the living room toward the kitchen, she tried to ignore the smoke-laden lace draperies and the fragile linen wallpaper that had been water stained. Several of the broken windows were now boarded, and a fine, gritty layer of ash still covered all of the elegant European antiques and the expensive burgundy carpet. No amount of vacuuming seemed to lift the soot from the interior of the manor.

The kitchen was in better shape. Sheila had taken the time to scrub it down with disinfectant before painting all of the walls. Even the countertop had been repaired, as the heat of the blaze had loosened the glue and caused it to buckle. The hot corn was just beginning to pop when Emily hurried into the kitchen. She was still soaked and attempting to put her wet arms and legs through the appropriate holes in her pajamas.

"It's easier if you dry yourself off first," Sheila reminded her daughter.

"Aw . . . Mom . . ." Emily's head poked through the soft flannel material, and her face, still rosy from the warm jets of shower spray, broke into a smile. "It's just about ready, isn't it?" she asked, running over to the popping corn.

"In a minute."

Emily stood on first one foot and then the other, eyeballing the kernels as they exploded in the hot-air popper.

"What were you doing down at the duck pond for so long?" Sheila asked.

"Talking. . . . I think it's done now."

Sheila looked up from the pan of butter on the stove. "Talking? To whom? Did Joey come over?"

"Naw . . . Joey couldn't come over . . . too much homework. Come on; let's put the butter on the popcorn."

Sheila's dark brows came together. "If it wasn't Joey, who were you talking to?"

Emily shrugged. "A man."

"A man? What man? Was it Joey's dad?" Sheila studied her young daughter intently, but Emily didn't seem to notice. She was too engrossed in fixing a bowl of her favorite snack.

"If it was Joey's dad, I would have told you. . . . It was just some guy."

Sheila could feel her face drain of color. "What guy?"

"Don't know his name." Emily replied with all the matter-of-factness of a confident eight-year-old.

Sheila attempted to sound calm, but the thought of a stranger talking to her young daughter made her quiver inside. "Surely it was someone you know . . . maybe someone you met in town. . . ."

Emily shook her dark, wet curls. "Nope." She began to attack the bowl of popcorn without another thought to the stranger.

Sheila didn't want to frighten her daughter. Emily had

grown up in a small, Northwest town where there were few strangers and nearly everyone knew each other on a first-name basis. "What did the man want to talk about?" she asked, pretending interest in the dishes.

"Oh, you know, all about the fire . . . the same old thing."

Sheila felt herself relax. "Oh, so a deputy from the sheriff's department came by. . . . He should have stopped at the house first."

"Wasn't a policeman or a deputy."

Once again Sheila's nerves tightened. She turned from the sink and sat in a chair opposite Emily's. "The man was a complete stranger, right?"

"Um-hum."

"Not a policeman?"

"I told you that already!"

"But maybe he was a detective? They don't always wear uniforms."

Emily sighed, and with a concern greater than her few years, looked at her mother. "Is something wrong?"

"Probably not . . . I just don't like the idea of you talking to strangers. From now on you stick a little closer to the house."

"I don't think he would hurt me . . . if that's what you're afraid of."

"You don't know that."

"But I like to go down to the duck pond."

"I know you do, sweetheart," Sheila said with more confidence than she actually felt, "but from now on I want to go with you."

"You're afraid of something, aren't you?" Emily charged, her innocent green eyes searching her mother's worried face.

"Not really," Sheila lied. It wouldn't help matters to

scare Emily, but the child had to learn to be more cautious. "But sometimes . . . it's better not to talk to strangers. You know that, don't you? From now on, if you see anyone you don't know hanging around, you come and tell me, before you talk to them, okay? No one should be on the property while the winery's shut down, so if someone comes, I want to know it immediately. Fair enough?"

"I guess so."

"Then you do understand why I don't want you to wander off too far from the house when you're alone?"

Emily nodded gravely. Sheila's message had gotten through.

"Good!" Sheila said, attempting to display a light-hearted enthusiasm she didn't feel. "We'll go feed the ducks together tomorrow. It will be lots of fun." Somehow she managed a confident smile for her daughter.

Emily continued to nibble at the popcorn while leafing through a math textbook. Sheila got up to clear the dinner dishes and turned on the radio to cover the sudden silence. Nightfall was imminent, and the lengthening shadows made Sheila nervous. She had always loved warm summer nights in the foothills of the Cascades, but tonight was different. She felt alone and vulnerable. The nearest house was over a mile away, and for the first time in her life the remote location of the winery put her on edge. A stranger had been lurking on the property, talking to her child. Why? Who was the man and what did he want from Emily? Information on the fire? Unlikely. Sheila let her gaze wander out the window and she squinted into the dusky twilight. She attempted to tell herself that the man was probably just an interested tourist who wondered why the daily tours of the winery had been suspended. But if that were so, certainly he would have come up to the main building. The entire incident put Sheila's nerves on edge.

That night, before going to her room, Sheila checked the bolts on all of the doors and windows of the house. When she finally got to bed, even though her tired body ached for sleep, it didn't come. Instead she found herself staring at the luminous dial of the clock-radio and listening to the soft sounds of the early summer night. Everything sounded the same. Why then was she so nervous and tense?

Lack of sleep from the previous night made Wednesday unusually tedious. The lengthy hours of teaching distracted students coupled with the forty-five minute drive from the community college seemed more tiresome than it usually was. Thank goodness there were only a few final days of the school year left. Next week was finals week, and after that Sheila could concentrate on the reopening of the winery. By the end of the summer the harvest season would be upon her.

Emily stayed with a friend after school. Since Oliver Lindstrom's death, Sheila hadn't allowed her daughter to stay at home after school because Emily would be alone. In light of the events the day before with the stranger, Sheila was more grateful than ever that she could trust Emily with Carol Dunbar, the mother of Emily's best friend, Joey. Emily was waiting for her when Sheila arrived, and after a quick stop at the market, mother and daughter finally headed home.

Sheila had contemplated calling the police about the trespasser, but had decided against it. No harm had been done, and if the man was still hanging around, Sheila hadn't seen any evidence of him. When he turned up again, then Sheila would alert the authorities, but right now, due to the unsolved arson and the suspicion cast upon her father, the last thing Sheila wanted to do was talk to someone from the local sheriff's department.

An unfamiliar car was sitting in the driveway near the house when Sheila and Emily arrived home. Sheila's thoughts turned back to the stranger and she felt her heart leap to her throat. Trying to appear calmer than she felt, she braked the small wagon to a halt near the garage and tried to pull together a portion of her poise. Who was he?

"That's the man I was talking to yesterday, Mom. You know, down at the duck pond." Emily was openly staring at the individual who was sitting, slump-shouldered, behind the wheel of an old Chevrolet.

The stranger had been waiting. At the sound of the approaching vehicle he had turned in his seat, pushed back the brim of his felt hat and blown out a final stream of smoke from his cigarette. He tossed the hat onto the front seat as he pulled himself out of the car.

"Wait here," Sheila told Emily.

"Why?"

"Just for a minute. Stay in the car." The authoritative ring in Sheila's voice gave Emily no room for argument. Sheila grabbed her purse and hurried from the car, intent on meeting the man out of earshot of her young daughter. Her gray eyes were cool as she focused on the rather average-looking, slightly built visitor.

"Ms. Lindstrom?" the man in the worn suit-coat asked. He strode boldly up to her and extended his hand.

Sheila nodded as she accepted the brief handshake. "I'm Sheila Lindstrom."

"Anthony Simmons," he retorted with a shadowy grin. He acted as if the name might mean something to her.

"Is there something I can do for you?" she asked calmly. The man looked trustworthy enough, but still she was jittery. It was his eyes, light brown and deepset over a nose that had obviously once been broken; they didn't quite meet her steady gaze. Instead, he seemed to be studying the angle of her face.

"I hope so," he replied, shifting from one foot to the other. His face broke slowly into a well-practiced and slightly uneven smile. "I work with Noah Wilder."

Sheila couldn't keep her heart from skipping a beat at the sound of Noah's name. This man standing before her was a friend of Noah's? Sheila doubted it.

"Mr. Wilder sent you?" she asked with a dubious and reserved smile.

"That's right. He wants me to look into that fire you had here a while back." Reading the skepticism on Sheila's even features, Simmons reached into his back pocket, extracted a wallet and withdrew a white card. He offered it to Sheila. Along with his name the card was inscribed with the nationally known logo for Wilder Investments.

Sheila kept the card and began to relax. "What is it exactly you're to do here?"

Simmons shrugged as if his job were entirely routine. "Mr. Wilder is hoping that I can speed up the investigation of the arson, help clear up the whole mess, in order for the insurance company to pay off on the policy. Didn't he tell you that I was coming?"

Sheila hedged. "He did mention that someone might be coming." Anthony Simmons was not what Sheila had expected.

The investigator's smile widened. "Then we're all set."

"For what?"

"Well, first I thought I'd check over the burned wing of the winery. Didn't the fire start in the aging room?"

"According to the fire department."

"I thought so. After I'm through poking around the burned building—"

"Are you sure you should go in there? What about the warnings posted by the sheriff's department?"

"I've taken care of that."

Sheila couldn't help but be dubious. The deputy had been adamant about the restraining orders surrounding the winery. "You have?"

"Sure. Don't worry about it. After I'm done with the building I'd like to take a look at Oliver Lindstrom's books," Simmons replied.

"Wilder Investments has copies of the winery's records. Didn't Mr. Wilder give them to you?" Sheila was puzzled.

Simmons nodded curtly. "I'm not talking about Cascade Valley. I need your father's *personal* records."

"Why?"

Simmons let out an exasperated breath. He hadn't expected any argument from this Lindstrom woman. Usually the crisp white card indicating that he worked for Wilder Investments gained him entrance to the most securely locked doors. But this lady was different. Even her sophisticated looks had surprised Anthony. He tried a different tactic with her. "Look, Ms. Lindstrom, it's no skin off my nose one way or the other. I just thought that your father's books might speed the investigation." He saw a look of doubt cross her gray eyes, and he pressed his point home. "Besides which, those records might possibly clear your dad's name."

"But the police have checked—"

"They might have missed something. It's my *job* to find what the police and the insurance company might have missed."

"I don't know . . ." But Anthony Simmons could tell that she would give him anything he wanted. He had found her weakness; he had read it in her startled eyes when he had mentioned her father's reputation.

"It's up to you," he called over his shoulder as he headed for the fire-damaged wing.

Sheila hurried back to the car and found an impatient child fuming in the front seat. "Well?" Emily queried.

"He's an investigator, sent by grandpa's business partners."

"Then it's okay if I talk to him?"

Sheila hesitated. Something about Anthony Simmons bothered her. "I guess so, but, try to stay out of his way."

"Why?"

"Because he's busy, honey. He's here to do a job and you might bother him. If he wants to talk to you again, I'm sure that he'll come up to the house."

Partially placated, Emily scrambled out of the car. "Then I can play by the duck pond again?" she asked.

Sheila managed a smile for the eager young face that was cocked upward at her. "Sure you can, dumpling, but not now. Let's wait until after dinner and I'll go down with you."

For the next few days it seemed to Sheila as if Anthony Simmons was forever underfoot. She couldn't turn around without running into him and having to answer questions that seemed to have little to do with his investigation of the fire. She tried to tell herself that he was just doing a thorough job, for which she should be grateful, but she couldn't help but feel that there was more than "leaving no stone unturned" to Anthony Simmons's overly zealous pursuit of the truth. Maybe that was what kept nagging at the back of Sheila's mind; she didn't really believe that Simmons was looking for the truth. He seemed to her to be more interested in finding a scapegoat for the fire. The pointed way he asked the questions, the quickly raised brown eyebrows, and his cynical remarks didn't live up to the professionalism Sheila had expected. The fact that

Simmons had been sent by Noah himself bothered Sheila even more than the short man's unprofessional attitude.

Simmons left within the week, and Sheila breathed a long sigh of relief. He hadn't explained what he had pieced together, and Sheila hadn't asked. She would rather hear Simmons's theories from Noah or even Ben Wilder. The less she had to do with a cockroach like Simmons, the better.

She waited to hear from Noah and was disappointed. Another week passed and school was out for the summer. She had turned in the final grades to the school administration and both she and Emily were home, able to spend a few weeks alone together until Emily left to spend four weeks with her father. In the custody arrangement, Jeff was allowed partial custody of his child. If he had wanted to see Emily more frequently, Sheila wouldn't have objected; after all, Emily *was* his only child. However, the four weeks he took Emily in the summer were generally more than he could stand. Jeff Coleridge wasn't cut out to be a father—or a husband.

Every summer, because of Emily, Sheila was forced to think about her ex-husband and the four years of her marriage. Fortunately, as time had worn on, the pain she had suffered at Jeff's hands diminished, and this year, because of the fire, Sheila had other thoughts to occupy her mind. This year Cascade Valley and its reopening were her main concern.

Sheila saw the situation concerning the winery: the clock was ticking and time was running out. With the passing of each successive day, she became more anxious about the business. Surely Noah had Simmons's report, and certainly the insurance company had come to some sort of settlement. Why hadn't she been notified? If only Sheila knew where she stood with Wilder Investments and the insurance company, she could begin to make plans for the fall harvest. As it was, her hands were tied. The fate of Cascade Valley Winery rested in the palms of Noah Wilder, and he hadn't had the decency to call.

The one time she had tried to reach Noah, she hadn't gotten through, and her stubborn pride forbade her from leaving her name or phone number. Surely Noah must know how desperate she was.

She tried another angle, but the telephone call to Jonas Fielding was a disappointment. Sheila had hoped that the attorney could prevail where she had failed, but it seemed that both the insurance company and Wilder Investments were stalling. Why? What had Anthony Simmons found out?

Despite her hopes otherwise, Sheila began to understand that there was no way Cascade Valley could put its label on this year's harvest. It seemed there was no other option but to sell this year's grapes to a competitive firm. For the first time in the nearly twenty years in which the Lindstrom name had been a part of the winery, Cascade Valley would be unable to bottle or ferment any wine. Not only would the winery's reputation be further tarnished, but also the potential income from the crop would be considerably reduced. It looked as if she would have to renew her contract to teach and counsel at the community college at least for another year, or until the winery was operating again—if ever. Maybe Noah had been right when he suggested that running a winery was too big a job for a woman, she thought idly to herself as she stacked her father's personal records back in the scarred oak desk. Or maybe it was more than that. Perhaps Noah was stalling for time to add just the right incentive, a little more pressure, all the while knowing that she couldn't possibly save the winery without his help. Would he be so callous as to wait her out, backing her into a trap she couldn't possibly avoid?

She slammed the rolltop desk shut with a bang. What was she thinking? Noah would never use her for his own benefit; he couldn't. She walked crisply into the kitchen and tried to ignore her suspicions. What had Jonas said about Wilder Investments and the reputation of Ben Wilder's firm? Something about forcing businesses on the brink of bankruptcy to their knees with the influence of money. Wasn't that how Ben Wilder had amassed his wealth, by purchasing failing businesses and, one way or another, turning them into profitable ventures for Wilder Investments?

Her growing suspicion crawled coldly up her spine. Without thinking, she picked up the telephone receiver and dialed the number for Wilder Investments. It was nearly five, but with any luck, Sheila would be able to catch Noah at the office. The pride that had kept her from calling him seemed small when compared with the grim fact that he might be using each passing day as a means of squeezing her out of ownership of the winery.

"Wilder Investments," answered a pleasant, if bored, voice.

"Yes . . . I would like to speak to Noah Wilder, please," Sheila said boldly.

"I'm sorry, Mr. Wilder is out for the day."

"Do you know where I could reach him? It's very important."

"I'm sorry, miss. As far as I know Mr. Wilder is out of town for the weekend and can't be reached until Monday. If you'll leave your name and number, I'll leave a message for him to call you back."

"No, thank you. . . . I'll try next week."

Sheila replaced the receiver and tried to think clearly.

Why hadn't he called? All of his questions and interest in the winery seemed to have passed with the one night she had shared with him. A flush rose in her cheeks as she considered the fact that the interest he had shown in the winery was probably little more than polite concern displayed as part of his seduction; a seduction that had trapped her completely. Unfortunately, it looked as if her entire trip to Seattle had been a waste. Not only had she lost precious time in her battle to save the winery, but she had also been played for a fool. Willingly she had begun to give her heart to a man who considered her only a passing interest that had faded with the dawn.

"What's for dinner?" Emily asked as she breezed into the kitchen and grabbed a cookie from the jar.

"Beef stroganoff," Sheila replied.

"That all?"

"No. I'm making a spinach salad, and if you don't demolish them all before dinner, we'll have cookies for dessert."

Emily, who was beginning to reach into the cookie jar again, quickly withdrew her hand. "I can take a hint," she mumbled.

"Good. Dinner will be ready in about half an hour. I'll call you when it's time to come in."

Emily hesitated and rubbed her fingers in distracted circles on the countertop. Sheila had begun to put water on the stove for boiling the noodles, but she stopped, noticing instead the droop in Emily's slim shoulders. "Is something wrong?"

Emily's head snapped up, and she took a deep breath. "I don't want to go to Daddy's place this summer," she announced.

"Oh, sure you do," Sheila said with a smile. "You love being with Daddy."

"No, I don't." Emily's slim arms crossed defiantly over her small chest. "And . . . I bet he doesn't want me to come."

"That's ridiculous. Your father loves you very much."

"Will you come with me?"

Sheila turned from the stove and faced her daughter. "If you want me to, I'll take you to Spokane, but you know that your dad likes to come and get you himself."

"You mean you're not going to stay with me?"

"I can't, honey; you know that."

"But maybe if you call Daddy and tell him you don't want me to go. He might understand."

"Emily, what brought all of this on?" Sheila asked, placing her arm over Emily's shoulders.

The young girl shrugged. "I just don't want to go."

"Why don't you think about it for a couple of weeks? You're still going to be here for a little while longer. Let's see how it goes and then we'll make a decision—okay?"

Emily's downcast eyes lifted to look out the kitchen window. "I think someone's coming."

Sheila turned her attention to the open window and the sound of a car's rapidly approaching engine. "You're right," she agreed, trying to focus on the sporty vehicle winding its way up the long gravel drive. As the silver car crested the final hill, Sheila felt her breath catch in her throat. The car belonged to Noah.

She was both ecstatic and filled with dread. Noah must have come here with his answer about the winery.

*Chapter Seven*

$\mathcal{T}$he lump in Sheila's throat swelled as she watched Noah's car approach.

"Who's that?" Emily asked, squinting into the sunset and straining to get a better view of the silver vehicle as she looked through the window. Noah braked the Volvo to a halt and got out of the car. He looked tired and hot. He was wearing tan corduroy pants and a loosely knit ivory sweater. The sleeves were pushed up over his forearms to display tanned skin and tight muscles. His dark hair was slightly windblown from the drive, and the shadow of his beard was visible against his olive skin. His mouth, set in a firm, hard line, tightened as the other passenger in the car said something that caught his attention. Sheila felt her pulse begin to race at the sight of him. No other man had ever affected her so deeply.

"Mom?" Emily asked, catching Sheila's attention. "Do you know that guy?"

Sheila managed a frail smile for her daughter. "I'm sorry, Em," she replied, realizing that she had ignored Emily's previous question. "Yes, I know him. His name is Noah Wilder, and he's in charge of the company that owns most of the winery."

"A big shot, huh?"

Sheila laughed. "I think his title is 'temporary president,' or something of the sort. Let's not call him a big shot. Okay?"

"If you say so."

"Just keep in mind that he is important. His decision on the winery is critical." Emily's puzzled expression was not lost on Sheila. "I'll explain more about him later. Right now let's go and meet him at the door." Sheila grabbed Emily's hand and hurried to the front entrance, hoping to forestall any more of Emily's questions about Noah.

When she opened the door, Sheila stood face to face with the one man who had touched her to the core, and she felt her poise beginning to slip. Noah wasn't alone. With him was a boy; his son, Sheila guessed. The resemblance between the man and teenager was strong. Though Sean's hair was blond, his skin was dark like his father's, and his eyes were the same piercing blue. Those blue eyes regarded Sheila intently with a deep-seeded, undisguised hostility.

"I tried the bell, but I didn't hear it ring," Noah explained

"It hasn't worked since the fire."

Noah seemed a little uncomfortable, but when his eyes found Sheila's, he held her gaze and spoke softly. "Earlier, you invited me to come and see the winery for myself. You asked me to spend a weekend here, and I've decided that there's no time like the present. Does the offer still stand?"

"Now? This weekend?" she asked.

"If it wouldn't inconvenience you. . . ."

Sheila was caught in the power of his gaze, the warmth and invitation in his eyes. She had to force herself to smile and keep her voice cool and professional. "Of course you're welcome, I'm sure if you stay and see the magnitude of the problem, you'll understand why we have to begin rebuilding the winery as soon as we can."

"I'm sure," he agreed, dismissing the subject. "I'd like you to meet my son, Sean."

Sheila's smile spread as she turned her attention to the boy at Noah's side. She had always had a way with kids, especially teenagers. She genuinely liked them, and it showed in the interest in her eyes. "Hi, Sean. How are you?"

"Fine," was the clipped, succinct reply. His expression of hostility didn't diminish.

Sheila didn't press the issue. "This is Emily." She touched Emily's shoulders fondly.

Noah bent his knees so he could talk to Emily at her level. "It's nice to meet you, Emily." He extended his hand, and when Emily took hold of it, he gave the girl a warm handshake. "I bet you're a big help to your mom, aren't you?"

"I guess so," Emily mumbled before retrieving her hand and stepping backward to put some distance between herself and the forceful man.

"We were just about to have dinner," Sheila stated as Noah rose back to his full height. "Could you join us?"

Sean rolled his eyes and looked away. Noah spoke for the two of them. "If it's not too much trouble. I should have called before I left the office, but I was running late, so I just headed out of town." The lie slipped so easily off his tongue that Noah had no trouble smiling disarmingly down at her. His conscience twinged, but he ignored it.

"It's fine," Sheila was saying emphatically. "I always

cook as if I'm expecting the army.'' She moved out of the doorway. "Come in. I still have a few things to do to get dinner on the table. Or, if you would prefer, you can look around the grounds. I'll give you a guided tour later.''

"I'll wait. I think I'd prefer a *personal* tour.''

Sheila felt the heat climbing up her throat. Somehow she managed to keep her voice level. "What about you, Sean? Dinner won't be ready for half an hour. You're welcome to come into the house; I've got several books and magazines you might be interested in, or you can do whatever you want out here.''

"I don't like to read,'' Sean replied curtly, but after receiving a dark and admonishing glance from his father, he amended his brusque response with a shrug of his shoulders. "I'll stay outside.''

Emily followed Sheila and Noah inside. Sheila busied herself with the finishing touches for the meal, and Noah lounged against the counter, watching her as she worked. Emily hovered near Sheila, uncertain about the upcoming evening.

"You out of school for the year?'' Noah asked the girl. "Uh-huh.''

Sheila could feel Emily's embarrassment. Ever since Sheila's divorce from Jeff, Emily was shy with men to the point of wariness, especially any man who showed attention to her mother. To ease Emily's discomfort, Sheila changed the subject. "Dinner's going to take a little longer than I thought, Emily. Why don't you take a couple of cookies and''—she paused to inspect the contents of the refrigerator—"some of this pop outside for you and Sean.''

Emily's wide brown eyes lit up. "Really? Before dinner?''

"Why not?" Sheila asked with a smile and handed the cans of ginger ale to her daughter. "Tonight's special."

Emily balanced the cans against her chest while she reached into the cookie jar and withdrew a handful of macaroons. "Great," she whispered, hardly believing her luck at receiving goodies before a meal.

When the back door slammed shut and Emily could be heard in the distance, Noah moved from his position against the counter to stand behind Sheila. She could sense his presence behind her, but she tried to maintain her interest in the sauce she was preparing. It was impossible. His hands wrapped around her waist and drew her close to him. She closed her eyes as she felt his breath rustle the hair at the nape of her neck.

"Is it?" he asked.

"What?"

"Is tonight special?" His words caressed the air.

She attempted to misread him. "Of course it is. It's not often Emily and I have guests for dinner."

"That's not what I meant."

Sheila sighed and turned the burner to the lowest setting. She rotated in Noah's arms and tried to step backward. He didn't let go. "I knew what you meant."

"Do you?"

"Of course I do, Noah. I'm not exactly a naive innocent. I think you were the one that pointed it out to me. I assume you came here to talk about the winery . . ."

"And?" His half smile showed just a seductive hint of white, straight teeth, and a gleam of fascination flickered in his blue eyes.

"And you probably expect to take up where we left off." Sheila's heart was pounding so loudly she was sure he could hear it.

"The thought did cross my mind."

"You're wicked," she accused teasingly.

"No, I wouldn't say that . . . *captivated* would be a better word."

"Oh, Noah," Sheila murmured. His words had a magical effect upon her, and she felt unable to resist the spell of tenderness he was weaving. Though she attempted to deny it, she still found something enigmatic and intimately alluring in Noah. A crazy feeling of exhilaration climbed steadily up her spine as she realized that he wanted to be with her. Perhaps she had misjudged him. Perhaps despite everything holding them apart, there was a chance that they could find happiness with each other.

"You look great," he said. His eyes caressed her face and dropped to the tempting white column of her throat.

"In jeans and an old blouse?"

"In anything. . . ." The pressure of his hands against her back drew her close to him; so close that she could feel the strength of his legs where they touched hers and the pressure of his chest against her breasts. "As I recall, you look incredible in absolutely nothing as well." His head lowered and his lips captured hers in a warm kiss that evoked passionate memories. In one instant she remembered his embrace in the rain and his touch in silent afterglow.

Without thinking she entwined her arms around Noah's neck and parted her lips under the soft pressure of his mouth. His tongue rimmed her lips, and all of the doubts of the last weeks fled with the promise of his kiss. "I've missed you," he groaned when he lifted his head and pulled her roughly against him. "God, how I've missed you."

At the sound of his confession, Sheila felt tears begin to pool in her eyes. "I've missed you too," she murmured into his sweater. Her voice caught, and she felt him stiffen. Slowly he released her.

"Is something wrong?" he asked.

"It's been a long day . . ." she hedged. How could she begin to explain the storm of emotions within her each time he held her closely?

"Is it a bad time for you? I should have called before I came racing over here."

"No . . . everything's fine. *Really*."

"Is dinner ready yet?" Emily called just as she was entering the room.

Sheila managed to brush her tears aside. "Just about. You can help by setting the table."

"In the dining room?" Emily asked as she reached in the drawer for silverware.

"No. We'll have to eat in here." Sheila withdrew a linen tablecloth and put it on the small kitchen table. Looking skeptically at the makeshift dining arrangements, her mouth pulled into a pouty frown. "It's not exactly elegant, but it will have to do. The dining room is still a mess."

"From the fire?" Noah asked.

"And the water that was used to put out the flames. I'll show you everything after we eat. Maybe then you'll appreciate my position about the winery."

The door opened and shut with a resonate thud. Sean strode into the room wearing cut-off jeans, a sloppy red sweat shirt and a look of bored indifference. His face was shaped similarly to his father's, except that the sharp planes of Noah's face were softer on his son. There was still a hint of boyish naiveté in Sean that he obviously tried to hide under a guise of insolence.

"Time to eat?" Sean asked, directing his question to his father.

"I think you can sit down."

"Good." Sean slid into the nearest chair and avoided looking at Sheila. His fingers tapped restlessly on the edge of the table. Emily took a seat next to Sean and began to chatter endlessly about a hike she hoped to take with him. Sean responded with adolescent nonchalance about the prospect of spending more time with the eager eight-year-old, but Sheila's practiced eye saw the interest he was trying to hide. Three years of counseling teenagers had helped her understand both the kids and their motives.

The dinner was eaten under a thin veil of civility. Sheila had hoped that as the meal progressed the strain of the impromtu get-together would fade and a comfortable feeling of familiarity would evolve. She had been wrong. Before the dinner was over, even Emily could feel the tension building between Sean and Sheila.

Sheila attempted to bridge the gap. "Are you out of school for the summer?" she asked Sean.

Silence. Sean continued to wolf down his food.

She tried another ploy. "Would you like anything else to eat? How about a roll?"

Nothing. Noah's anger had been simmering throughout the meal, but he had decided not to discipline his son in front of Sheila and Emily. Sean's rude behavior forced the issue.

"Sheila asked you a question, Sean," he stated sternly.

"Yeah . . . I heard."

"Then could you be polite enough to answer."

Sean bristled. "Sure." His cool blue eyes sought Sheila's. "Naw . . . I don't want another roll." He turned his gaze back to his father. "Satisfied?"

Emily's eyes widened as father and son squared off.

"No, I'm not. I don't expect much from you, son, but I do think you can be civil."

"Why?" Sean demanded.

"Out of respect."

"For what? *Her?*" He cast his disdainful gaze at Sheila.

"Cut it out!" Noah stated tersely.

Sean ignored him. "Look, Dad, I don't need this."

"What you need is to learn about acting with just a modicum of decency and common curtesy." A muscle in Noah's jaw began to tense.

"Back off, Dad. What I don't need is some lady trying to be my mother!"

"Don't worry about that, Sean," Sheila interjected. "I have no intention of trying to become your mother." With that, she turned her attention back to her dinner and finished eating. Sean cast a skeptical glance in her direction, and Noah's dark eyebrows cocked. However, he didn't interfere. When finished with her meal, Sheila again looked at Sean. "No, I'm sure you've done very well without a mother for the past sixteen years, and I, for one, have no intention of changing that." She rained her most disarming smile upon the confused boy. "Now, is there anything else I can get you?"

"No!"

"Good." Sheila placed her napkin on the table. "Then, if we're all finished, you can clear the table while Emily gets the dessert."

Sean's face fell and his blue eyes sought those of his father, entreating Noah to help him. "Good idea," Noah agreed amicably, but the glint of determination in his eyes demanded that his son obey.

Sheila wasn't finished. She began stacking the plates and handing them to Sean. "Just put the dishes on the counter near the sink, and don't worry about washing them, I'll take care of that later. Let's see, the leftovers go in the refrigerator. Use the plastic wrap to cover them. Can you handle that?"

Sean's hot retort was thwarted by his father's stern glare.

Rather than press the issue, Sean scowled and nodded curtly.

"All right, now, Emily; it's your turn." Emily fastened her frightened eyes on her mother. Never had she witnessed such hostility at a meal. Nor had she ever seen her mother so tough with a guest.

Sheila smiled at her daughter, and Emily's anxieties melted a bit. "You can bring the cookies out to the back patio. I'll bring the coffee and Noah will get the milk." If Noah was surprised that he, too, was issued an order, he didn't show it.

Sean's chair scraped insolently against the tiled floor as he rose from the table. His handsome face was clouded in an expression of disdain, but he managed to clear the dishes. Emily was uncommonly silent as she arranged the macaroons on a small plate. The tension that had been building throughout dinner continued to mount. Noah poured two glasses of milk and escaped out the back door. Emily soon followed. Sheila waited for the coffee to perk, while Sean put things away, making as much noise as he possibly could.

Just as Sheila was pouring the hot, black liquid, Sean exploded. "Maybe you can fool my dad, but you can't fool me!"

Sheila was startled and sloshed some of the coffee on her wrist. The scalding brew burned her skin, but she remained calm. As Sean watched her reaction, she set the cup down and put her hand under cold water from the tap. Her voice was even when she addressed him. "I have no intention of trying to fool you, Sean."

"Sure," he sneered.

Sheila turned to face the tall boy, and she leveled her cool gray eyes on his face. "Look, Sean, I'm not trying to deceive anyone, and I expect the same in return. I don't really care if you like me or not. You have the right to your own opinions, just as I have the right to mine. . . ."

"Don't give me any of your psychiatric lines! I know you're a school counselor, and I'll just bet Dad dragged me up here so you could do a number on me; you know, analyze me—try and straighten me out." He threw up one of his hands in disgust. "I just want you to know that it won't work on me. Save your breath!"

Sheila managed a smile. "Do you really think that I would bother wasting my time or expertise on someone who didn't want it?"

"It's your job."

"No. I'm sorry, Sean, but you're wrong. I'm not going to beat my head against the wall for someone who doesn't want my help, and that includes you. As for what your father expects from me, it has nothing to do with you. We're business partners."

"Sure."

"I think I will take your advice," Sheila agreed. Sean tensed. The last thing he had expected was for this woman to concur with him. "I'm going to save my breath. I would like to try and convince you to relax and enjoy the weekend—"

"Fat chance," Sean interrupted under his breath.

"Pardon me?"

"This isn't my scene," he spat out, and turned to glare out the window.

"That's too bad, because it looks like you're stuck here for the duration of the weekend." Sean rolled his eyes heavenward, and Sheila poured the coffee into the second cup. When she picked up the tray, she cast a final glance in Sean's direction. "Why don't you come out to the patio and join the rest of us? Emily already took out the cookies."

Sean whirled angrily to face Sheila. "I'm here, okay?

That's the end of it. I'm not going to sit with the rest of you and eat milk and cookies. That might be all right for Emily, but not for me. I'm not wasting my time baby-sitting your kid!'' he shouted.

The screen door slammed shut and Emily came into the room. From the expression on her face it was evident she had heard Sean's final words. Tears sprung to her soft brown eyes as she stared at Sean.

''Damn!'' Sean muttered, and slammed his fist onto the counter. His face burned in his embarrassment as he strode angrily from the room.

''Why doesn't he like me?'' Emily asked Sheila. The little girl tried vainly to swallow her tears. Sheila set the tray down.

''It's not that he doesn't like you, Em,'' Sheila replied, hugging her child. ''He's just not sure of himself here. He doesn't know you or me, and he's not really sure how to act.''

''He's mean!'' Emily sniffed.

''He's not trying to be. Maybe he's jealous of you,'' Sheila whispered into her daughter's thick, dark curls.

''Why?''

''Sean doesn't have a mother.''

Emily was puzzled. She pulled out of her mother's embrace and with a childish imitation of adult concern, looked deeply into Sheila's eyes. ''I thought everybody had a mommy.''

''You're right, sweetheart. Everybody does have a mother, including Sean. But, I think he's unhappy because he doesn't see her very much.''

''Why not?'' Emily was clearly perplexed, and Sheila wondered if she had broached a topic she couldn't fully explain. After all, what did she know of Sean's mother? If she had interpreted Noah's story correctly, Sean may never have met his mother. No wonder the kid had a chip the size of a boulder on his young shoulders. Sheila felt her heart go out for the stubborn boy with the facade of bravado. Emily was still staring at Sheila, and she knew she had to find a suitable answer for her daughter. "Sean's parents don't live together," she whispered.

Emily's sober expression changed to one of understanding. "Oh, they're divorced. Like you and Daddy."

Sheila's expression clouded. "Sort of," she replied vaguely. Emily seemed satisfied for the moment, and Sheila changed the subject quickly. "Let's go out on the patio and see Noah before this coffee gets cold."

"He's not there."

"He's not?"

Emily shook her head. "He's just walkin' around."

"Then we'll wait for him." Again Sheila picked up the tray, and with Emily in tow, walked out to the brick patio that was flanked by Oliver's rose garden.

Noah had been familiarizing himself with the layout of the winery. His walk also gave him the excuse to vent some of the frustration and tension that had been boiling within him since he had left Seattle. The trip over the mountains had been strained; Sean had brooded because his weekend plans were canceled by his father's hastily organized trip. Sean had pleaded to be left alone in Seattle, and when Noah had refused, Sean had ridden the entire distance with his head turned away from his father while he pretended interest in the passing countryside. He had responded to Noah's questions with monosyllabic grunts. By the time they reached the winery, Noah's tension was wound tighter than the mainspring on a watch.

Noah had hoped that Sean would loosen up by the time they had come within sight of the winery, but he had been wrong—dead wrong. Sean was more petulant than ever. It was as if he were intent on punishing his father with his abrasive behavior.

Noah's frown twisted into a wry grin as he thought about Sheila's reaction to his strong-willed son. The embarrassment Noah had experienced at the table had faded into admiration for Sheila as he had witnessed the effective manner in which she had handled Sean. Even Sean had been set on his heels by Sheila's indifferent and cooly professional attitude. She had refused to be goaded by anything Sean had done. Noah had to hand it to her: She knew how to handle kids, her own daughter was proof of that. It occurred to him that perhaps he would never be able to control his son. It was all too evident that Sean needed a mother as well as a father. Noah had been a fool to think that he could raise a son of his own. Ben's warning, issued sixteen years before, rang in his ears. "You want to raise that bastard on your own? You're an even bigger fool than I thought!"

The screen door slammed, breaking into Noah's thoughts. He lifted his eyes to observe Sean racing angrily from the house. There had obviously been another battle and it seemed as if Sean had lost one more round to Sheila. Noah shook his head as he watched his athletic son run across the back yard, hoist himself effortlessly over a pole fence without once breaking stride, and continue at a break-neck pace into the fringe of woods beyond the orchard.

Noah's thoughts returned to Sheila. There was more grit to her than met the eye. Stunningly beautiful, she was also independent and intelligent. Noah raked his fingers impatiently through his hair as he wondered if he had made a grave mistake in seeking her out. She was more intriguing than he had remembered, and seeing her in the setting of the burned winery seemed to add an innocent vulnerability to her large eyes. Noah felt as if he wanted to protect her, when in fact he had come to Cascade Valley expecting to confront her with the knowledge that her father did, in fact, start the fire at the winery. As yet, Noah hadn't found the right opportunity to broach the subject. The more he was with Sheila, the less he wanted to talk about the fire.

Anthony Simmons's report had been short and concise. Though the detective had produced no concrete evidence to name Oliver Lindstrom as the arsonist, the case Simmons had built against Sheila's father had been complete. Noah knew that the insurance company was bound to reach the same conclusion as he had: Based on circumstantial evidence, it was proven that Oliver Lindstrom set fire to Cascade Valley hoping to collect the insurance settlement and pay off a sizable debt to Wilder Investments. Inadvertently Mr. Lindstrom got caught in his own trap, was overcome by fumes of noxious gas and died in the blaze.

Noah's stomach knotted as he wondered how involved Sheila had been in her father's scheme. Had she known about it beforehand? Was she involved? Or was she, as she claimed, looking for a solution to the dilemma? According to Simmons, Sheila had been polite, but hadn't gone out of her way to help with the investigation. It had been like pulling teeth to get her to divulge anything personal about her father . . . or herself. Was she hiding something? Simmons seemed to think so. Noah didn't. Still, it didn't matter, the bottom line was that he had to tell her about her father and then gauge her reaction to the news. It wasn't going to be easy. Either way she lost. If she already knew that her father was a fraud, she would come out of this mess at the very least a liar; at the most an accomplice. If she didn't know that her father had started the fire, her dreams and respect for the dead man would be shattered. No doubt she would blame Noah for digging up the dirt on Oliver Lindstrom.

As Noah walked back to the patio he tried to find a way to help her rather than hurt her.

# Chapter Eight

$\mathcal{N}$oah paced back and forth across the red bricks of the patio. The anxieties of the day were etched across his face in long lines of worry. It was nearly ten, the sun had set over an hour before and Sean hadn't returned. He was obviously back to his old tricks of vanishing without a word of explanation.

Emily was already asleep in her bed. Since overhearing Sean's unkind remarks, she had been quiet. The girl hadn't even put up an argument about going to bed, and Sheila's heart broke when Emily reasserted her earlier assessment of the situation. "Sean doesn't like me, and it's not because I've got a mommy. He doesn't like anybody."

"He's just trying to find out who he is," Sheila had responded.

"That's silly. He's Sean. He just doesn't like me."

"Maybe he doesn't like himself."

Emily hadn't been convinced as she snuggled under her comforter. Sheila had attempted to hand the child her favorite furry toy, but Emily pushed it onto the floor. "I don't need Cinnamon," Emily had stated. "Toys are for *little kids.*" Sheila hadn't argued, wisely letting her child cope with the struggle of growing up. Instead she picked up the toy dog with the floppy ears and set him on the nightstand near Emily's bed.

"Just in case you change your mind." After her parting remarks she had kissed Emily lightly on the cheek and left the room.

"Is she all right?" Noah asked.

"I think so."

"What was bothering her?"

"She took offense to Sean's notion that she was a little kid. She thinks she has to grow up all in one evening."

"Sean's the one who has to grow up," Noah argued. "I don't know if he ever will!"

"It will get better," Sheila said quietly.

"How do you know?"

"It has to. Doesn't it?" The gray intelligence in her eyes reached out to him.

"What makes you so certain? How do you know I don't have the makings of a hardened criminal on my hands?"

Sheila smiled, and her face, captured in the moonglow, held a madonnalike quality that was only contradicted by the silver fire of seduction in her eyes. "Sean's not a bad kid," she pointed out. "He's just not certain of himself."

"He could have fooled me."

"That's exactly what he's trying to do."

Noah strode over to the chaise lounge where she was sitting. "How did a beautiful woman like you get so wise?" He sat next to her and his hand touched her thigh as he leaned over her to kiss her forehead.

"Don't you remember what it was like when you were in high school?"

"I try not to."

"Come on, admit it. Didn't you give your parents a few gray hairs?"

"I don't remember ever getting into as much trouble as Sean has."

"Maybe you were smarter and just never got caught," she suggested.

"Now you're beginning to sound cynical."

"Realistic."

"Yeah, so it's all business, is it?" Sean jeered, walking out of the darkness into the circle of light surrounding the patio. Noah, still leaning over Sheila, barely moved, but Sheila could feel all the muscles in his body become rigid. Slowly he turned to face his son.

"It's about time you got back. Where were you?"

Sean shrugged indifferently. "Around."

"I was beginning to worry about you."

"Yeah. I can see that," the boy snorted. His blue eyes sought Sheila's in a condemning gaze. "You told me you were business partners with him, nothing more!"

"I said that we were business partners and that I didn't think your father brought you up here for a counseling session. I should have added that your father and I are friends," Sheila explained calmly.

"Yeah. *Good* friends."

"Sean, that's enough!" Noah shouted, rising to his full height. Sean's defiance wavered under his father's barely controlled rage. "You apologize to Sheila!"

"Why?" Sean asked, managing to pull together one last attempt at asserting his pride.

"You tell me," Noah suggested.

Sean shifted from one foot to the other as he measured his

father's anger. Noah didn't take his eyes off of his son. Realizing he had no other choice, Sean mumbled a hasty apology before entering the house.

"I'll show him his room," Sheila offered. "There's a hide-a-bed in my father's office. I just put clean sheets on it yesterday."

Noah objected. *"I'll* take him to the room. He and I have a few things to get straight. I'm not putting up with his cocky attitude any longer." He rubbed the tension from the back of his neck and followed his son into the house.

Pieces of the argument filtered through the thick walls of the château. Sheila began to clear the dishes off the patio and tried not to overhear the heated discussion. Noah's voice, angry and accusatory, didn't drown out Sean's argumentative tones.

The night was sultry and still. The tension from the argument lingered in the air, and Sheila felt beads of moisture beginning to accumulate on the back of her neck. She wound her hair into a loose chignon and clipped it to the top of her head before she carried the dishes into the house.

Noah and Sean were still arguing, but the hot words had become softer. In order to give them more privacy, Sheila turned on the water in the kitchen and rattled the dishes in the sink. It wasn't enough to drown out all of the anger, so she switched on the radio. Familiar strains of a popular tune filtered through the kitchen and Sheila forced herself to hum, hoping to take her mind off the uncomfortable relationship between Noah and his son. Just as Noah couldn't get along with Ben, Sean shunned his father. Why? Her loose thoughts rambled as she began to wash the dishes. She didn't hear the argument subside, didn't notice when Noah entered the room.

He leaned against the doorjamb and watched her as she

worked. Her hair was piled loosely on her head, and soft tendrils framed her delicate face. A thin trickle of perspiration ran down her chin and settled below the open neck of her blouse. He could almost visualize it resting between her breasts. Her sleeves were rolled over her elbows, and her forearms were submerged in water so hot it steamed. A vibrant rosy flush from the hot night and the even hotter water colored her skin. She was softly humming to the strains of music from the radio, and though the sound was slightly off-key, it caused Noah to smile. She had to be the most beautiful woman in the world.

"Don't you have a dishwasher?" he asked, not moving from the doorway. He enjoyed his vantage point, where he could watch all of her movements.

She laughed. "Oh, I've got one all right, but it doesn't work."

"Can't it be repaired?"

Sheila turned to face Noah, while still wiping her hands with the dish towel. "I suppose it can."

"But you haven't called a repair man?"

"Not yet."

"Why not?"

"Because I enjoy washing dishes," she snapped sarcastically.

Noah finally understood. "You're waiting for the insurance money, right?"

"Right." Sheila's expression softened. "A dishwasher is the last thing we need right now. Emily and I use very few dishes, so it's not exactly a hardship."

"That kind of thinking will send you back to the nineteenth century," he teased.

"That kind of thinking will keep me out of debt . . . at least for a little while." Sheila's eyes clouded with worry for an instant, but she bravely ignored her problems. The best way to solve them was to apprise Noah of the hopeless condition of the winery. She tossed the dish towel over the back of a chair and boldly reached for Noah's hand. "I promised you a tour of the grounds."

"I can think of better things to do," he suggested huskily.

"Not on your life." She pulled on his hand and attempted to ignore the laconic gleam in his eyes. "Now that I've got you on my territory, you're going to see exactly what I've been talking about." She led him to the front of the house. "Let's start with public relations."

"Public relations? For a winery?"

"Not just any winery, Noah. This is Cascade Valley, the Northwest's finest. My father always ran the winery with the opinion that the public comes first. Anyone who was even the slightest bit interested in Cascade Valley has always been treated as if he were an important dignitary." She led him down an asphalt path that led from the château toward the park grounds of the vast estate. Though the grass was overgrown, Noah could tell that in the past the grounds had been immaculately groomed. Stands of dark pine trees surrounded the long grass and the untrimmed shrubbery. The air was fragrant with the scent of pines and lilacs. A hazy moon gave an iridescent glow to the shadowy night.

"Sounds as if your father spent a lot of time and money humoring tourists."

Sheila refused to be baited. "It paid off, too. Word of mouth was our first form of advertising." Sheila glanced at Noah to interpret his reaction. Though it was dark, she could read the hardening of his gaze, feel the tensing of his hand over hers, sense the clenching of his teeth as his jaw tightened.

"What kind of tours did your father give?" Noah asked, pressing the issue.

"At first they were nothing out of the ordinary. One of the staff would just show the tourists around. But, as public interest grew, Dad had to hire a woman to pass out literature about the winery and give tours of the buildings every afternoon in the summer." Sheila motioned her hand toward a small lake shimmering in the moonlight. "Dad had the duck pond built about six years ago. Then he added the gravel paths through the woods. Later he installed the picnic tables and the benches."

"I'm surprised he didn't give away bottles of Cabernet Savignon, too," Noah muttered caustically.

"You didn't approve of my father, did you?" Sheila accused.

"I didn't know him."

"But you're passing judgment."

"Not on the man," Noah pointed out. He took his hand away from Sheila's and rubbed his chin. How could he explain to her that her father was an arsonist who had only wanted to get money from the insurance company to pay his debts? If Oliver Lindstrom had been a little more daring and a little less clumsy, it might have worked. "I'm only questioning some of his business practices. Public relations is usually sound, but not when it devours all of a company's profits. What's the point? If your father had paid less attention to putting on a show for anyone who happened to wander by and had more concern for his profits, maybe he never would have had to borrow money from Wilder Investments in the first place!"

Sheila felt the hairs on her neck prickle with anger. "The reason he borrowed the money had nothing to do with the tourists or the duck pond, Noah. That nearly paid for itself in the gift shop alone," she argued. Indignation flashed in her eyes as she came to the defense of her father. "Dad took a survey of all the people who came here one summer and it proved him right; nearly seventy percent of the tourists bought more than one bottle of Cascade Valley a month."

"What about the other thirty percent?"

"I don't know."

"Do you think those people, those who bought your product, were swayed because of a duck pond, or picnic tables?"

"No . . . but . . ."

"Of course not! Those people would probably have bought the wine without all of this . . . grandstanding. The money would have been better spent in production or research, even advertising. Sure, these grounds look impressive, but it's the quality of the product that counts! Wouldn't it be wiser to use this acreage for cultivation?"

"I don't know if the soil is right . . ." she hedged.

"So check it out."

Her simmering anger began to boil. "I guess you don't understand, Noah. We're not only selling the best wine on the West Coast, we're creating an image for the consuming public. We're not competing with cheap Muskatel. Our opposition is the finest European wine on the market. Every summer we provide samples of our product at a wine-tasting celebration and the public is invited. We introduce the newest varieties, invite a few celebrities and generally promote the image of Cascade Valley wines as sophisticated, yet reasonably priced.

"Sounds expensive."

"It is," she admitted reluctantly. "But, most often, we get national media attention. That kind of advertising we can't afford to lose."

"But you didn't get any national attention for the last few years, did you?"

She shook her head as if she had expected this question and seemed resigned to a fate she couldn't avoid. "No."

"Why not?" He knew the answer, but he wanted to hear it from her.

Sheila bit her lower lip nervously. Her words rang with honesty and despair. "Dad was afraid. With all of the news coverage on the tampered bottles of Chardonnay found in Montana and the problems with the crop because of the early snowfall, Dad thought it would be best for Cascade Valley to keep a low profile." She paused for a moment to study the ribbon of silver moonglow on the pond. "This was the year he had hoped would change all of that."

"How?"

"Because we planned to introduce our reserve bottling of Cabernet Sauvignon."

"Reserve bottling?" Noah repeated. "Something new?"

"For Cascade Valley, yes." She turned to face him, her expression sincere. "It could be the biggest breakthrough we've had."

"Tell me about it." Noah was interested. This was the first hint of good news at the winery.

Sheila shook her head. "Not now. On Monday Dave Jansen will come by. He can tell you all about it . . ." She stopped midsentence, as if she'd assumed far too much about him. "You can stay until Monday, can't you?" Why was it so imperative that he remain for more than just one night? Now that he was here, she desperately wanted him to stay.

"Is it that important?" he asked, his voice as low as the soft breeze that had begun to whisper through the pines.

"Yes, it's important," she admitted, but lied about the reason. "I think you should see for yourself. . . ."

His fingers lightly touched her shoulders, and through the light cotton fabric they warmed her skin. "What I meant was, is it important that I stay with you?"

Her lips felt desert dry. She had to lick them in order to

find the courage for her truthful reply. "I'm glad you came here, Noah," she admitted with only a trace of reluctance. "And I'd like you to stay, not just to witness the damage from the fire, nor just to evaluate the winery. I *want* you to stay here with me, for *me*." Her honesty filtered softly through the warm night air. The words of confession surprised her. After Jeff, she thought she had lost the *need* of a man's embrace. She had never expected to admit how much she wanted a man, because she thought that part of her had died. She had assumed that Jeff had ruined her for a relationship with any man, that the cynical feelings he had created in her would remain forever.

But she had been wrong, hopelessly mistaken. The strong man touching her lightly on the shoulders had changed her mind about many things, one of which was love. Though she couldn't yet admit it to him, Sheila knew that she loved Noah as she had never loved before.

"Then I'll stay," he whispered. His thumbs smoothed the fabric over her collar bones. "I want to stay with you, sweet lady."

Sheila sighed through trembling lips as Noah reached up and unclasped her hair. It billowed down in a chestnut tumble to frame her face in copper-tinged curls. Noah gently kissed her eyelids, and Sheila felt her knees begin to give way. His arms came protectively around her waist and pulled her achingly against the length of him. Her thighs touched his, her breasts were crushed against his chest, her heartbeat echoed with his in the still night.

His lips caressed her eyelids before moving slowly downward, leaving a moist trail of midnight dew on her cheekbones and the soft skin below her chin. A warm passion uncurling within her made a shudder pass through her body, and her skin quivered under the touch of his hands. His lips moved gently against her throat, and his tongue stroked the white skin, leaving a heated, wet impression. Sheila sighed dreamily into the night, unconsciously asking for more from him.

Her lips quivered when met by his and her gentle moan of pleasure blended warmly with his answering sigh. Their breath mingled and caught, heated by the fires dancing in their bloodstreams. When his tongue touched hers, the tempo of her heartbeat quickened and she opened her mouth in a gasp, wanting all of him, craving more of his bittersweet love.

He felt her surrender, knew the moment when the passion began to thunder in her ears and her bones began to melt. Her tongue stroked his, teasing and flirting with him until he could stand no more of the painless agony. Gently he pushed against her until the weight of his body forced her to fall on the soft bed of grass beneath the towering Ponderosa pines. He let his weight fall against her, imprisoning her with the power of his body and the strength of his desire.

The ground felt cool against her back, a welcome relief to a sultry night. Noah's kisses inflamed her blood and awakened a savage beast of passion slumbering quietly within her. She felt hot blood pumping through her racing heart until she thought she would explode from the powerful surge of desire sweeping through her. She wanted him—all of him. There was a desperation to her need, an untamed craving that knew no bounds.

"Make love to me," she pleaded through fevered lips. He lifted his head and slowly extracted himself from her embrace.

After opening one of the buttons of her blouse, he kissed the warm skin between her breasts, tasting the salt of her perspiration on his tongue. His hand shook as he smoothed the hair away from her face. "I thought I'd go crazy," he confessed, watching the play of moonlight on her red-brown hair. "I wanted to follow you back here that first night I met you." His face was grave, his eyes earnest. "It was hell staying away."

"Why didn't you come sooner?" she asked, trying to keep her mind on the conversation. With his free hand he was toying with the collar of her blouse, letting his fingers dip deliciously below the lapels. Her skin still burned where he had planted the wet kiss between her breasts. Heat waves washed over her skin, which flushed a rosy hue.

"You were the one who needed time," he reminded her. "I didn't want to push you into anything you might regret later."

"I could never regret spending time with you," she confessed.

His forefinger circled the hollow of her throat, creating a whirlpool of sensitive longing deep within her. "Is . . . is that why you decided to come now, because you thought I might have come to some decision . . . about our relationship?" Why couldn't she keep her wandering mind on the subject? It was important that she learn more about this man, and yet all of her thoughts were centered on his slow, seductive touch at the base of her throat.

"No . . . I came because I couldn't wait any longer," he admitted. It wasn't a lie; he had felt an urgency to be with her again, but there was that sordid little business about Anthony Simmons's report and her father's implication in the arson. Dear God, how would he be able to tell her? He promised himself that he would find a way to break the news—when the timing was right. Just now, beneath a dusty sprinkling of midnight stars, he could only think of how hopelessly he wanted her.

She grabbed his finger, stopping its wandering journey on her neck. "I can't think when you touch me like that."

"Don't think," he persuaded, but she ignored the husky invitation in his voice.

"Why couldn't you wait?"

"I had to see you again."

She released his finger, and a smile crept slowly across the smooth contours of her face. Shadowy moonlight lingered in her gaze as she looked up at him. "It doesn't matter," she whispered, kissing his hand. "The only important thing is that you're here, *now*." Her fingers curved around the back of his neck, ruffling his coffee-colored hair and pulling his head down to meet hers in a kiss of naked longing. She willingly parted her lips, inviting him to touch her most intimate reaches.

"Oh, Sheila," he groaned, damning himself inwardly for his deception. How could he make love to her without telling her everything he knew about her, her father, the fire? A bothersome guilt nagged at him like a broken vow, and yet he pushed it savagely aside. "Some other time," he promised himself.

"What?" Her hand stopped caressing his head. "What are you talking about?"

His grip on her tightened. "Nothing, my darling . . . nothing that can't wait."

His lips came to hers in a kiss that dismissed her fears. She was conscious of the hot breeze singing through the trees as it carried the sweet scent of pine and honeysuckle to her. She could taste the salty masculinity that passed from his lips to hers and she felt the protective strength of his hands as they quickly unbuttoned the remaining buttons of her blouse. The fabric parted, letting her breasts caress the night air. Noah pushed the blouse off her shoulders and never took his eyes from hers as he unclasped the filmy bra and tossed it recklessly to the ground.

Sheila's breasts, unbound by clothing, glistening with a

dewy film of sweat, were swollen from the flames of passion Noah had aroused within her. They stood out in the darkness as two white globes, small and firm, perfectly proportioned to her petite body. Noah held first one and then the other in his caressing hands. At his softly insistent touch, the dark nipples hardened.

Sheila sighed when he took one of the moonlit mounds of feminine flesh into his mouth. His fingers gripped the soft skin of her back, drawing her closer to him, letting him devour more of her. She felt the tip of his tongue and the ridges of his teeth against her sensitive skin, and she had the sensation of melting deep within her being. His fingers kneaded her back, persuading her muscles to respond to his intimate touch.

"You're gorgeous," he sighed, taking his head away from her breast long enough to capture her passion-drugged gaze with his knowing blue eyes. His hand took one of hers and guided it to the button above the zipper of his cords. "Undress me," he commanded, "and let me make love to you until the sun comes up."

"I want to," she admitted, removing her hand.

Once again he pulled her fingers against him, lifting the edge of his sweater and letting her hand touch the taut muscles of his abdomen. "Trust me," he whispered into her hair. "Come on, love, take my clothes off. Show me that you want me."

"Noah—"

"I'll help." In one quick movement he pulled the sweater over his head and discarded it against the trunk of a tree. Blue fire flamed in his eyes. She let her gaze travel slowly down his chest, taking in the ripple of each muscle, the mat of dark hair, his tanned skin, darker because of the night. "Now it's your turn," he coaxed with a wicked smile.

She raised her hand and placed it on his chest. Her fingers tentatively stroked the rock-hard muscles, tracing the outline of his male nipples. He groaned in pleasure and she let her finger slide down his torso to rest on his belt. She told herself she was being wanton, but she didn't believe it, not for a moment. Her love for this man stole all of the guilt from her mind.

The heat in his loins ached with restraint. The fires within him burned with a savage flame, and he had to use all of his willpower to control himself and the urge to rip off the remaining clothes that kept him from taking her. He wanted this night to be as important for her as it was for him. He wanted to love her as she had never before been loved. He wanted to take the time to draw out every feminine urge in her body and satisfy it. Beads of perspiration collected on his forehead and the back of his neck from the frustration of his self-imposed restraint.

"Take them off," Noah pleaded as her fingers hesitated at his belt buckle. Obediently she withdrew his belt and tossed it into the air. It landed silently on the sweater. Her fingers touched the button of his pants—it slid through the hole noiselessly. Every muscle in Noah's body strained with nearly forgotten control.

The zipper tab dropped easily and Noah let out a groan. "Dear God, woman, do you enjoy tormenting me?" He opened his eyes to search hers and saw the reckless gleam of pleasure in her eyes. "You're going to regret this," he warned, and a wicked smile of seduction curved his lips.

Picking up the pieces of his shattered self-control, he began extracting the same sweet agony from her as she did from him. Slowly, with barely concealed deliberation, he lowered her jeans inch by inch over her hips. He let his fingers graze the warm flesh of her inner thighs only to withdraw them. He again took her breast in his mouth and rekindled the passion that had earlier driven her mad with longing.

She arched against him, moaning into the night. Her fingers traced the contours of the lean muscles in his back, pulling him closer to her, letting him know without speaking how much she needed him, how deep the ache within her was. "Please, Noah," she cried into the night, her desire for him chasing away all other thoughts.

Her desperate cry ended the agony. With a groan he settled upon her, letting his weight fall against her, making her feel that the need in him was as great as hers. His lips caressed her and his breath warmed her skin. He threw off the last thin pieces of his self-control and found her, became one with her and joined her in the exquisite union of body and soul. His body fused with hers completely, and his rhythm was as demanding as the ceaseless pounding of waves upon the shore. The tempo increased, pushing her to higher crests of rapture as they blended together in a rush of naked passion.

She shuddered beneath him, a quake ripping through her body as the final wave crashed her wildly in sublime surrender. His answering explosion sealed their union, and he let his weight fall gratefully against her body, flattening her breasts. Their arms entwined, the rapid breathing slowed, and they clung together, hoping to capture forever the moment when the two became one.

Words of love, honest thoughts that needed to be shared, came unbidden to her lips. "Noah . . . I . . ."

"Shhh, darling. Just listen to the sounds of the night," he whispered against her hair.

# Chapter Nine

*Tell* me about yourself," Noah coaxed, whispering into Sheila's ear. They had managed to get dressed and were sitting together, propped by a pine tree. Noah's arms were wrapped protectively around her as she leaned against him, and his chin rested on her head.

"There's not much to tell." She snuggled deeper into his arms while she watched ghostly clouds move across the moon. It was a still night, with a mere hint of a breeze. The soft drone of insects and the occasional cry of an owl were the only sounds she could hear, aside from Noah's steady breathing and the rhythmic beating of his heart.

"Why don't you start by telling me why you want to stay on at the winery?" He felt her body become rigid.

"I think it's obvious."

"Good. Then you can explain it to me."

"It was my father's lifeblood, Noah. He spent his whole

life dreaming of producing the best wines possible. I can't just give it up.''

"I haven't asked you to.''

"Not yet.'' She could feel the muscles in her jaw tensing. Not now, she thought to herself, don't ruin it now. We just made beautiful, heavenly love. I love you hopelessly. Don't betray me! Not now.

"But you think I will.''

She ran a trembling hand through her hair. "You already offered to buy me out.''

"And that bothers you. Why?''

He seemed sincere. She didn't want to think that he had the ugly ulterior motives of which her attorney had warned her. She didn't want to believe he was like his infamous father. "It's just too soon . . . after my father's death. I don't want to give up everything he believed in. Not yet.''

His thumb persuaded her to turn her head and look at him. "Does it mean that much to you—what your father wanted?''

"We were very close.''

Noah rubbed his thumbnail under his lower lip. "Close enough that you're willing to sacrifice everything in order to prolong his dream?''

"It's not a sacrifice. It's what I want to do.''

Noah sighed and his breath ruffled her hair as he tightened his grip around her waist and pulled her closer to him. "Oh, beautiful lady—what am I going to do with you?'' She was a puzzle to him; an intriguing, beguiling puzzle for which he had no answers.

"Trust me,'' she replied in answer to his rhetorical question.

"I do,'' he admitted fervently.

She wanted to believe him, but couldn't forget the dark shadows of doubt she had seen in his clear blue eyes.

"Tell me about your husband," Noah suggested, carefully changing the topic of conversation. The faceless man who had married Sheila, impregnated her, and then left her had been eating at Noah since the first night they had been together.

"I don't like to talk about Jeff." It was a flat statement, intent on changing the subject.

"Why not?"

Her fingers curled into tiny fists, and she had to force them to relax. "It still bothers me."

"The divorce—or the marriage?"

"The fact that I made such a big mistake." She pulled herself out of Noah's warm arms.

"Then you blame yourself."

"Partially, I suppose—look, I don't want to talk about it."

"I didn't mean to pry . . ."

Sheila waved his apology aside. "No . . . you didn't. I don't know why it bothers me so much."

"Maybe it's because you're still in love with him."

Sheila's head snapped back as if his words had slapped her in the face. "You're wrong. The answer is probably just the opposite. I don't know if I ever loved him. I thought I did, but if I had loved him enough, perhaps things would be different."

"And you would still be married?"

She nodded mutely, trying to repress the urge to cry.

"Is that what you want—to be married to him?"

Sheila felt as if the blood were being drained from her as she told Noah her innermost thoughts, the secrets she had guarded from the rest of the world. "No, I don't want to be married to him—marrying Jeff might have been my biggest mistake. But, because of Emily, I wonder if I did the right thing."

"By divorcing him?"

"He divorced me," she sighed, rubbing her fingertips pensively over her forehead. "But maybe I should have fought it, tried harder for Emily's sake." ·

"Oh, so you think that it would be better for the child if the two of you hadn't split up." His voice sounded bitter in the dark night.

"I don't know what would have been right. It was difficult. I thought he was happy."

"Were you?"

"In the beginning, yes. And when I found out I was pregnant, I was ecstatic. Jeff wasn't as thrilled as I was, but I thought his reaction was normal and that he would become more involved with the child once she was born." Sheila paused, as if trying to put her emotions into some kind of order. Noah felt an intense dislike for Jeff Coleridge.

"It didn't happen," Noah guessed.

"It wasn't the baby so much . . . as the added strain on him to support the family. I couldn't work, not even in the part-time job I had kept before Emily was born. The cost of a good sitter would have eaten up all my salary. I guess the financial burden was too much for him." Sheila stopped, and the heavy silence enveloped her. Noah was waiting to hear the end of her story, but she found her courage sadly lacking. What she had hidden from her father and the rest of the world, she found impossible to say to the man whose fingers still touched her arm.

"He left you because of the money? What kind of man would leave a wife and a child when he couldn't support them?"

Sheila felt herself become strangely defensive. "He wasn't born to wealth, like you. He had to struggle every day of his life."

"That has nothing to do with a man's responsibility."

His fingers dug into her arm. "What happened? There's something you're not telling me."

Sheila swallowed back her tears. "Jeff . . . he became . . . involved with another woman." She lowered her head, ashamed of what she had admitted.

When confronted with the truth he had suspected, Noah felt a sickening turn in his stomach. He gritted his teeth to prevent a long line of oaths from escaping.

Compelled to continue, Sheila spoke again in the barest of whispers, as if the pain were too intense to be conveyed in a normal tone of voice. "This woman—her name was Judith—she was older than Jeff, midforties, I'd guess. Divorced and financially secure. She wanted a younger . . ."

"Stud?" Noah asked sarcastically.

"Man."

"Your husband was no man, Sheila!" he swore. "He's a bastard, and a stupid one at that."

Sheila bravely held her poise together, admitting to Noah what no one else had ever known. She had kept her secrets locked securely within her, hoping to keep any of her pain or anger from tainting Emily's image of her father. "It doesn't matter. Not now. Anyway, Jeff demanded a divorce, and when I realized that there was no hope for the two of us, I agreed. The only thing I wanted was my child. That wasn't much of a problem; Emily would only have gotten in Jeff's way."

Noah's fingers tightened and pulled her closer to his chest. "You don't have to talk about any of this. . . ."

"It's all right. There's not much more to tell, but I think you should hear it," she stated tonelessly. "When the marriage failed, I went off the deep end. I didn't know where to turn. Dad encouraged me to move to California and go to school for my master's."

Sheila smiled wistfully to herself when she recalled how transparent her father had been. "I'm sure that he expected me to find some other man to take my mind off Jeff. So"—she let out the air in her lungs with her confession—"I took money from my dad, a lot of money that he probably couldn't afford to lend to me, and accepted his advice. I didn't know that payment for my out-of-state tuition and living expenses was more than Dad could afford. I thought the winery was profitable. But, it wasn't, and Dad had to borrow the money he loaned to me."

"From Wilder Investments," Noah guessed. Noah's frown deepened and the disgust churning in his stomach rose in his throat. So this was how Ben had cornered Oliver Lindstrom, by using the man's love of his daughter and capitalizing upon it. The muscles in the back of Noah's neck began to ache with the strain of tension.

"There are two mortgages on the winery," Sheila admitted. "Dad had nowhere else to borrow."

"And of course Ben complied."

"You make it sound as if he instigated the whole thing."

Noah's nostrils flared, and his eyes narrowed. "I wouldn't put it past him."

"Your father had nothing to do with the fact that my marriage fell apart. It's my fault that I hadn't paid back the loan. . . . I just thought there was more time. I never even considered the fact that my father was mortal." Her grief overcame her and the tears she had been fighting pooled in her eyes. "I thought he'd always be there."

"Don't," he urged, kissing her lightly on the top of the head. "Don't torture yourself with a guilt you shouldn't bear."

The little laugh that erupted from her throat was brittle with self-condemnation. "If only I could believe that."

"You're being too hard on yourself."

"There's no one else to blame."

"How about your ex-husband to start with?" Noah spat out, surprised at the hatred he felt for a man he didn't know. "Or your father. He should have told you about his financial problems."

She shook her head, and the tears in her eyes ran down her cheeks. "He didn't want to burden me, and I didn't even ask!"

"Shhh . . . love, don't," Noah whispered, holding her shaking form against him, trying to quiet a rage that burned within him. How did so beautiful a creature, so innocent a woman, get caught in the middle between two men who only meant to hurt her? Her husband was a wretch, and her father, while trying to shield her, had wounded her in the end. The fire and Oliver Lindstrom's part in its conception waged heavy battles in Noah's tired mind. If only he could tell Sheila what he knew about her father, if only he could bare his soul to her. But he held his tongue, fearful lest he reinforce her feelings of guilt.

Noah had never guessed why Sheila's father had borrowed against his interest in the winery. He had assumed that the money was used for personal use or folly, but he didn't doubt the authenticity of Sheila's tale. Too many events correlated with the ledgers at Wilder Investments, ledgers he had studied for hours before coming to the Cascade Valley. If the ledgers weren't evidence enough, the guilt-ridden lines on Sheila's face testified to her remorse and self-incrimination.

"Come on," he murmured, rising and pulling her to her feet. "Let's go back to the house. You need some sleep."

"Will you stay with me?" she asked, cringing in anticipation of possible rejection. She felt as if her confession would destroy any of the feelings he might have had for her.

"For as long as you want me," he returned, slowly walking up the hill toward the house.

Sheila woke to find herself alone in the bed. The blue printed sheets that she loved seemed cold and mocking without Noah's strong embrace. She knew why he wasn't with her. He had held her and comforted her most of the night, but sometime near morning, when she was drowzily sleeping, he had slipped out of her room to wait for dawn on the uncomfortable couch. It was somewhat hypocritical, but the best arrangement possible because of Emily and Sean.

The day began pleasantly, and even a makeshift breakfast of sausage and pancakes went without much of a hitch. Sean was still sullen and quiet, but at least he seemed resigned to his fate, and for the most part didn't bait Sheila.

After breakfast, while the kids washed the dishes, Sheila took Noah through the rooms of the château. It was a large building; it had originally been built as the country resort of a rich Frenchman named Gilles de Marc. Viticulture had been his hobby, and it was only when he discovered the perfect conditions of the Cascade Valley for growing wine grapes that he began to ferment and bottle the first Cabernet Sauvignon.

Other than a few rooms on the first floor that had been spared, the damage to the main house was dismal. Noah's practiced eyes traveled over the smoke-laden linen draperies and the gritty layer of ash on the carpet. It was obvious that Sheila had tried to vacuum and shampoo the once-burgundy carpet to no avail. Huge water stains darkened the English wallpaper, and a few of the window panes were broken and covered with pieces of plywood. The elegant European antiques were water stained, and with the grateful exception of a few expensive pieces, would have to be refinished.

Everywhere there was evidence that Sheila had attempted to restore the rooms to their original grandeur, but the task had been too overwhelming.

Later, sitting in the office looking over Oliver Lindstrom's personal records, Noah noted they coincided with the events in Sheila's story. He pondered the entries in Oliver's checkbook, noting dismally when the money borrowed from Wilder Investments had come in. Some of the funds had been sent in quarterly installments to Sheila in California; other money had been used for the day-to-day operation of the winery in lean years. As far as Noah could tell, Oliver had used none of the funds for himself. That knowledge did nothing to ease his mind; it only made it more difficult to explain to Sheila that her father was involved with the arson.

Sheila attempted to help Noah, explaining what she knew of the winery. Noah sat at her father's desk, jotting notes to himself and studying her father's books as if they held the answers to the universe. She felt as if she were growing closer to him, that she was beginning to understand him. She knew that she could trust him with her life, and she quietly hoped that the love she was feeling for him would someday be returned. Perhaps in time the shadows of doubt that darkened his eyes would disappear and be replaced by trust.

Even Emily was beginning to open up to Noah, and the little girl's shyness all but disappeared by midafternoon. Though he was busy looking over the books, he always took the time to talk to her and show an interest in what she was doing. By late afternoon Emily seemed completely at ease with Noah.

The most surprising relationship that began to evolve was Emily's attraction to Sean. She adored the teenager and followed after him wherever he went. Though Sean tried vainly to hide his feelings, Sheila suspected that Sean was as fond of the tousled-headed little girl as she was of him. Things were going smoothly—too smoothly.

"Enough work," Sheila announced, breezing into Oliver's study. Noah was at the desk, a worried frown creasing his brow. One lock of dark hair fell over his forehead. As he looked up from the untidy stack of papers on the desk and his eyes found hers, a lazy grin formed on his lips.

"What have you got in mind?" A seductive glint sparked in his eyes as they caressed her from across the room.

She lowered her voice and dropped her eyelids, imitating his look of provocative jest. "What do *you* have in mind?"

"You're unkind," he muttered, seeing through her joke.

"And you're overly optimistic."

He leaned back in the leather chair and it groaned with the shifting of his weight. "*Expectant* might be a better word."

"I was hoping to hear that you were hungry."

His smile broadened. "That might apply," he admitted, his voice husky.

"Good." She threw off her look of wicked seduction and winked at him. "We're going on a picnic."

"Alone?"

"Dream on. The kids are joining us."

Before Noah could respond, an eruption of hurried footsteps announced Emily's breathless arrival into the study. "Aren't you ready yet?" she grumbled. "I thought we were going on a hike."

"We're on our way," Sheila laughed. "Did you pack your brownies?"

"Shhh . . ." Emily put her finger to her lips and her face pulled into a pout. "They're supposed to be a surprise!"

"I promise I won't tell a soul," Noah kidded, his voice hushed in collusion with the excited child. "This will be our secret, okay?"

Emily smiled, and Sheila couldn't help but wonder how long it had been since she had seen her daughter so at ease with a man. Emily was shy, and even when her father visited, it took time for her to warm up to him. But with Noah it was different; a genuine fondness existed between the man and child. Or was it her imagination, vain hopes that Emily would take to Noah. . . .

Emily raced out of the room, and Sheila cocked her head in the direction of the retreating child. "I think we'd better get going before Emily's patience wears out."

"I can't believe that little girl would ever lose her temper."

"Just wait," Sheila warned with a warm laugh. "You'll see, only hope that you're well out of range of her throwing arm if you ever cross her."

"Emily? Tantrums?"

"The likes of which haven't been seen in civilization," Sheila rejoined.

Noah rose from the chair. "I wonder where she gets that temper of hers?" he mused aloud. The corners of his eyes crinkled in laughter as he stared pointedly at Sheila. He crossed the room and encircled her waist with his arms. His fingers touched the small of her back, pressing her firmly against him. He pushed an errant lock of copper hair behind her ear as he stared down at her, a bemused smile curving his lips. His clean, masculine scent filled her nostrils.

She lifted an elegant eyebrow dubiously. "Are you accusing me of being temperamental?"

He shook his head. "Temperamental is far too kind. Argumentative is more apt, I think." His lips caressed her forehead and his voice lowered huskily. "What I wouldn't give to have just an hour alone with you," he growled against her ear.

"What would you do?" she asked coyly, playing with the collar of his shirt.

"Things you can't begin to imagine."

She felt a tremor of excited anticipation pierce through her. "Try me."

His eyes narrowed in frustration. "You're unbelievable, you know, but gorgeous. Just wait, you'll get yours," he warned as he released her and gave her buttocks a firm pat. "Let's go—we don't want to keep Emily waiting."

The hike up the steady incline of the surrounding hills took nearly an hour, but Sheila insisted that the view from the top of the knoll was well worth the strain on their leg muscles. Noah appeared openly doubtful, Emily was an energetic bundle of anticipation and Sean had once again donned his role of bored martyrdom.

The picnic spot Sheila had chosen was one of her favorites, a secluded hilltop guarded by a verdant stand of tamaracks and lodge-pole pines. After selecting an area that afforded the best view of the surrounding Cascade Mountains, she spread a well-worn blanket on the bare ground and arranged paper plates and sandwiches haphazardly over the plaid cloth. The tension of the previous night was subdued, and Sheila relaxed as she nibbled at a sandwich and sipped from a soft drink. Even Sean began to unwind, letting his mask of sullen rebellion slip.

"I know a good place to catch trout," Emily stated authoritatively. She was still trying to impress Sean.

"You do, do you?" Sean kidded, rumpling Emily's dark curls. A mischievous twinkle lighted his blue eyes. "How would a little kid like you know about catching trout?"

Emily's face rumpled in vexation. "I'm *not* a little kid!"

"Okay," Sean shrugged dismissively. "So how do you know how to fish?"

"My grandpa taught me," Emily declared.

Sean's indifference wavered as he sized up the little girl. She was okay, he decided, for a little kid. His expression was still dubious. "What kind of trout?"

"Rainbow . . . and some brook."

Sean's interest was piqued. "So how do you catch them?"

"With a pole, stupid," Emily replied haughtily.

Once again Sean was defensive. "But we didn't bring any poles."

"You think you know everything, don't you?" Emily shot back. She reached into Sheila's backpack and extracted two tubes; within each was an expandable fly rod.

"You need more than a pole to catch a fish."

Emily shot him a look that said more clearly than words, *Any idiot knows that much.* Instead she said, "Give me a break, will ya?" Once again she reached into the open backpack and pulled out a small metal box full of hand-tied flies. She flipped open the lid and held it proudly open for Sean's inspection. "Anything else?"

Sean smiled, exposing large dimples as he held his palms outward in mock surrender. "Okay, okay—so you know all about fishing. My mistake. Let's go." He looked toward Noah and Sheila sitting near the blanket to see if he had parental approval.

Sheila, who had been witnessing the ongoing discussion with quiet amusement, grinned at the blond youth. "Sure you can go. Your dad and I can handle the dishes—such as they are. Emily knows how to get to the creek; she and her grandpa used to go up there every evening." Sheila's smile turned wistful. "Just be sure to be back at the house before it gets too dark."

Emily was already racing down the opposite side of the hill, her small hand wrapped tightly around the fly rod. "Come on, Sean. Get a move on. We haven't got all day," she sang out over her shoulder.

Sean took his cue and picked up the remaining pole and the box of flies before heading out after Emily.

Sheila began to put the leftover fruit and sandwiches into the basket. "You can help, you know," she pointed out, glancing at Noah through a veil of dark lashes.

"Why should I when I can lie here and enjoy the view?" His blue eyes slid lazily up her body. He was lying on his side, his body propped up on one elbow as he studied her. As she placed the blanket into her backpack, his hand reached out to capture her wrist. "Explain something to me."

The corners of her mouth twitched. "If I can."

His dark brows blunted, as if he were curiously tossing a problem over in his mind, but his thumb began to trace lazy, erotic circles on the inside of her forearm. "Why is it that you and that precocious daughter of yours can handle my son when I can't even begin to understand him?"

"Maybe you're trying too hard," Sheila answered. She bit into an apple and paused when she had swallowed. "Do you really think that Emily's precocious?"

"Only when she has to be."

"And when is that?"

"When she's dealing with Sean. He's a handful."

Sheila rotated the apple in her hand and studied it. "She's never had to deal with anyone like Sean before."

Noah seemed surprised. "Why not?"

Sheila shrugged dismissively. "All of my friends have children just about Emily's age. Some are older, some younger, but only by a few years. The winery's pretty remote and she hasn't run into many teenagers. That might be because they tend to avoid younger kids.''

''Certainly you've had baby-sitters.''

Sheila shook her head, and the sunlight glinted in reddish streaks on her burnished curls. ''Not many,'' she explained, tossing the apple core into the trash. ''I usually trade off with my friends, and when that doesn't work out, there's always Marian.''

''Marian?''

''Jeff's mother. Emily's grandmother.''

Noah's thumb ceased its seductive motion on her inner wrist. ''Right,'' he agreed, as if he really didn't understand. He stood up abruptly and dusted his hands on the knees of his jeans. A dark scowl creased his forehead. As if dismissing an unpleasant thought, he shook his head and let out a long gust of wind. ''You're still very attached to your ex-mother-in-law, aren't you?'' he observed.

Sheila jammed the cork back in the wine bottle and stashed it in the backpack. ''I suppose so,'' she said. ''She's Emily's only living grandparent.''

''And that makes her special?''

''Yes.''

Noah snorted his disagreement as he picked up his pack and the light basket.

''Marian Coleridge is very good to Emily and to me. She adores the child, and just because Jeff and I split up doesn't mean that Emily should have to sacrifice a good relationship with her grandmother.''

''Of course not,'' was Noah's clipped reply.

''Then why does it bother you?''

''It doesn't.''

''Liar.''

''I just don't like being reminded that you were married.''

"You're reminded of it every time you see Emily."

"That's different."

"How?"

"Your child can't be compared to your ex-husband's mother."

Sheila sighed to herself as they began walking back to the house. "I don't want to argue with you. It's pointless. I'm a thirty-year-old divorced woman with a child. You can't expect me to forget that I was married."

"I don't. But then, I don't expect you to constantly remind yourself of the fact."

"I don't."

They came to a bend in the path, and Noah stopped and turned to face Sheila. He set down the basket and gazed into the gray depths of her eyes. "I think you're still hung up on your ex-husband," he accused.

"That's ridiculous."

"Is it?"

Sheila's anger became evident as she pursed her lips tightly together. "The only reason I don't like to talk about Jeff is that I'm not proud of being divorced. I didn't go into that marriage expecting it to end as it did. I thought I loved him once, now I'm not so sure, but the point is, I had hoped that it wouldn't have turned out so badly. It's . . . as if I've *failed*." She was shaking, but tried to control her ragged emotions. She sighed as she thought of her daughter. "I am glad I married Jeff, though."

"I thought so." His blue eyes narrowed.

"Because of Emily!" Sheila was becoming exasperated. "If I wouldn't have married Jeff, I would never have had Emily. *You* should understand that."

"I didn't get married to have Sean!"

"And I wouldn't have a baby without a father."

Noah's jaw clenched, and the skin over his cheekbones

stretched thin. "So you think Marilyn should have gotten an abortion, as she had planned."

"No!" Didn't he understand what she was saying? "Of course not. I don't even understand the circumstances surrounding your son's birth."

"Is that what you want, to hear all the juicy details?"

"I only want to know what you're willing to tell me and to try and convince you that I'm not in the least 'hung-up' on Jeff. That was over long before the divorce."

The anger in Noah's eyes began to fade. His mouth spread into a slow, self-deprecating smile. "It's hard, you know."

"What?"

"Dealing with jealousy." He looked into the distance as he sorted his thoughts. It was late afternoon; a warm sun hung low in the sky, waiting to disappear beneath the ridge of snow-capped mountains and he was with the only woman who had really interested him in the last sixteen years. Why did he insist on arguing with her? Why couldn't he just tell her everything he felt about her—that he was falling in love with her and couldn't let himself fall victim to her? Why couldn't he find the courage to explain about her father? Why couldn't he ignore the look of pride and love in her eyes when she spoke of her father? What did he fear?

Sheila was staring at him, her eyes wide with disbelief. "You're trying to convince me that you're jealous . . . of what . . . not *Jeff?*" If Noah hadn't seemed so earnest, so genuinely vexed with himself, she might have laughed.

He was deadly serious, his voice low and without humor. "I'm jealous of any man that touched you."

She reached down, picked up the basket and handed it to him. "Now who's exhibiting 'latent Victorian morality'?"

His dimple appeared as he carefully considered her accusation. "Okay, so you're right. I can't help it. I get a little crazy when I'm with you." He reached for her, but because he was hampered by the picnic basket, she managed to slip out of his grasp. A few feet ahead of him, she turned and walked backward up the sloping, overgrown path. "Is that such a crime?"

"That depends,'' she murmured, tossing her rich chestnut hair before lowering her lashes and pouting her lips provocatively.

He waited, his smile broadening, his dark brows arching. "Upon what?" he coaxed while striding more closely to her.

She touched her finger to her lips and then pressed it fleetingly to his. "On just how crazy you want to get. . . ."

"You're wicked," he accused, "seductively wicked." This time, when he reached for her with his free hand, his steely fingers wrapped possessively over her forearm.

"Only when I'm around you," she promised. A smile quirked on her full lips. "That makes us quite a pair, doesn't it? Crazy and wicked."

"That makes for an indescribably potent attraction," he stated, drawing her closer to him. "Just where are you taking me? Didn't you take the wrong turn back at the fork in the path a little while ago?"

"I wondered if you would notice."

"Did you think that you had captivated me so completely that I would lose my sense of direction?"

"Hardly," she whispered dryly.

"Is it a secret?"

"No."

"Then why are you being so mysterious?"

"Because I've never taken anyone up here before . . . aside from Emily."

"What is it, your private part of the mountains?"

Sheila smiled broadly, slightly embarrassed. "I guess I

kind of thought of it that way. It's just a place I used to go, as a kid, when I wanted to be alone.''

Noah's hand strengthened its grip on her arm. They followed the path around pine trees that had fallen across it and over a summit, until they entered a small valley with a clear brook running through it. The water spilled over a ledge from the higher elevations of the mountain, creating a frothy waterfall with a pool at its base. From the small lake the stream continued recklessly through the valley and down the lower elevations of the foothills.

They walked around the small pond together, arms linked, eyes taking in the serenity of the secluded valley. Noah helped her cross the stream, nearly slipping on the wet stones peeking from the rushing water. Once on the other side of the brook, Noah spread the blanket. They sat together near a stand of Ponderosa Pines, close to the fall of cascading water and able to feel the cool mist of water on their skin.

"Why did you bring me here?" Noah asked, his eyes following the path of the winding mountain stream.

"I don't know. I guess I just wanted to share the beauty of this place with you. . . . Oh, Noah, I just don't want to lose it.''

Grim lines formed at the corner of his mouth. ''And you think that I'll take it away from you.''

"I think you have that power.''

Noah rubbed his thumbnail over his lower lip. "Even if I did, do you honestly think I would use it?''

Her eyes were honest when they looked into his. Lines marred her forehead where her brows drew together. ''I don't know.''

"Don't you trust me?''

She took in a steadying breath. ''Yes . . .''

"But?''

"I don't think you're telling me everything."

Noah tossed a stone into the pond and watched it skip, drawing circles on the clear surface of the water. "What do you want to know?"

"About Anthony Simmons's report on the fire."

"What if it isn't complete?" he heard himself ask, damning himself for hedging. The truth should be so simple.

"It has to be. He hasn't been here in two weeks. He strikes me as the kind of man who doesn't give up until he finds what he's looking for."

"And you think he has?"

"I think that if he hadn't, he would still be knocking on my door, digging through Dad's records, asking his inane questions."

Noah rested his forearms on his knees. "You're right about that much."

"And I'm right that his report is complete?" she asked, barely daring to breathe.

"Right again."

"Well?"

"Well, nothing."

"I don't understand."

"I'm not convinced that Simmons's report was conclusive. There are a few discrepancies."

"Such as?"

Noah found himself lying with incredible ease. Was this how it started, with a single deception that multiplied and compounded until it became an intricate network of lies? Is this what had happened to his father? "Nothing all that important . . . it's just that the insurance company needs some more documents to support his theories. Until Pac-West is satisfied, the entire report isn't considered valid."

Doubts darkened her eyes and her confidence in him wavered. The trust he had worked so hard to establish was flowing from her as surely as sand through an hourglass.

"I assume that means that Mr. Simmons and his questions will be back."

"Maybe not."

"Noah." Her voice was amazingly level for the sense of betrayal that was overwhelming her. "You're talking in circles. Just tell me the truth . . . all of it."

One lie begat another. "There's nothing to tell."

"Then why did you come here? I thought you had news about the winery. I thought we could finally put the fire behind us."

This time he didn't have to lie. His eyes were a clear blue, filled with sincerity. "Don't let the fire stand between us. I came here because I wanted to see you. Can't you believe that?"

"Oh, God, Noah, I want to," she whispered fervently. She let her forehead drop into the open palm of her hand. Noah's heart turned over, as he witnessed her defeat. "It's just that I feel that you're holding back on me. Am I wrong? Aren't there things you know that you should be sharing with me?"

He traced the sculpted line of her jaw with his finger. The curves of her bones neared perfection. "Just trust me, Sheila," he stated, feeling the traitor he was. He tilted her head with the strength of one finger and pressed his lips against hers. His lips were gentle but persuasive. His seduction began to work. Against her will, she thought less of the fire and the damage to the winery and concentrated with a growing awareness of the man. She realized that he was pushing against her, that she was falling backward, but she knew that his strong arm would break her fall and before her back would encounter the plaid blanket and cold earth, he would catch her. She wanted to trust him with her life.

His hands parted her blouse, slipping the cotton fabric easily over her shoulders, and his tongue rimmed her lips, which opened willingly to his moist touch. His fingers grazed her breast and finally settled against it, warming her skin and causing her to moan. She trembled with need of him and felt contentment welling from deep within her when he unclasped her bra and pressed his flesh against hers, molding his skin to hers.

Her nipple hardened under his erotic touch, and he growled hungrily in the back of his throat. "You do make me crazy, you know," he whispered against the pink shell of her ear. "You make me want to do things to you that will bind me to you forever," he admitted raggedly. "I want to make love to you and never stop. . . . Damn it, Sheila, I love you."

She swallowed the lump in her throat that had formed during his tortured admission. How could she possibly sort the fact from fiction? Tears began to collect in her eyes. "You . . . you don't have to say anything," she stammered, bracing herself for the denial that was sure to come once his passion had subsided.

"I don't want to love you, Sheila . . . but I just can't seem to help myself." His black brows knit in confusion as he looked down upon her, witnessing her tears and misreading them. "Oh, no, Sheila, darling, don't cry."

To still him and prevent any more half-truths to form on his lips, she kissed him, holding his head against hers and letting him feel the depth of her desire.

Her heart began to thud in her chest, and the blood rushing through her veins turned molten. His hands smoothed the skin over her breasts and down her rib cage, pressing against her with enough force to mold her skin tightly over her ribs and inflame the skin when his fingers dipped below the waistband of her jeans.

His lips followed the path of his hands, and his hungry mouth caressed each breast moistly as his tongue massaged a nipple. She felt the convulsions of desire rip through her body as he trailed a dewy path of kisses across the soft skin of her abdomen. Still, his hands kneaded her breasts. Involuntarily she sucked in her breath and arched against him. Her fingers pushed his shirt off his shoulders and dug into the hard, lean muscles of his upper arms.

When he removed her jeans, he tossed them aside and she sighed in contentment. Slowly he rose and took off his jeans, discarding them into a pile near hers. She stared at him unguardedly, devouring the contours of his tanned muscles as if her eyes were starved for the sight of him.

The sun was beginning to set, casting lengthening shadows across the valley. The fading light played over his skin, adding an ethereal dimension to the oncoming evening.

Noah was silent as he settled next to her and began caressing her with his lips and hands. He stroked her intimately, forcing the tide of her desire to crest, making the blood within her throb with fiery need as it pulsed through her body. They lay together, face to face, man to woman, alone except for the hungry need that controlled them.

He took her slowly, coupling with her as gently as if she were new to him. He waited until he felt her demand a faster rhythm, until he saw passion glaze her eyes, until the pain in his back where her fingernails had found his flesh forced him to a more violent, savage union.

Her breath came in short, uneven gasps, her body broke into a glow of perspiration, and the ache within her deepest core began to control her, until she was rising with him, pushing against him, calling his name into the wilderness.

She began to melt inside, and convulsive surges of fulfillment forced her to cling to him. He groaned her name against the silken strands of her hair as he shuddered in an eruptive release of frustrated desire that turned his bones to liquid.

"I love you, Sheila," he whispered over and over again. "I love you."

## Chapter Ten

"You're out of your mind," Noah stated emphatically. Twilight was rapidly approaching and the last thing he wanted to do was take a quick dip in an icy lake.

"Come on . . . it's not that cold."

"Save that for someone who'll believe it, Sheila. That water is runoff from the spring melt on the Cascades. You've got another think coming if you think you can talk me into swimming in ice water."

"It could be fun," she suggested. He could see her body through the ripples in the water. The firm contours of her limbs were distorted against the darkening pool. He would catch a glimpse of one breast as she treaded in the water, and then it would be gone, covered by her arm as she kept herself afloat. Her hair was damp and tossed carelessly off her face. Dewy drops of water clung to her eyelashes and cheeks. "Come on."

"I've never done anything this irrational in my life," he admitted, testing the water and withdrawing his foot.

"Then it's time." She shoved her hand through the clear ripples and set a wave of cold water washing over his body. His startled look was replaced by determination as he marched into the lake. Quickly she dove under the water and swam near the bottom, to resurface behind the waterfall. Just as she took in a gulp of air, her legs were pulled out from under her by strong arms. When she came up again, she was sputtering for air. Noah's arms encircled her waist.

"You lied," he accused. "This lake is *too cold*."

"Refreshing," she bantered back.

"Frigid." He captured her blue lips with his and kissed the droplets of water off her face. His hands and legs touched her intimately beneath the surface of the water; his kiss deepened and their tongues entwined. Her skin heated, but was cooled by the chilly temperature in the water.

His fingers touched her thigh, smoothing the soft skin and caressing her as they stood, waist deep in the pond. The waterfall was their flowing curtain of privacy as Noah kissed a hardened nipple and pushed her against the ledge.

"We should be going," she pleaded.

"Not now, you little witch. You coerced me into this lake with you, and you're going to suffer the consequences."

"And just what consequences are you talking about?"

"I'm going to make you beg me to love you."

"But Sean . . . Emily . . ." His hand continued its exploration, warming her internally while her skin was chilled by the water.

"They'll wait for us."

He kissed her again, his hand still extracting sweet promises from her. Her breasts flattened against him, and he licked the moisture from them.

Despite the temperature of the water, Sheila began to warm from the inside out. She felt her legs part and wanted more than the touch of cold lapping water on her skin. She yearned to be a part of the man she loved, ached for him to join with her. His kisses upon her neck enticed her. The dewy droplets of cold water on her breasts made her skin quiver. And his hands, God, his hands, gently stroking her, driving all thoughts from her mind other than the desire welling deep within her body.

"Oh, Noah," she whispered as she felt the excruciating ache within her beg for release.

"Yes, love," he whispered thickly.

"Please . . ."

"What?"

"Please love me," she murmured against his chest, stroking her tongue against the virile male muscles, wondering if it were possible ever to get enough of him. How long would it be before her love for him would consume her?

"I do love you, Sheila. I will forever," he vowed as he pushed her gently against the ledge beneath the water's surface. He placed his legs between hers, and the spray from the waterfall ran in lingering rivulets down her face and neck. The water lapped lazily around her hips and thighs and Noah came to her, burying himself in her with savage strokes.

She found herself clutching him, clinging to him, surging with him over the final barrier until satiation and exhaustion took its toll on her.

"I love you," she whispered, licking a drop of water from his temple, and the strength of his arms wrapped her more tightly to him, as if he were afraid that in releasing her he would lose her.

They shivered as they got dressed, packed their belongings, and hiked down the path. Dusk began to shadow the hills in darkness, but when they were within sight of the château, they could see that no lights burned in the windows. It was obvious that Sean and Emily hadn't returned. Sheila became uneasy.

"I thought the kids would be back by now," she said, voicing her thoughts. "I told Emily to be home before dark."

"She might have had trouble convincing Sean," Noah muttered. "It's quite a hike, and the best fly fishing is in the evening."

Sheila wasn't convinced. "They should be home."

"They will be. Don't worry. I bet they'll be here within the next half hour."

"And if they're not?"

"We'll go looking for them. You do know where Emily was headed, don't you?"

Sheila nodded and smiled in spite of her apprehension. "It's the same place Dad used to take me."

"Then let's not worry until we have to. There's something I want to talk about." He settled upon a rope hammock in the yard and indicated with a gesture that he wanted her to lie next to him.

She slid into the rope swing, careful not to lose her balance. "Okay—so talk."

"I think I should tell you about Marilyn."

"Sean's mother?"

Noah's lips twisted wryly. "I don't think of her as his mother, merely the woman who gave him birth."

"You don't have to explain any of this to me." Sheila wanted to know everything about him, and yet was unwilling to know his secrets more intimately. The past was gone; what was the point in dredging up bitter memories?

"I don't have to tell you anything, but I want to. Maybe

then you'll understand my feelings for my son . . . and my father.''

"Ben was involved.''

Noah's entire body became rigid. "Oh, yes, he was involved all right—he couldn't help himself. You don't know my father, but if you did, you'd realize that he tries to dominate everyone or everything he touches.''

"Your father's ill," Sheila reminded him gently.

Noah relaxed a little and stared at the stars beginning to peek through the violet-gray dusk. "He wasn't ill sixteen years ago," Noah asserted as he squinted in thought. "As a matter of fact he was in his prime."

Noah paused, conjuring up the period in his life he had tried to forget. "Marilyn was only seventeen when we first met. She came to a fraternity dance with a friend of mine. I thought at the time she was the most beautiful girl I had ever seen. Long blond hair, clear blue eyes and a smile that could melt ice. I was captivated.

"It wasn't long before I was dating her, and Ben told me to 'dump her.' In the old man's opinion, Marilyn wasn't quite up to par, socially speaking." Noah shook his head at his own young foolishness.

"You know that I haven't ever gotten along with Ben?" Sheila nodded, afraid to break the silence. "Well, Ben considered Marilyn a 'gold digger,' after the family fortune. Maybe she was. Hell, she was just a kid, barely seventeen. Anyway, I suppose that because my father was so hell-bent against her, it made her all the more attractive to me . . . at least for a while. We dated for about four months, I guess, and then we started arguing, over stupid little things. We never got along."

Noah absently ran his hand across his chin, rubbing the beard shadow that had begun to appear. "Anyway, just as I decided to break things off with her, she turned up pregnant. She was probably scared, but she didn't have the guts to tell me about it. I heard the news secondhand, through a friend of mine who was dating her sister.

"At first I was angry—furious that she hadn't come to me with the news. When I found out that she intended to have an abortion, I thought I would kill her myself. I drove around for four hours, and I had no idea where I'd been, but I had managed to calm down. By the time I went to her house, I knew that I wanted my child more than anything in the world and that I was willing to pay any price to get it.

"I tried pleading with her to keep the baby, but she didn't even want to talk about it. I told her that I would marry her, give my name to the child, whatever she wanted, if she would reconsider."

Noah closed his eyes, as if hiding from the truth. "She finally agreed and I thought I'd won a major victory because it was pretty evident that she was more concerned about being cheerleader to the football squad than being a mother to my unborn child. And maybe I've been too rough on her—she wasn't much older than Sean is now. Just a kid. And I was just as foolish. Although we'd made one mistake, I thought we could correct it. Given time, I was sure that Marilyn would mature and learn to love the baby. I even thought she and I had a chance."

Bitterness made his voice brittle. "But I was wrong. Dead wrong. Ben couldn't leave it alone . . . and maybe it was better that he didn't . . . I don't know. Anyway, Ben was against the marriage from the first, baby or no baby, and he offered Marilyn a decent sum of money to go quietly away and give the baby up for adoption. The offer was attractive to her; she had no other means to afford college.

"I was outraged at my father's proposal and sickened by Marilyn's transparent interest in the money. I tried to talk her out of it and insisted that she marry me and keep the child. If she wanted to go to school, I was sure we could afford it, at least part-time. She was adamantly against any solution I provided. I didn't understand it at the time; not until she told me what she had come up with as an alternative solution.''

Sheila was breathless as she watched the angry play of sixteen-year-old emotions contort Noah's face in pain. ''In Marilyn's beautiful, scheming mind, she found the answer. The price was considerably higher of course, but she agreed to give the baby up for adoption to me, his father, for a discreet and large sum of money. Although Ben didn't like the idea of being manipulated by a girl he considered socially off-limits, he seemed to almost . . . enjoy her sense of values.

''It was obvious that a marriage to Marilyn under the best circumstances would be a disaster for both the baby and myself, so I swallowed my pride and pleaded with my father to agree to her demands, in order that I could gain custody of Sean. Sixteen years ago father's rights were virtually unheard of, and without Marilyn's written consent, I could never have gotten custody of my son. I wanted the only decent thing I could retrieve from that relationship with Marilyn—my unborn son.

''Ben thought I was completely out of my mind, but finally agreed. In the past sixteen years, every time he and I would disagree, Ben would remind me that it was *his money and his power* that gave me custody of Sean.''

Noah ran an angry hand through his dark hair and uttered an oath under his breath. Sheila knew she was witnessing a rare side of him. As she watched the cruel emotions tighten his jaw, she understood that she was learning things about him that he kept hidden from the rest of the world. He was letting her become closer to him, divulging his innermost secrets. She leaned her head against his shoulder and listened to the steady beat of his heart.

"Ben even has the stubborn pride to think that he saved me from an unhappy marriage. . . . Maybe he did. Who can say? The point is that he's held it over my head for sixteen years. Finally, I've paid him back in full." He spat the words out with a vehemence that sent a shiver skittering down Sheila's spine.

"Because you've taken over the business while he's been recuperating in Mexico?"

"That's right. It took me this long to get out of the old man's debt." Sheila could see the emotional scars of pain etched on Noah's broad forehead; she could read the agony in his blue eyes.

Her voice caught as she began to speak. "I'm sorry."

"Don't be. It's over."

"It bothers you."

"I said, it's over." He shifted on the hammock and seemed to notice the darkness for the first time. His eyes searched the hillside. "The kids should be home."

Sheila, too, had been caught up in the complexity of his story. Panic began to take hold of her as she realized that night had descended and Emily was missing.

"Oh, my God," she whispered, clasping a hand over her mouth. "Where could they be?"

"You tell me. Do you have any flashlights?"

She nodded, and was on her way to the house before he could tell her to get them. She fumbled with the lightswitch in the kitchen in her hurry. Within two minutes she was back outside, listening for a response to Noah's shout. Nothing interrupted the stillness of the night.

"Damn," Noah muttered as he pinched the bridge of his

nose. "I should have listened when you wanted to search for them earlier."

"You didn't know they wouldn't come home."

"But you did." He turned to look at her as they followed the bobbing circles of lights flashing on the ground before them. "Why were you worried—is it part of being a mother?"

"Emily's never late," Sheila asserted breathlessly. They were climbing the hill at a near run.

"Next time I'll pay more attention when you begin to worry."

"A lot of good that does us now," Sheila snapped back. She knew she was being short with Noah and that it was unfair, but her concern for her daughter made her irritable.

Noah stopped and cupped his hands around his mouth to call Sean's name. From somewhere in the distance they heard his answering shout. Sean's voice sounded rough and frightened.

"Oh, my God," Sheila whispered, listening for Emily's voice and hearing nothing. "Something's happened." Fear took a stranglehold on her throat, and she started running up the path, jumping to conclusions and imagining scenarios of life without her daughter.

She stumbled once on an exposed root. Noah reached for her, but couldn't break the fall that tore her jeans and scraped her knee. Wincing in pain, she continued to race up the hill, mindless of the blood that was oozing from the wound.

Sean's shouts were louder, and within minutes his anxious face came into range of the flashlights. Sheila choked back a scream as she saw Emily in his arms. The child was dripping wet, her face was covered with mud and there were several scratches on her cheeks.

"Mommy . . ." Emily reached her arms out to her mother and tears formed in Sheila's eyes as Emily clung, sobbing to her.

"Hush . . . Emily, it's all right, Mommy's here." Emily burrowed her nose into Sheila's shoulder. The girl was visibly shaking and her teeth were chattering. Noah took off his shirt and placed it on Emily's small shoulders. "Shhh . . . Sweetheart, are you all right . . . are you hurt?"

"It's her ankle," Sean interrupted. His face was ashen as he looked down at Emily.

"Let's take a look at that." Noah took the flashlight and illuminated Emily's right ankle. Gently he touched the swollen joint. Emily wailed in pain.

"Shhh . . . Em, Noah's just seeing how bad it is," Sheila whispered into Emily's bedraggled curls. Sheila's eyes drove into Noah's with a message that he had better be careful with her daughter.

"I don't think it's broken . . . but I can't really tell," Noah said softly. "Here, Emily, let me carry you back to the house. We'll call a doctor when we get there."

"No! Mommy, you hold me. *Please.*" Emily clung to Sheila's neck as if holding on for dear life.

"Emily." Noah's voice was firm as he talked to the little girl.

"Don't, I can handle her."

"Forget it, Sheila." The beam of light swept from Emily's ankle to Sheila's torn, bloody jeans. "You'll be doing well if you can get back to the house on your own. I'll carry Emily."

"Mommy . . ." Emily wailed.

"Really, Noah, I'm sure I can manage," Sheila asserted, her gray eyes glinting like daggers.

"Forget it . . . Sean, you carry the gear and the flash-lights." Noah carefully extracted Emily from Sheila's arms, but still gave orders to his son. "Then you walk with Sheila; she's cut her leg. Now let's go. The sooner we get Emily home, the better."

Not even Emily argued with the determination in Noah's voice. Sheila pursed her lips together and ignored the urge to argue with him. The most important thing was Emily's well-being, and Sheila couldn't find fault with Noah's logic.

"Tell me, son," Noah said sternly, when the lights of the Chateau were visible. "Just what happened?"

"We were fishing."

"And?"

"Well, it was getting dark, and I guess I was in kind of a hurry," Sean continued rapidly. "Emily kept getting be-hind, and when we crossed the creek, she slipped on a rock. I threw down the gear and reached for her, but the current pushed her off balance and pulled her under the water. It was lucky that the creek was shallow, and I got to her. Then she started crying and screaming about her ankle and, well, I just started carrying her down the hill as fast as I could."

"You should have been more considerate, Sean. If you weren't always hurrying to get where you should have been an hour ago, this might never have happened!" Noah declared gruffly.

"I didn't think . . ."

"That's the problem, isn't it?"

"Noah, don't," Sheila interjected. "It's not Sean's fault. Arguing isn't going to help anything."

It seemed an eternity to Sheila, but eventually they got Emily to the house. While she cleaned and dried the child, Noah called a local doctor who was a friend of Sheila's.

Sean paced nervously from the living room to the den and back again until Emily was propped up in bed and the doctor arrived.

Doctor Embers was a young woman who had a daughter a couple of years younger than Emily. She was prematurely gray and wore her glasses on the end of her nose as she examined the child.

"So you took a tumble, did you?" she asked brightly as she looked into Emily's pupils. "How do you feel?"

"Okay," Emily mumbled feebly. Her large brown eyes looked sunken in her white face.

"How about this ankle . . . does this hurt?"

Emily winced and uttered a little cry.

The doctor continued to examine Emily while Sheila looked anxiously at the little girl, who seemed smaller than she had earlier in the day. Lying on the white pillow, Emily seemed almost frail.

Dr. Embers straightened, smiled down at the child and gave her head an affectionate pat. "Well, I think you'll live," she pronounced. "But I would stay off the ankle for a while. And no more jumping in creeks for the time being, okay?"

Emily smiled feebly and nodded. Dr. Embers took Sheila into the kitchen and answered the unspoken question hanging on Sheila's lips. "She'll be fine, Sheila. Don't worry."

"Thank goodness."

"She shouldn't need anything stronger for the pain than aspirin, but I do want you to bring her into the clinic on Monday for X-rays."

Alarm flashed in Sheila's eyes. "But I thought . . ."

Donna Embers waved Sheila's fears away with a gentle smile and a hand on her arm. "I said don't worry. I'm sure the ankle is just a sprain, but, I want to double-check, just in case there's a hairline fracture hiding in there.''

Sheila let out a relieved sigh. ''I really appreciate the fact that you came over tonight.''

''No problem; what are friends for? Besides, you'll get the bill.''

Sheila smiled. ''Can you at least stay for a cup of coffee?''

Donna edged to the door and shook her head. ''I'd love to, really, but I left Dennis with dinner and the kids, which might be just a shade too much responsibility for him.''

Sheila leaned against the kitchen door frame and laughed. The last thing she would call Donna Ember's loyal husband was irresponsible. A feeling of warm relief washed over her as she watched the headlights of Donna's van fade into the distance.

''Is Emily going to be all right?'' Sean asked when Sheila walked back into the kitchen and began perking a pot of coffee.

''She's fine.''

Sean swallowed and kept his eyes on the floor. ''I'm really sorry.''

''It's not your fault,'' Sheila maintained.

''Dad thinks so,'' Sean replied glumly.

''Well, your dad is wrong.''

Sean's head snapped upward, and his intense blue eyes sought Sheila's. ''But I thought you liked Dad.''

''I do . . . I like him very much,'' Sheila admitted, ''but that doesn't mean he can't be wrong some of the time.''

Sean sank into a chair near the table. ''I should have been more careful.''

''Even if you had, the accident might still have occurred. Just be thankful it wasn't any worse than it was.''

Sean's face whitened at the thought. "I don't think it could have been worse."

"Oh, Sean, it could have been a dozen times worse." Sheila took a chair near Sean and touched him lightly on the shoulder. "Emily could have struck her head, or you could have fallen down, too . . . a thousand different things could have happened." Sheila fought the shudder of apprehension that took hold of her when she considered how dangerous the accident could have been. "Look, Sean, you did everything right. You got Emily out of the water and carried her to me. Thank you."

Sean was perplexed and confused. "You're thanking me . . . why?"

"For clear thinking, and taking care of my little girl."

"Miss Lindstrom—"

"Sheila."

Sean shifted uncomfortably on the chair. He was still carrying the weight of guilt for Emily's accident and had transformed from a tough punk teenager into a frightened boy. "Okay . . . Sheila . . . I'm . . . sorry for the way I acted last night."

"It's okay."

"But I was crummy to you."

Sheila couldn't disagree. "You were."

"Then why aren't you mad at me?"

"Is that what you want?" Sheila inquired, taking a sip from her coffee.

Noah had heard the end of the conversation and stood in the door awaiting Sean's response to Sheila's question.

Sean looked Sheila in the eye, unaware that his father was standing less than five feet behind him. "I don't know." He shrugged, some of his old bravado resurfacing. "I just didn't want to like you."

Sheila's eyes flicked from Sean to Noah and back again.

"Because you were afraid that I might take your father from you?"

Again the blond youth shrugged.

"I would never do that, Sean. I have a daughter of my own, and I know how important it is that we have each other. No one could *ever* take me away from my child. I'm sure the same is true of your father."

Sean looked at Sheila, silently appraising her. His next words shattered the friendliness between them. "My dad still cares for my mom!" His look dared her to argue with him.

"I'm sure he does, Sean," Sheila agreed, silencing Noah with her eyes. "And I don't intend to change that." Knowing that Noah was about to break in on the conversation, and hoping to avoid another confrontation, Sheila changed the topic. "Emily made some brownies for you earlier, but she must have forgotten them with all of the excitement about fishing." She rose from the table and began putting the chocolate squares on a plate. Noah entered the room, but Sheila ignored him. "Why don't you take these into Emily—cheer her up?"

"Do you think she'll want to see me? She might be sleeping or somethin.' "

"She's awake," Noah stated. "I just left her, and believe it or not, I think she's hungry."

Sean grabbed the plate of brownies and, balancing them between two glasses of milk, left the kitchen in the direction of Emily's room. Without asking if he wanted any, Sheila poured Noah a cup of coffee.

"How's *your* leg?" Noah asked, eyeing Sheila skeptically.

"Never better. I cleaned it and it's okay. A little of the skin is scraped off, that's all."

Noah took an experimental sip from his coffee as he

looked dubiously at her white slacks. "Did Dr. Embers look at it."

"No."

"Why not?"

"I told you I cleaned it and bandaged it. Look, it's really no big deal."

Noah didn't look convinced. "I'm just sorry that you and Emily had to suffer because of Sean's neglect."

"Noah, please. Don't blame him. He's just a child himself."

"He's sixteen and has to learn responsibility some time. He should have been more careful."

"He knows that—don't reprimand him. It would be like rubbing salt into his wound. He feels badly enough as it is."

"He should."

"Why? Because he was careless? Noah, accidents will happen. Give the kid a break, will you?"

Noah set his cup down on the table and walked over to the sink. For a few silent moments he stared out the window into the night. "It's not just the accident, Sheila. It's his attitude. You were there the night he came home drunk. It wasn't the first time." He breathed deeply and tilted his head back while squinting his eyes shut. "He's in trouble at school and I've even had to pick him up downtown. Since he's a minor, he hasn't been in jail, but he's been close, damned close. He missed a couple of probation meetings, and so now he's walking a very thin line with the law."

"A lot of kids get into trouble."

"I know. I should count myself lucky that he doesn't use dope, I guess."

Sheila approached Noah and wrapped her arms around his waist. How long had he tortured himself with guilt for his son? "Sean will be all right, Noah. I've seen more kids than you'd want to count in my job, some easier to deal with than Sean, others more difficult. Sean will come through this.''

He put his large hands over hers, pressing her fingertips into his abdomen. "Why did you let him lie to you?"

"About what?"

"His mother. You know how I feel about Marilyn."

"Sean probably does, too. But he can't admit it to me, not yet. He still considers me a threat."

"I think you're reading more into this than there really is."

"Adolescence is tough, Noah, or don't you remember? Add to that the fact that Sean knows his mother rejected him. It makes him feel inferior."

"Lots of kids grow up without one parent . . . even Emily."

"And it's hard on her too," Sheila sighed against his back.

Noah turned around and faced her. One hand pushed aside her hair as he studied her face and noticed the thin lines of worry that dimmed her smile. He pressed a kiss to her forehead. "You're a very special woman, Sheila Lindstrom, and I love you." He traced the edge of her cheekbones with his finger. "It's times like these that I wonder how I managed to live this long without you."

Sheila warmed under his unguarded stare. "I guess you must have a will of iron," she teased.

"Or maybe it's because I'm a stubborn fool." He draped his arm possessively over her shoulder and guided her out of the kitchen. "Let's go check on Emily."

"In a minute. . . . You go look in on her, I'll be there shortly." She moved out of his embrace and pushed him down the hall. "I've got to make a phone call."

Noah looked at his wrist watch. "Now? To whom?"

She was ready for his question. "I think I'd better call Jeff."

"You're ex-husband?" Noah was incredulous. "Why?"

"He has the right to know about the accident," Sheila attempted to explain. Before she could get any further, Noah cut her off and his mouth pulled into a contemptuous scowl. A thousand angry questions came to his mind.

"Do you think he would even care?"

"Noah, he's Emily's father. Of course he'll care."

"From what you've told me about him, he hasn't shown much fatherly concern for his daughter!"

"Keep your voice down!" Sheila warned in a harsh whisper. "Jeff has to know."

Noah's face contorted with disgust. The skin stretched tightly over the angled planes of his features. "Are you sure the accident isn't some handy excuse?"

Sheila's gray eyes snapped. "I don't need an excuse. He has to know and I can't have him hear it through the grapevine."

"Why not?"

"How would you feel if it were Sean?"

"That's different. I care about my son. I would have done anything to have him with me. It was a little different with your husband, I'd venture to guess."

"He's still her legal father. This is a rural community, but word travels quickly. I either have to call Jeff or his mother, and I'd prefer not to worry Marian. If I call her now, she'll be over here within a half hour."

"And what about Coleridge? Is that what he'll do—come racing over here to check on his daughter and his ex-wife. Is that what you're hoping for?"

"You're impossible!" Sheila accused. "But you're right about one thing, I would be thrilled to pieces if Jeff came over here."

"I thought so," he commented dryly as he crossed his arms over his chest and leaned against the wall, looking as if he were both judge and jury. She, of course, was the unconvincing defendant.

"But not for the reasons you think," she continued, trying to stem her boiling anger. "Jeff is Emily's father, for God's sake. She's just been through a very traumatic experience, and I think she could use a little support from Daddy."

"A little is all she'd get, at the very best," Noah pointed out in a calm voice. His blue eyes looked deadly. "Jeff Coleridge is no more Emily's father than Marilyn is Sean's mother! I can't believe that you're still hanging onto ideals that were shot down years ago when he walked out on you and your kid, Sheila. You don't have to paint the picture any rosier than it really is. It's not good for you, and it's not good for Emily."

"So look who's handing out free advice—*Father of the year!*" The minute her words were out, she wanted to call them back. She hadn't meant to be cruel.

Noah's hands clenched and then relaxed against his rib cage. "Once again, the sharp tongue cuts like a whip, Miss Lindstrom. I'm not trying to hurt you, I'm only attempting to suggest that genetics has nothing to do with being a parent. Oh, sure, Coleridge *sired* your child, but where was he when the chips were down? Or have you conveniently forgotten that he walked out on you and took up with another woman? A man like that doesn't deserve to know that his child was hurt. Face it, Sheila, he just doesn't give a damn."

Sheila's nerves were strung as tightly as a piano string, her voice emotionless. "Each summer Emily spends a few weeks with Jeff. He's expecting her by the end of next week."

"Does she want to see him?"

Sheila wavered. "She's confused about it."

Noah's lips twisted wryly. "What you're saying is that she knows he doesn't want her, and you're hoping that when he learns of the accident, he'll rush to her side and reestablish himself as a paragon of virtue in her eyes. Don't delude yourself, Sheila, and for Emily's sake, don't try to make your ex-husband something he's not. Let her make up her own mind."

"She will," Sheila said softly, "whether I call him or not. But I am going to call, you know. It's his right as a father."

"He has no rights—he gave them up about four years ago, wouldn't you say?"

For a moment they stared across the room at each other, trying to repair the damage their argument had caused, but it was impossible. "Excuse me," Sheila said shakily, "but this is my decision." She turned to the telephone and dialed the long-distance number to Spokane.

Noah turned on his heel, uttered a low oath, and headed down the hall toward Emily's room. Women! Would he ever live to understand them?

# Chapter Eleven

*Though* never mentioned again, the argument hung over Noah and Sheila like a dark, foreboding cloud. Noah had decided to spend another week at the winery to double-check Anthony Simmons's conclusions concerning the fire. Sean was entrusted with Noah's car and sent back to Seattle to pick up a couple of changes of clothes and some documents from the office of Wilder Investments. The boy was back at Cascade Valley as he had promised, the car intact.

For his part, Noah was a whirlwind. He decided it was in the best interests of Wilder Investments to reopen the winery, and he began a full-scale clean-up of the estate. It took some fast talking, but even the local sheriff's department had reluctantly complied with his demands that the west wing be completely reconstructed. By late Friday afternoon D & M construction, a subsidiary of Wilder

Investments, had moved in, and the foreman was working with an architect to redesign the building.

Days at the winery were spent preparing for the autumn harvest; the nights making love. Noah didn't mention Jeff again, and Sheila hoped that the harsh words shouted in the heat of anger would soon be forgotten.

Noah began a furious study of viticulture, with Sheila and Dave Jansen as his tutors. Dave was a young man whose serious, plain face was offset by laughing brown eyes. He took Noah on a tour of the vineyards and explained, endlessly, the reasons that wine production was suited for the valley.

"Thirty years ago, few people thought that western Washington could hold a candle to California for wine production," he declared, proudly showing off a hillside covered with vinifera wine grapes.

"But you're changing their minds, right?" Noah asked.

"You got it. Everybody thinks it rains all the time in Washington, or that it's overcast, but that's because they haven't seen the eastern part of the state. Over here our summers are warm and dry with extremely low precipitation and cloud cover. This allows for a unique combination of moderate heat, high light intensity and long days that produce vinifera fruit with an excellent sugar-acid balance. All of our wines have a distinctive varietal character."

"But what about the winters? A couple of years ago the late snow just about wiped out the crop."

Dave nodded gravely. "That can happen," he admitted. "We try to select our vineyard sights as close as possible to the Columbia River. We use southern slopes above the valley floor to further decrease the risk of low temperatures. Recently we've been planting a hardier grape, a vinifera that can stand colder temperatures."

Noah's gaze ran skeptically over the vineyards.

"Really, this is a great place to produce wine," Dave stated firmly. "Look, Mr. Wilder—"

"Noah."

Dave smiled and inclined his head. "I know that Sheila's had a run of bad luck here, but for my money, Cascade Valley will produce the best wine in the country."

"That's a pretty broad statement."

Dave pursed his lips and shook his balding head. "I don't think so." He held up his fingers to add emphasis to his point. Eastern Washington has a good climate, the right amount of light, loamy soils and is relatively free of pests and disease. I don't think you can do better than that."

Noah squatted and ran his fingers through the soil. "So what's to prevent a competitor from building next to Cascade Valley?"

"Name familiarity and reputation," Dave replied quickly.

"A reputation that has been tarnished over the last few years."

"Yeah. I can't deny that, much as I'd like to," Dave conceded, opening the door to his pickup. "Want a lift back to the house? I'd like you to take a look at our latest investment, French oak barrels for aging instead of American white oak. They were Oliver's idea. He used a few of them several years ago and the end result is our reserve Cabernet Sauvignon, which we hope to market late this year.

"I think I'll walk back to the house," Noah decided. "I'll catch you tomorrow because I would like to see the reserve bottles."

"All right. See you then." The battered old pickup took off, leaving a plume of dust in its wake. Noah placed his hands, palms outward, in the back pockets of his jeans as he walked back to the house. He was lost in thought, considering all of the disasters that had struck Cascade Valley in the past few years. No one could be blamed for the volcanic eruption of Mount St. Helens. The tonnage of ash and soot that had fallen on Cascade Valley and destroyed the harvest would have to be attributed to an act of God, or natural disaster. But the tampered bottles found in Montana were a different story. The contamination had been planned rather than accidental. Needle marks found in the corks of some of the damaged bottles proved that someone had to have been behind the sabotage.

Originally Noah had assumed that Oliver Lindstrom had executed the poisoning of the bottles; now he wasn't so sure. The image painted by people he had spoken with told him that Oliver Lindstrom wasn't the kind of man who would destroy all that he had worked so hard to build. If, as Sheila and the staff maintained, Cascade Valley Wines and the winery itself were Oliver Lindstrom's lifeblood, why would he want to tarnish a reputation it had taken years to establish?

Noah squinted against the setting sun and kicked a stone out of the rutted dirt road. It just didn't make sense. If a man needed money, he wouldn't consciously taint his product, thereby causing an expensive recall and losing consumer trust. Could Lindstrom really have been as desperate as Anthony Simmons wanted Noah to believe: desperate enough to take his own life in an arson attempt? The damned fire—always that damned fire—continued to plague Noah with doubts. As he walked up the final crest of the hill supporting the château, he stopped to look at the wreckage.

A disappearing sun cast red-gold rays over the charred timbers of the west wing. A yellow bulldozer was parked near the blackened building, waiting to raze the sagging skeleton. Noah ran his fingers through his hair as he studied the destruction. If only he didn't care about Sheila, it would be much easier.

Sheila was tearing the old wallpaper off the walls in the dining room when the doorbell rang.

"Emily," she called, pulling at an obstinate strip, "could you get that? Emily?" There was no immediate response, and Sheila remembered Emily mentioning something about going outside with Sean. Her ankle was much better and she was feeling more than a little cooped up in the house.

The doorbell rang again impatiently. "Coming," Sheila called as she wiped her hands on a nearby towel. Who could be calling today, she wondered. It was nearly the dinner hour, and she was a mess. Her jeans and blouse smelled like the sooty walls she had been cleaning, and her hair was piled in a bedraggled twist on the top of her head. She pulled out the pins and ran her fingers through it as she made her way to the door.

Before she could open it, the door swung open and Jeff Coleridge poked his head into the foyer. "So there is someone home after all," he remarked dryly, his eyes giving Sheila a quick head to heels appraisal.

Sheila managed a thin smile. "Sorry—I thought Emily would get the door."

"And I thought she was laid up," he replied with a smirk. "Or was this just one of your rather obvious attempts to see me?"

Sheila's gray eyes didn't waver. "That was a long time ago."

"Not that long."

Sheila stood in the entryway, not letting him pass. "I assume you came here to see Emily."

"Who else?" His smile was as devilish as ever, his dark eyes just as flirtatious. He was still handsome; living the good life seemed to suit him well. His lean torso reflected hours on the tennis courts, and his devil-may-care attitude added to his cunning charm. After all of these years, Sheila was immune to it.

"I hope no one. Emily's outside. I'll go and get her."

"Sheila, baby." He reached out a hand and touched her wrist. "What is our darling daughter doing out of bed—I thought she had some horrible ankle sprain. At least that's the story you gave me."

Trying desperately not to be baited, Sheila withdrew her wrist and pasted a plastic copy of his saccharine smile on her face. "That was no story, and if you would have shown up a few days ago, you would have found her in bed. Fortunately she's young and heals quickly."

"Now, now," he cajoled, noting the sarcasm dripping from her words. "Your claws are showing, sweetheart. You know I couldn't come any sooner."

"You could have called."

"Is that what you wanted?"

"What I wanted was for you to show some interest in your child. She's not a baby anymore, Jeff, and she's beginning to understand how you feel about her."

"I'll just bet she does," he snapped, losing his calm veneer of self-assurance. "With you poisoning her mind against me."

"You know I don't do anything of the kind." Sheila's face was sincere, her gray eyes honest and pained. "You handle that part of it well enough on your own."

Jeff's frown turned to a pout. "I thought we were supposed to have a 'friendly divorce,' isn't that what you wanted?"

"When I was naive enough to believe it."

"I suppose you think that's my fault, too."

"Not really. We couldn't get along while we were married; I should never have expected that the divorce would change anything."

"You act as if it's carved in stone."

"I wish I thought it wasn't," Sheila sighed, leaning against the door.

"So what do you want now, Sheila?" His eyes narrowed suspiciously as he looked down upon her.

"I want you to be an interested father, Jeff. And I don't want it to be an act. Is that too much to ask?"

Jeff took in a deep breath, attempting to stem the rage that took hold of him every time he saw Sheila and was reminded of her quiet beauty. It unnerved him. Perhaps it was her fiery spirit coupled with her wide, understanding eyes. There had been a time in his life when he had been proud to show her off as *his* wife. But she wanted more—she wanted a child, for God's sake. Not that Emily wasn't a great kid . . . he just didn't like the idea of fatherhood. It made him feel so *old*. If only Sheila would have given a little more, seen things his way, maybe the two of them would have made it.

Even in dusty jeans and a sooty blouse, with a black smudge where her hands had touched her cheek, she looked undeniably beautiful. Her hair fell in a tangled mass around her face, the way he liked it, and she still carried herself with an elegance and grace he had never seen in another woman—even Judith. Whereas Judith's beauty was beginning to fade, Sheila's was just beginning to blossom.

Jeff cleared his throat and tried to ignore Sheila's intent stare. He coughed before answering her question. "You know I care about Emily," he said with a shrug of his shoulders. "It's just that I've never been comfortable with kids."

"You've never tried. Not even with your own."

Jeff shook his head, and he looked at the boards of the porch. "That's where you're wrong, Sheila. I did try, honestly . . ."

"But you couldn't find it in your heart to love her."

"I didn't say that." His eyes lifted to meet the disgust and rage simmering in hers.

"You have never loved anyone in your life, Jeff Coleridge, except yourself."

"That's what I've always liked about you, Sheila: your sweet, even-tempered disposition."

Sheila was shaking, but she attempted to regain her poise. If only she could look at Jeff indifferently. If only she didn't see a man who rejected his infant when she looked into his eyes. "This argument is getting us nowhere," she said through tight lips. The strain of trying to communicate with Jeff was getting to her. "Why don't you come into the kitchen and wait while I get Emily. She's just on the patio."

Jeff hesitated, as if he wanted to say something more, but decided against it. Sheila stepped backward, allowing him to pass, and tried to calm her anxious nerves. When she found Emily, she didn't want to infect the child with her worries about the disintegrating relationship between father and daughter.

She stepped onto the patio and drew in a steadying breath. Emily was watching Noah and Sean trying to outdo one another in a Frisbee throwing contest. Emily was giggling in excitement, Noah was concentrating on the returning Frisbee and Sean was smiling with satisfaction, sure that the plastic disc would elude his father. It was a tender scene, a family scene, and it pulled at Sheila's heartstrings knowing she had to destroy it.

"Emily," she called softly. "Someone's here to see you."

"Who?" Emily demanded, riveted to her spot and eyeing Noah's ungraceful catch. He flipped the Frisbee back at his son.

"Daddy's come to see you."

Emily's smile faded. "My daddy?"

Sheila's grin felt as phony as it was. "Isn't that great?"

"He's not going to take me with him to Spokane, is he?"

"Of course not, honey," Sheila said with unfelt enthusiasm. "He just came to see how you're doing with that ankle of yours." Pushing aside an errant curl around her daughter's face, Sheila continued. "Come on. He's waiting in the kitchen."

"No, I'm not," Jeff's cheery voice called as he walked out the door. He smiled down at his daughter. "It's been a long trip, and I couldn't wait any longer." It was then, when his eyes lifted from his daughter's serious gaze, that he noticed Noah and Sean. The game had ended and Noah was staring intently at the man who had once been Sheila's husband. "Pardon me," Jeff announced with a wary, well-practiced smile. "I don't believe we've met."

Noah strode slowly up to the patio, his blue eyes challenging Jeff's dark ones. Sheila could see that every muscle in Noah's body had become rigid, the skin drawn taut. "The name's Wilder," he stated. "Noah Wilder. This"—he cocked his head in the direction of the blond boy in cut-off jeans—"is my son, Sean." He extended his hand, took Jeff's, and gave it a short, but firm, shake.

"Jeff Coleridge."

Noah's smile twisted as if smiling at a private irony. "I assumed as much."

"Wilder?" Jeff's eyes followed Noah's movements as he placed his body between those of ex-husband and wife. The move was subtle, but not lost on either Sheila or Jeff. "You're connected with Wilder Investments?"

"My father's company."

"Ben Wilder is *your* father?" A note of genuine respect and surprise entered Jeff's voice.

"That's right." Noah didn't return Jeff's growing smile.

"Oh . . . so you're here because of the winery . . . as a business partner to Sheila?" Jeff assumed. He seemed relieved.

"Partly."

"I don't understand."

"Noah is Mommy's friend," Emily interjected.

"Is that right?" Jeff's thin eyebrows raised, and his accusing dark eyes impaled Sheila.

There was an awkward silence while Sheila struggled with the proper words. Both men regarded her intently. From the corner of her eye, Sheila noticed that Sean was walking toward the orchard, away from the uncomfortable scene. An embarrassed flush crept up her neck, but her eyes never wavered, and her voice was surprisingly steady. "Yes, that's right. Noah is a friend of mine, a very good friend."

The nasty retort forming on Jeff's lips died under the power of Noah's stare and the innocent, wondering eyes of his child. He didn't want to appear the fool. "I see," he returned vaguely, as if he really didn't understand at all. Then, as if dismissing the entire conversation as something that should have been swept under the rug, he pulled at the crease in his pants and bent on one knee to talk to his daughter. He took one of Emily's little hands and pressed it between his own. He considered it a very fatherly gesture. "So tell me, Emmy, how're you feeling?"

"Fine." Emily was suddenly shy as she found herself the center of attention.

"You're sure now? How about that ankle?"

"It's okay."

"Good . . . that's good. Are you going to tell me all about your fall in the creek?"

"Do you really want to know?" Emily asked skeptically.

Jeff's thin smile wavered. "Of course I do, precious," he replied, patting the top of her hand nervously. He led her over to the chaise lounge and indicated that she should sit with him. "Why don't you tell me all about it?" He pressed the tip of his finger awkwardly against her nose.

Noah felt his stomach lurch at Coleridge's stumbling attempts at paternity. While the man turned all of his attention upon his child, Noah took his leave, heading in the direction of the west wing.

Sheila watched Noah stride angrily across the yard, and she had to suppress the urge to run after him. Until she was assured that Emily was comfortable with Jeff, Sheila felt her responsibility was to remain with her child.

Noah was soon out of sight and Sheila swung her eyes back toward Jeff and Emily. Her gaze met the brittle dark stare of her ex-husband. "How long has *he* been here?" he sneered.

"About a week."

"Do you think that's such a good idea?"

"He's helping me reestablish the winery."

"I bet he is." The insinuations in Jeff's flat statement couldn't be ignored.

"Look, Jeff. I like Noah . . . I like him a lot. Not that it's any concern of yours."

"He's an arrogant s.o.b., don't you think?"

Sheila's eyes flew to Emily's young face and then back to Jeff, silently warning him against any further derogatory remarks while Emily was close at hand.

"I think he's a very kind and considerate man."

"And I'm not?"

"I didn't say that." Sheila shot Jeff another threatening glance. "Would you like a cup of coffee?" Somehow she had to change the course of the conversation, for Emily's sake.

Jeff tried to relax and appear comfortable. "Got anything stronger?" he inquired, running a shaky hand through his neatly combed hair.

"I think so."

"Good." He let out his breath. "Make it a vodka martini."

"All right. It will take me a few minutes." He didn't argue. He, too, must have been looking for a way to avoid further disagreement. Sheila turned toward the house, her eyes still searching for Noah, when Jeff's voice reached her. "With a twist, okay?"

She nodded curtly without glancing back in his direction, muttering under her breath, "With a twist . . . with a twist." Sheila had forgotten how demanding Jeff could be—a real pain in the neck. Damn him for ruining the peaceful afternoon. Damn him for interrupting what she had hoped would be an intimate *family* meal.

That was the problem, wasn't it? She considered Noah and Sean as part of the family, while she looked upon Jeff as an outsider; an intruder who would only cause trouble.

Her chestnut hair swept across her shoulders as she shook her head at her own foolishness. What had she expected? she asked herself as she walked into the den.

She was startled to find Noah sitting at the desk, going over the original blueprints for the west wing of the château. A pencil was in his hand, its lead point tapping restlessly on the yellowed paper. He didn't move when he heard the sound of Sheila's sandaled feet enter the room, nor did he speak. Instead he stared broodingly at the blueprint, seemingly engrossed in the faded drawing. Sheila could feel the rift between them deepen, and she wondered if she had the courage to bridge it.

"I'm sorry you had to witness all of that," she began as she moved across the room to the bar to pull out a bottle of vodka. The pencil stopped its erratic tapping on the desk.

Noah's voice was controlled to the point of exasperation. "Don't apologize to me. It's none of my concern."

"But it is," she disagreed. "And I didn't mean for it to turn into a circus."

"Didn't you? Don't kid yourself, Sheila. You were the one who invited him here. How could you possibly expect things to turn out differently?"

"I had no choice. I had to tell him about Emily and invite him to visit her."

"Save it, Sheila. I've heard all this before."

She could read the anger in the crunch of his shoulders, feel his questions begging for answers, see the pride in the lift of his chin. "Please, Noah," she pleaded, setting the mixed drink aside. "Don't shut me out."

"Is that what I'm doing?" He tossed the pencil down on the desk and rubbed his hands wearily against the back of his neck.

"Aren't you?"

"No!" He got out of the chair and faced her for the first time since she entered the room. Ignoring the pain in her eyes, he wagged an accusing finger in her face. "I'll tell you what I'm doing," he stated hoarsely, "I'm sitting on the sidelines, hoping to hold on to my patience, which isn't exactly my long suit to begin with, while the woman I love clings to some faded, rose-colored memories of a past and a marriage that didn't exist."

"I'm not—"

"I'm trying *not* to throw out a conniving jerk whose fumbling attempts at being a father border on the pathetic, for the sake of holding up appearances!"

"Jeff's just trying to—"

*"And,"* his voice increased in volume, "I'm attempting, Lord knows I'm not good at this sort of thing, but I'm trying damn it, to understand how a beautiful, sensitive woman like you could have ever gotten tangled up with a creep like Jeff Coleridge in the first place." The cords in Noah's neck were bulging, the muscles in his shoulders tight, the line of his mouth curled in distaste. He looked as if at any moment all of his simmering anger might explode.

Sheila picked up the martini with trembling hands. "I think that's enough," she whispered, her wide eyes unseeing. Her voice shook with the wounded tears of pride that had settled in her throat as she turned toward the door.

Noah was beside her in an instant, and his powerful arm reached out to impede her departure. He twisted her back to face him and the drink fell to the floor, breaking the glass and spilling the colorless liquid.

"No, Sheila," he stated through clenched teeth, "you're wrong." He ignored the shattered glass and the pooling liquid. He gave her arm a shake to make sure she was giving him all of her attention. "I love you," he admitted, the hardness in his gaze beginning to soften. "I didn't want to fall in love with you. I fought it . . . I fought it like hell . . . but I lost." His grip loosened on her arm, but she didn't move as she was spellbound by the honesty in his eyes. "And I have no intention of letting you go—not to that snake you once called a husband. Not to anyone."

Sheila felt her anger beginning to wither. Her gray eyes were colored by her conflicting emotions. "Then, please

. . . please try and understand that I'm only putting up with Jeff because of Emily.''

"Do you think you're fooling that child?"

"I'm not trying to fool her. I'm just trying not to bias her opinion of her dad.''

"By letting him intrude where he's not wanted?" His eyes left hers to stare at the spilled drink. "By jumping at his every whim?" He touched her cheek tenderly. "Or by covering up his mistakes and omissions?"

"By letting her make her own decision.''

"Then let her see him as he really is.''

The muscles in his jawline tensed. "How important to you is Jeff Coleridge?" he demanded.

"He's the father of my child.''

"Nothing more?"

"He once was," she admitted. "I can't deny that, and I wouldn't try to. But that was a long time ago. Please believe me, Noah, I'm not in love with him. I don't know if I ever was.''

Noah wrapped his arms tightly around her slim shoulders, and she could feel the warmth of his body where his arms touched her. Tenderly he brushed the smudge of soot from her cheek. "All right, Sheila," he said with a reluctant sigh. "I'll try and tolerate that jerk. But, believe me, if he gets obnoxious with you *or Emily,* I'm not going to apologize for throwing him out on his ear. Fair enough?"

Sheila's smile spread slowly over her lips, showing just a hint of her white teeth. "Fair enough," she agreed.

"Now, why don't you work on dinner, let Jeff and Emily alone, and I'll finish up with the blueprint.''

"Only if you promise to clean up this mess," she suggested, flipping her open palm toward the spilled drink, "and pour Jeff another vodka martini.''

"Not on your life, lady. Doting on that man is where I draw the line. If he wants a drink badly enough, he can damn well come in and mix his own."

Sheila laughed and clucked her tongue. "Not very hospitable, are you?" she teased.

Noah raised an inquiring eyebrow. "Can you blame me?"

"No," she admitted with a trace of wistfulness, "I really can't. But, do *try* to be civil."

"If that's what you want," he conceded. "But for the life of me, I don't understand why."

She wrapped her arms around his neck and stood on her toes. "It won't kill you," she pointed out.

"No, I suppose not. But watching him drool over you might."

"You're imagining things." She kissed him lightly on the lips.

The muscles in his body reached out to hers. She felt his thighs straining against hers, his chest flattening her breasts, his arms pressing against the small of her back. "The kinds of things I imagine with you are very private. They have nothing to do with your ex-husband." His lips brushed against hers and his tongue rimmed her lips. "Let's get rid of him and put the kids to bed early."

Sheila laughed against his mouth. "Somehow I don't think Sean would take kindly to going to bed at six thirty."

"Spoilsport." Slowly he released her.

She started toward the door, but paused to look over her shoulder at him and give an exaggerated wink. "Later," she promised throatily.

The rest of the evening was uncomfortable but tolerable. Jeff stayed for dinner and looked stiff and ill at ease with Noah, Sean and Emily. His perfectly pressed suit had become wrinkled, his hair unruly and his eyes begged

Sheila to find some excuse to get him away from Noah's intense, uncompromising stare. Noah was polite but quiet, and his blue eyes very rarely strayed from Sheila's ex-husband. It made Jeff uncomfortable; the man's stare bordered on the eery.

Jeff made his excuses, begged off dessert and was back on his way to Spokane long before eight o'clock. Even Emily seemed relieved that she didn't have to go back to her father's sterile apartment and persnickety old wife, Judith, at least for a few more weeks.

For the first time in over a week the dark cloud of argument between Sheila and Noah had disappeared, and they made impassioned love without the shadow of Jeff Coleridge hanging over their heads.

# Chapter Twelve

The end of Noah's stay came much too quickly for Sheila. The fact that he hadn't been clear about his decision concerning the status of the winery worried her. She knew that he wanted to rebuild the west wing—the construction crew that had been razing the old structure was proof enough of that—but still he was hesitant. It was as if he were keeping something from her. She could feel his reluctance whenever she would broach the subject of the fall harvest. As far as she could tell, it had to be something to do with the fire.

It was morning on Noah's final day at Cascade Valley when Sheila summoned the courage to bring up the fire and Anthony Simmons's report. Over the past week Noah had managed to dodge the issue, but this morning Sheila told herself she had to have answers—straight ones.

The first rays of dawn filtered through the terrace doors to bathe Sheila's room in a golden aura of dim morning light. Dewdrops clung to the underside of the green leaves of the climatis that grew against the glass doors, and the chill of the mountain night hadn't disappeared.

Noah was still asleep, his face pressed against the pillow. Sheila slowly extracted herself from his embrace, and while still lying near to him on the antique bed, stared at his sleeping form. The dark profile of his face, etched in relief against the ice blue sheets, seemed innocent in slumber. The powerful muscles were relaxed, the corners of his eyes soft. His near-black hair was unruly and would seem almost boyish if it hadn't been for the contrast of his shadowy beard.

Sheila felt her throat tighten at the sight of him sleeping, oblivious to any of the anxieties that aged his face. He seemed incredibly vulnerable, and it touched the deepest, most feminine part of her. She wanted to smooth back his hair and comfort him. *I love him,* she thought to herself. I love him too much. This is the kind of blind love that can be dangerous, the kind of self-sacrificing, unreturned love that can only cause pain. It's a love that causes dependency and inspires jealousy, like a drug addiction. More than anything else in the world, I want to be with this man, to be a part of him. I want my life to blend with his, my family to be one with his, my blood to run in his body.

She bent over and kissed him softly on the forehead. I know he cares for me—he says he loves me—but I know that he is hiding something from me. He won't let himself trust me.

She drew herself away from him and got out of the bed. After snuggling into the downy folds of a cream-colored velour bathrobe, she once again sat on the edge of the bed, content to watch the even rise and fall of Noah's chest as he lay entwined in the sheets. Why won't you tell me, she wondered. Why won't you tell me everything about the fire? What are you hiding from me?

Noah rolled over onto his back and raised an exploratory eyelid against the invading morning sunlight. His dimpled smile slowly emerged as his gaze focused on her. "God, you look incredible," he growled as he wrapped an arm around her waist and pulled her down beside him on the bed.

"Noah," she whispered, trying to ignore the deliciously warm feel of his lips against her throat. "We have to talk."

"Later." His fingers found the zipper on her bathrobe and slowly lowered it.

Against the yearnings of her body, she put her hand over his to impede the zipper's progress. "Now."

"Let's not waste time with talk," he grumbled as he kissed the exposed tops of her breasts. The zipper slid lower, and the downy robe parted. "This is my last morning here," he murmured against her bared skin. Sheila felt her pulse jump and the blood begin to heat in her veins.

She attempted to clutch the robe together. "Precisely why we have to talk now." She tossed her hair away from her face and looked him steadily in the eye as she disentangled herself from his persuasive grip. Her breath was uneven as she eased her body off the bed.

After somewhat shakily taking a seat in one of the chairs near the terrace, she nervously ran her fingers over the open neckline of her robe. Noah propped himself on one elbow, raked his fingers through his dark hair and stared at her with amused, but smoldering, blue eyes. The sheet was draped across his body, exposing the hard muscles of his chest and leaving his lower torso covered. "All right, Sheila, out with it."

"What?" She really didn't know where to begin.

"The inquisition."

"You're expecting one?" She was surprised.

"I'd have to be a fool not to know that before I went back to Seattle, you and I would have a showdown about the fire. That is what this is all about, isn't it?"

Sheila's eyes narrowed suspiciously, and her fingers stopped toying with the collar of her robe. "I just want to know why you've been avoiding the issue of the fire and the rebuilding of the west wing."

"Because I hadn't made a decision." His honest blue eyes begged her understanding and patience.

"But you have now?"

"I think so."

*"Well?"*

The corners of Noah's eyes twitched. "I'm going to transfer a quarter of a million dollars into an escrow account from Wilder Investments when I get back to Seattle. The money will be in escrow for the express purpose of rebuilding Cascade Valley."

Sheila's smile froze on her face as she read the hesitation in his gaze. "But what about the insurance company . . . and that report by Anthony Simmons?"

Noah waved off her questions as if they were bothersome insects. "Don't worry about that end of it; that's my problem."

Sheila held back a million questions, but the one nagging doubt in her mind refused to die. Her voice was hoarse. "But what about my father's name? Will you be able to clear it?" she asked cautiously. The look of sincere concern in her light gray eyes pierced him to the soul, and he found his deception entrapping him. He had decided not to tell her anything about the fire or Simmons's report, knowing full well that what he would have to disclose to her would only cause her more pain. In his mind she had borne more than her share. He couldn't add to it.

"I hope so," he whispered, damning himself for his duplicity.

She sighed with relief and closed her eyes.

"We do have another problem to consider."

She smiled wryly and opened her eyes to study him. "Only one?" she asked sarcastically.

He laughed aloud. How long had it been since he'd laughed in the dawn? The thought of leaving Sheila sobered him, and he realized it was an impossible task. She sat across the room from him, her toes peeking out from the folds of creamy fabric, her hair beautiful in its coppery disarray. And her eyes, a warm gray, the color of liquid silver, surrounded by thick, sexy black lashes, watched his every movement. "Maybe we have two problems," he acquiesced with a slow smile. "The first is simple. If construction of the west wing is incomplete by harvest time, I'll lease a facility nearby and we'll still bottle under the Cascade label. It will be expensive, but better than selling our crop to the competition."

Sheila thoughtfully nodded her silent agreement.

"So that brings us to our next dilemma."

"If you come up with another blockbuster solution, like you did for the first problem, I doubt that there will be any dilemma at all," she quipped, smiling radiantly. At last she knew for certain that the winery would reopen. She couldn't help but smile.

Noah rubbed the edge of his chin before he tossed off the sheet, stood up and strode over to the chair in which she was sitting. Positioning his hands on either arm of the chair, he imprisoned her against the peach-colored cushions. "The solution depends entirely on you."

The corners of her mouth twitched, and a light of interest

danced in her eyes. She cocked her head coquettishly and let the chestnut sheen of her hair fall over one cheek. "On me? How?"

His voice was low and serious, his gaze intent as it probed her eyes. "Sheila, I want you to marry me. Will you?"

Her playful smile disappeared as the meaning of his words sunk in. An overwhelming sense of ecstasy overtook her as her heart flipped over. "You want to get married?" she repeated, her voice filled with raw emotion.

"As quickly as possible."

Her self-assurance wavered. "Of course . . . I mean, I'd love to . . ." She shook her head. "This is coming out all wrong. I guess I just don't understand what's going on here."

"What's to understand?" His lean muscles entrapped her, and his lips nuzzled softly behind her ear. When he spoke, she could feel his warm breath against her hair. "Because I love you, Sheila. Haven't you been listening to what I've been saying to you for the better part of the week?"

"But . . . married?" she stammered. Visions of her first marriage filled her mind. She remembered the hope and the love, a gorgeous ivory lace gown that had yellowed with the lies and the faded dreams. She had rushed into marriage once, and though she loved Noah with all her heart, she was wary of making the same mistake again. The thought of losing him was too agonizing to her. "I . . . I don't know," she said, and the confusion she felt was reflected in the gray depths of her eyes.

The muscles of his arms tensed as he gripped the chair more savagely. "Why not?"

There were probably more than a dozen reasons, but Sheila couldn't think of them. Memories of Jeff closing the door in her face kept closing in on her. "Have you thought about the kids? How is this going to affect them?" She was grasping at straws, and they both knew it. He provided the perfect response.

"Can you honestly think of any better arrangement for Sean or Emily?"

"But that's no reason to get married . . . to provide another parent for your child."

"Of course it isn't. Think of it as a fringe benefit," he suggested. His hand had been touching the collar of her robe, gently rubbing the delicate bones surrounding her neck. Suddenly he stopped touching her and took a step backward. "Are you trying to find a polite way of telling me no?" he challenged, his features growing hard.

Sheila shook her head, tears of happiness welling in her eyes. He misread them.

"Then what is it? Certainly you're not satisfied with a casual *affair?*"

"No, no, of course not."

He crossed his arms over his chest, his blue eyes intent on hers. "Has this got something to do with Coleridge? Damn it! I knew he was still in your blood."

"He isn't. . . . It's just that I'm overwhelmed, Noah. I didn't expect any of this. . . . I don't know what to say."

"A simple yes or no will do."

"If only it were simple." She wrapped her arms around herself as if protecting her body from a sudden chill. "I'd love to marry you . . ."

"But?"

"But I think it's all a little sudden." Why was she making up excuses? Why couldn't she just accept his vow of love?

As she looked into Noah's brooding eyes and honest, angular face, Sheila's doubts fled. If she knew nothing else, she realized that Noah Wilder wasn't the kind of man who would stoop to deceit. She shook her head as if shaking out the cobwebs of unclear thought that had confused her. "I'm sorry," she apologized shakily as she touched her fingertips to the solid wall of his chest. "It's just that you surprised me. The truth is that I love you and I can't think of anything I'd rather do than spend the rest of my life with you."

"Thank God," he declared prayerfully. He folded her into the strength of his arms and pressed his hungry lips to hers. A warm glow of happiness began to spread through her as her lips parted to accept the promise of his love. She closed her eyes and sighed against his mouth as she felt the robe slip off her shoulders and the chill of morning touch her skin when Noah guided her to the bed.

"Woman," he groaned against her skin, "I need you so desperately." She shivered in anticipation as she fell against the cool sheets and was warmed only by the gentle touch of the man she loved.

Sheila's life became a whirlwind. Between scanning blueprints submitted by architects, attempting to organize the interior designers sent by Wilder Investments and working with Dave Jansen on the fall harvest, Sheila had little time to dwell on the distance that kept her apart from Noah. She fell into bed exhausted each night and was up at the crack of dawn each morning. One hot summer day bled into another as June flowed into July.

Though Sheila was working herself to the bone, it was worth it. Everything seemed to be going her way. Jeff had called earlier in the week, and when Sheila had explained that Emily had reservations about visiting with him in Spokane, Jeff didn't press the issue. In fact, he had almost sounded *relieved* that he wouldn't have to entertain his child until later in the summer.

Emily missed Sean, but Sheila took that as a positive sign. She prayed that the two children would continue to get along after the marriage, whenever that was. Noah had been pressing Sheila for a date, even had gone so far as to suggest eloping. Sheila admitted to herself that running off to get married might be the best solution for all involved. She had once been married in an elaborate ceremony; it hadn't guaranteed success.

Perhaps this weekend, she mused to herself as she pressed her foot more heavily on the throttle of the car. The auto responded and climbed the Cascade mountains more quickly. For the first time in four weeks, there had been a break in the work. The interior of the château was nearly completely restored to its original regal design. Only a few details remained unfinished. The fabric for the draperies was woven in Europe, hence the delay. But the walls had been resurfaced and painted, new wallpaper hung and the old stained burgundy carpet replaced by a new, elegant champagne-colored pile.

Emily was spending the weekend with her grandmother, and Sheila decided to visit Noah. He would be surprised, no doubt, as he hadn't expected to see her until all of the legal papers surrounding the refurbishing of the winery were complete, but when she hadn't been able to reach him by telephone, Sheila had thrown caution to the wind, packed a few clothes and jumped in her car.

It was a beautiful summer day, the mountain air fresh with the scent of wildflowers and pine trees, and Sheila had the confident feeling that nothing could ruin the feeling of exhilaration that claimed her. The prospect of spending a quiet weekend alone with Noah made her smile to herself and hum along to the pop music coming from the radio.

Nothing can possibly go wrong, she thought to herself as she turned up the circular drive of the Wilder Estate. This weekend is going to be perfect. She smiled when she saw the familiar silver Volvo sitting near the garage. At least she had caught Noah at home.

She knocked on the door and waited for it to be answered. The mysterious smile that had spread across her face froze in place when the door was opened by a well-mannered, gray-haired man of near fifty. He was dressed in formal livery and displayed not one shred of emotion as he inquired as to the nature of her call.

*A butler,* Sheila thought wildly, not really understanding. Noah employed a butler? He hadn't mentioned hiring any servants in his telephone conversations. An uneasy feeling began to grip Sheila. Something was wrong.

"I'm here to see Mr. Wilder," Sheila explained to the outwardly skeptical butler.

"Is he expecting you?"

"No. You see, this is kind of a surprise."

The butler cocked a dubious gray eyebrow and his lips pressed into a thin, firm line. "You do know that Mr. Wilder isn't well. He isn't seeing visitors."

Sheila's eyes widened, and her heart leapt to her throat. What was this man saying? "What's wrong with him?" she demanded, fear claiming her emotions.

"Pardon me?"

Sheila forgot all sense of civility. "What's wrong with Noah? Was he hurt in an accident?" Her hands were shaking. "What happened?" How could this character out of *Upstairs Downstairs* take Noah's health so casually? She looked past the butler into the stone house, her eyes searching for some evidence that Noah was all right.

"Miss, if you will calm down! I wasn't speaking of Noah Wilder, but his father."

Sheila's eyes flew back to the butler. "Ben? Ben's here?"

The man in the doorway raised his nose a bit higher, but Sheila sensed kindliness in his sparkling hazel eyes. "Would you kindly state your name and business?"

"Oh, I'm sorry. I'm Sheila Lindstrom," she replied rapidly. Thank God Noah was safe. Her breath released slowly. "I'm . . . a friend of Noah's. Is . . . is he in?"

"Yes, of course, Miss Lindstrom. This way please." The butler seemed pleased that he had finally made sense of her appearance. He turned on a well-polished heel and escorted her into a formal living room.

It was a cold room, not at all like the warm den where she had met Noah. It was decorated in flat tones of silver and white, with only a sprinkling of blue pillows on the expensive, modern furniture. White walls, icy gray carpet and tall, unadorned windows. In the middle of it all, sitting near the unlit flagstone fireplace, was a man Sheila guessed to be Ben Wilder. He didn't bother to rise when she entered the room, and his smile looked forced, as cold as the early morning fog that settled upon Lake Washington.

"Miss Lindstrom," the butler announced quietly. "She's here to see your son."

At the mention of her name, Ben's interest surfaced. His faded eyes looked over her appraisingly, as if she were a thoroughbred at auction. Sheila felt an uncomfortable chill.

"Pleased to meet you, Miss Lindstrom. I'm Noah's father."

"I thought so. I think I met you once, years ago . . ."

Ben was thoughtful for a moment. "I suppose you did. I came to the winery to see Oliver—by the way, please accept my condolences."

"Thank you." Sheila anxiously fingered the clasp on her purse. Where was Noah? The man sitting in the snowy chair was not anything she had expected. When she had met Ben Wilder he was robust and bursting with energy. Though it had only been nine years, Ben Wilder had aged nearly thirty. The pallor of his skin was gray, and his hair had thinned. He still appeared tall, but there was a gauntness to his flesh that added years to his body. Ben Wilder was gravely ill.

"Did I hear someone at the door?" a female voice asked. Sheila turned to see a woman, younger than Ben by several years, walk into the room. She was graceful, and the smile that warmed her face seemed sincere.

"This is Sheila Lindstrom," Ben said. "My wife, Katharine."

Katharine's smile wavered slightly. "Noah's mentioned you," she stated vaguely. "Would you care to have a seat?"

"Thank you, but I really did come to see Noah."

"Of course you did. He was outside with Sean. I think George has gone to find him."

Thank God, Sheila thought to herself as she settled onto the uncomfortable white couch. Katharine attempted to make conversation. "I was sorry to hear about your father, Sheila." Sheila nodded a polite response. "But I hear from Noah that you've made marvelous strides toward rebuilding the entire operation."

"We're getting there," Sheila replied uncomfortably.

"A big job for a young woman," Ben observed dryly.

Sheila managed a brave smile and turned the course of the conversation away from Cascade Valley. "I didn't know that you had come back from Mexico," she explained. "I should have called and let Noah know that I was planning to visit him here."

The silence was awkward, and Katharine fidgeted with the circle of diamonds around her thin neck while she studied the young woman in whom her son had shown such an avid interest. An interest that had taken him away from his duties of managing the business. Sheila Lindstrom was pretty, she thought to herself with amusement, but beautiful women had held no interest for her only son. What was so special about this one? She heard herself responding hollowly to Sheila's vague apology. "Don't worry about that," Katharine stated with a dismissive wave of her slim, fine-boned hand. "Noah's fond of you. Therefore, you're welcome any time. No invitation is necessary."

"Did Noah tell you all the details that Anthony Simmons dug up on the fire?" Ben asked, bored with social amenities. It was time to get down to business. He reached for a cigar and rotated it gently in his fleshless hand.

Sheila felt her spine stiffen. "Only that the report was inconclusive," she replied, meeting his gaze squarely.

Ben smiled, still watching her over the cigar. He reached for a match, but was halted by his wife's warning glare. "I figured as much."

"Pardon me?" Sheila inquired, pressing the issue.

"I didn't think he told you everything. . . ."

"Ben!" Katharine's smooth voice held a steely note of caution. She lowered it slightly. "Let's not bore Miss Lindstrom with all this talk about business. Sheila, would you like to stay for dinner? It really would be no imposition. . . ."

Her voice faded as the sound of heavy, quick footsteps caught her attention. A wavering smile broadened her lips. "Noah, guess who dropped by?" she asked.

"What are you doing here?" Noah asked fiercely. Sheila turned to see if his question was intended for her. It was. His face was hard, set in rigid lines. A muscle near his jaw pulsed.

"I wanted to surprise you."

"You did!"

Sheila felt something wither inside her under his uncomfortable stare. He appeared more gaunt than the last time she had been with him. The circles under his blue eyes gave his face a harsh, angular appearance. His inflamed gaze moved from her face to that of his father's. Ben's old lips twisted with private irony. "What have you been telling her?" he demanded, advancing upon his father.

"Noah, please . . ." Katharine interjected.

"I asked you a simple question," Noah said through tightly clenched teeth. "If you won't answer it, then fine. I'd like to talk to her . . . alone." He looked away from his father to meet Sheila's confused gaze. For a moment his face softened, and the defeat in his eyes seemed to fade. "Let's go into the den and talk," he suggested softly.

Sheila understood. He had changed his mind about her and the winery and the marriage. He was going to tell her that all of her dreams had turned to dust. A sinking sensation of doom, like that of falling into a bottomless black hole, enveloped her. Noah's persuasive hand was on her shoulder, encouraging her to her feet. Slowly, she rose. She felt dizzy, sick.

"No reason to shuffle her out of here, son," Ben said with sarcastic familiarity. "One way or another, she's got to know."

"I'll handle it," Noah spat. The pressure on Sheila's back increased as he tried to guide her out of the sterile living room.

"I'm sure you will, my boy," Ben agreed with a mirthless laugh.

"What's he talking about?" Sheila asked impatiently.

"Tell her," Ben demanded.

"Ben . . . let Noah handle this his own way," his wife whispered.

The pressure in Sheila's head got to her. She stopped her exit from the long living room with the cold carpet and announced in a calm, hushed voice. "Don't talk as if I can't hear you, because I can. What's this all about?"

She had to know, had to hear his words of rejection, waited with head held high for the final blow. Noah's lips compressed into a thin, uncompromising line. "I'll tell you everything, but it will be best if we're alone."

"Oh, hell, boy! Stop pussy-footin' around, for God's sake." The old man rose shakily from his chair and rubbed his freckled scalp. "What Noah is trying to tell you, honey, is that your father started that damned fire and it cost the company one helluva lot of money, let me tell you. The insurance company hasn't paid us a dime; there's a doubt that they ever will!"

Sheila's face turned ashen, her stomach lurched and she thought she might faint. She turned her eyes to Noah's and read the guilt and remorse in his look. He had known. From the time that Anthony Simmons had turned in his preliminary report Noah Wilder had known about her father and the fire.

"No!" she attempted to shout. But no sound escaped from her constricted throat. His deceit was too much for her to accept.

Ben enjoyed the scene. It was hard for an old man with a heart condition to get many thrills out of life. He enjoyed the intrigue of passions and deceit. It didn't matter that it was his own son. The sanctimonious heir had been looking down his nose at his father's morals for the last sixteen years—even to the point of refusing to work for the company, until he was forced to by Ben's most recent attack. It did old Ben's failing heart good to see the tables turned for once.

"Sheila," Noah said softly, touching her chin. She drew away, repelled by his touch. "Things aren't exactly what they seem."

"But you knew about Dad!" she accused.

"Yes," he admitted loudly.

"And you didn't tell me!"

"I thought I could prove the report wrong . . . I was convinced that with a little time, I could sort things out, and the results would be different."

*"But you knew!"* Her heart sank to the blackest depths of despair. "And you wouldn't tell me. . . ."

"I didn't want to hurt you."

"So you *lied* to me?"

His response was quick. "I've never lied to you."

"Just omitted the facts, avoided the issues. . . ."

"Tried to stop your pain."

"I don't want a man to *protect* me from the truth. I don't want anyone who can't trust me. . . ." The ugliness of the situation became blindingly apparent to her, and another wave of nausea took all of the color from her pale face. *"You thought I was involved, didn't you?"*

"No."

*"Didn't you?"*

"No!" he screamed. He shook his head, and his blue eyes pleaded with her to understand him. "Not after I met you. I couldn't."

"Oh, Noah," she whispered, shaking her head, running her fingers through her long, chestnut hair. "What has happened to us?"

She had forgotten there were other people in the room. When she looked up, she met Katharine's sorrowed gaze. "I'm sorry," Katharine murmured. "Come on, Ben, let's leave them alone." She tried to help her husband out of the living room, but he refused.

Ben yanked his arm out of Katharine's grasp. "I think you should understand something, Miss Lindstrom." Sheila raised her head to meet his cool, laughing eyes. It was as if he were enjoying some private joke at her expense. "I'm a businessman, and I can't let you continue to operate the winery."

"What do you mean?"

"I mean that I'm not prepared to invest the money Noah promised you to rebuild the winery."

"Don't worry about it," Noah interjected. "I'll handle it."

Ben continued, unruffled by his son's visible anger. "The most prudent thing for you to do, Sheila, would be to sell out your portion of Cascade Valley to Wilder Investments."

"I can't do that. . . . I won't."

Ben's toothy smile slowly turned into a frown. "I don't think you'll have much of a choice, considering the information in Mr. Simmons's report—"

"Stop it!" Noah shouted, taking Sheila by the arm and nearly dragging her out of the living room. "Don't listen to him . . . don't pay any attention to any of his suggestions."

She pulled what little shreds of dignity she could find and turned her cold eyes on Noah. "I won't," she assured him cooly, while extracting her arm out of his fingers. Her eyes burned, her throat ached, her heart bled, but she held her face as impassive as possible. "Nothing you or your father can say will convince me to sell my father's winery."

"I know that," he admitted softly.

"But you were the first one to suggest that I sell."

"At that time I thought it would be best."

The unhappy smile that twisted on her lips was filled with self-defeat. "And now you expect me to believe that you don't?"

"You know that, Sheila." His fingers reached out to cup her chin, and they trembled as he sought to rub his thumb along her jawline. She had to turn away from him; she was too numb to feel the tenderness in his caress.

"Leave me alone, Noah," she whispered tonelessly. "I'm tired."

"Don't go," he begged, his hand dropping impotently to his side. The pain in his eyes wasn't hidden as he watched her move slowly toward the door. "Don't let the old man get to you."

"The 'old man' isn't the one that got to me."

"Sheila!" He reached for the bend of her elbow, clutching at her arm and twisting her to him. He held her so savagely that she wondered for a moment if she could breathe . . . or if she really cared. The tears that had slid over her lips to warm them with drops of salt told her she was crying, but she couldn't feel them. She didn't feel *anything*. Empty. Hollow. It was as if the spirit she had once owned had been broken.

"Let go of me," she said through her sobs.

"You can't go. You don't understand. . . ."

"I understand perfectly! You may have been able to get what you wanted from Marilyn by paying her off, but you can't buy me, Noah Wilder! No man can. I'll go bankrupt before I'll sell you one bottle of my cheapest wine!" She wrenched free of his hold on her and backed toward the door.

He watched her leave, not moving from the foyer where he had held her in his arms. They felt strangely empty as his eyes followed the path of her flight. The door slammed shut, closing her out of his life. He fought the vain urge to follow her and tried to convince himself that everything was for the best. If she trusted him so little, he was better off without her.

# Chapter Thirteen

For five long weeks Sheila tried futilely to get the image of Noah Wilder out of her mind. It had been an impossible task. Everywhere on the estate she was reminded of him and the bittersweet love they had shared. There wasn't a room in the château where she could hide from him or the memories of the nights of surrendered passion they had shared together. She couldn't even find solace in her own room, the sanctuary where they had held each other dear until the first stirrings of dawn. Now the room seemed pale and empty, and Sheila was alone. She attempted to convince herself that she never had really loved him, that what they had shared was only a passing fancy, an affair to forget. It was a bald-faced lie, and she couldn't deceive herself for a minute. She had loved Noah Wilder with a passion time and deceit couldn't erase. She loved him still.

The winery had become a ghost town. Reconstruction of the west wing had been halted by one fell stroke: an executive order from Ben Wilder himself. Gone was the whine of whirring saw blades consuming wood, vanished were the shouts and laughter from the construction crew. The air was untainted with the smell of burning diesel or the scent of freshly cut lumber. The west wing of the winery was as defeated as her dreams.

Sheila had tried, ineffectively, to tell Emily about Noah. As comfortingly as possible she had mentioned that Noah and Sean wouldn't be back to Cascade Valley as they had originally planned and that her marriage to Noah would probably never happen. If Sheila had hoped not to wound her child, she had failed miserably. Emily was heartbroken. When Sheila had explained that she doubted if Noah and Sean would return to the winery, Emily had burst into tears, screamed that it was all her mother's fault and raced from the dinner table to hide in her room. It had taken several hours for Sheila to get through to her and calm her down. The child had sobbed on her shoulder bitterly, and it was difficult for Sheila to hold back the tears stinging the backs of her eyes.

Part of Emily's reaction was due to incredibly bad timing. The girl had just returned from a dismal trip to visit her father, a vacation that was to have lasted a week and was cut down to five regretful days. It seemed as if Jeff and his wife Judith just didn't have the time or the inclination to take care of a busy eight-year-old. Emily felt rejected not only by her father but by Noah as well.

The final blow to Sheila's pride had come from a local banker she had dealt with for years. Regardless of the winery's past record, Mr. Stinson couldn't justify another loan to Cascade Valley. It had no reflection on Sheila, but the winery just didn't qualify. There was simply not enough collateral to back up a quarter of a million dollars of the bank's money. He was kind and told her that he would talk to his superiors, although he was sure that her request was next to impossible. There was a distinct note of inflexibility in his even voice.

Sheila found it increasingly difficult to sit idle. Time seemed to be slipping by without purpose or meaning. Within a few short weeks Emily would be enrolled in the fall semester of school and the autumn harvest of grapes would be ripe. Sheila had no alternative but to sell the crop despite Dave Jansen's protests. He was convinced that this was the best year Cascade Valley had seen in a decade. The yield per acre was ten percent better than the previous year's, and the grapes held the highest sugar and acid content he had seen in several years. All in all it looked like a bumper crop. But Sheila had no choice. She was backed into a corner by Ben Wilder and his son.

She sighed wearily and ran her fingers through her hair as she picked up the telephone and dialed the number of Mid-Columbia Bank. A cheery receptionist put Sheila through to Jim Stinson. Shiela could envision the perplexed look of dismay that must have crossed his features when he learned that she was calling. He probably wanted to avoid this conversation as much as she did.

"Good afternoon, Sheila," Jim greeted heartily. "How've you been? Busy, I'll bet."

Sheila was taken aback at his friendly response to her call. "It's about that time of the year," she agreed.

"How's the construction going?" Jim asked good-naturedly. "Are you going to get the west wing finished before harvest?"

Sheila choked on her response. Jim, better than most people, knew of her plight, and it wasn't like him to rub salt into a wound. He actually sounded as if he thought she were running the winery as she had planned. "I can't do that, Jim, because construction was stopped on the west wing."

There was a moment's hesitation before Jim laughed. "Is this some kind of a joke? Haven't you begun to rebuild yet?"

"As a matter of fact, no. I was hoping that Mid-Columbia would give me a loan, remember?"

"But that was before you got your other loan."

Once again silence.

"Other loan?" What the devil was Jim talking about? He wasn't usually one to talk in circles.

He acted as if she were incredibly dense. "You know, the quarter of a mil."

"The loan I requested from you."

She heard an exasperated sigh. "Just a minute." She was put on hold for a minute and then he was on the phone again. "Is there some mistake?"

Before she could ask what in the world he was muttering about, he spoke again. "No . . . no, everything looks right. You do know that a deposit of two hundred and fifty thousand dollars was made to the winery's account on the thirtieth of August, don't you?"

Sheila's mind was reeling, her voice faint. "What deposit?" she asked.

"Let's see . . . it was a cashier's check drawn on Consolidated Bank of Seattle. Didn't you get a loan from them . . . Sheila?"

Sheila felt as if she were melting into the kitchen floor. Noah! Noah had deposited the money. From somewhere in her conscious mind, she was able to respond to Jim Stinson. "Of course I did . . . I just wasn't aware that they had transferred the money so quickly. My statement hasn't come yet."

"But didn't they call you?" Stinson asked.

"I've been out a lot lately . . . down in the vineyards."

She lied, trying to find a way to get off the phone politely. "Thank you very much."

"No trouble, but you might think about putting some of that money into savings or another account. Deposits aren't insured for that large a sum."

"You're right. I will. Thanks, Jim."

She hung up the phone and leaned against the wall. Hot beads of perspiration dampened the back of her neck. "That bastard!" she muttered between her teeth. Why couldn't he leave her alone? He must have deposited the money out of a guilty conscience from the coffers of Wilder Investments, perhaps as incentive for her to sell. But that didn't explain everything. Why would she have to sell anything? The money was hers, or so it appeared.

Her anger grew white hot. Ben Wilder might have bought Marilyn Summers sixteen years ago, but no man, not even Noah, could purchase her or her father's dream. She balled a small fist and slammed it into the wall. "Emily," she called as she raced to the back door.

Emily was playing distractedly with a fluffy white kitten. She turned her head to watch her mother nearly run out of the back door. "What?"

Sheila tried to hold her fury in control. "Get your overnight case and pack your pajamas and a change of clothes. We're going to Seattle."

"Seattle?" The girl's dark eyes glittered with expectation. "To see Noah and Sean?" she asked hopefully.

"I . . . I don't know if we'll see Noah, honey." The trembling in her voice belied her calm. "And I really doubt that Sean will be where we're going."

The smile on Emily's face fell. "Then why are we going to Seattle?"

"I have some business to discuss with Noah and his father."

Emily's brows drew together, and her rosy cheeks flushed. "Then why can't we see Sean? Won't he be with Noah?" She was genuinely concerned . . . and expectant.

"Another time. But we're going to Noah's office. Sean's probably at home."

Emily's lower lip stuck out in a pouty frown. "Can't we go see him? We don't go to Seattle very often."

Sheila shook her head but muttered a quick "We'll see," hoping to change the subject. "Hurry up and get your things." She left Emily in her room, packing, and did the same herself. She was out the door before she remembered the checkbook. Cascade Valley's checkbook. The one with a balance of over a quarter of a million dollars in it.

She tried to smile as she imagined herself self-righteously scribbling out a check for two hundred and fifty thousand dollars and dropping it theatrically on Noah's desk. Her smile faded as she visualized the scenario. Where was the justice she would feel? Where the triumph? And why, dear God, why wouldn't this ache leave her heart?

It was nearly five o'clock when they arrived in Seattle. The drive had been tedious due to the combination of road work on the winding mountain roads and Sheila's thinly stretched nerves. Her palms were damp on the steering wheel, her lips tight over her teeth. Emily had been quiet for most of the trip, but as they got closer to the heart of the city and she caught a few glimpses of Puget Sound, she began to chatter, asking Sheila questions about Seattle. The questions were intended to be innocent. Each one wounded Sheila anew.

"Where does Sean live?"

"Not down here. His house is near Lake Washington."

"Have you been there?"

"A couple of times."

"Can we go to Sean's house together?"

A pause. The lump in Sheila's throat made speech impossible. She tried to concentrate on shifting down as the car dipped along the hillside streets.

"Can we? Will you take me?" Emily repeated, looking at her mother with the wide-eyed innocence of only eight years.

"Maybe someday."

The water of Puget Sound shimmered in the brightness of the warm summer sun. Seagulls dipped and dived over the salty water; huge, white-hulled ferries with broad green stripes down their sides plowed through the water, churning up a frothy wake and breaking the stillness with the sound of their rumbling engines.

Sheila parked the car across from the waterfront and stared out at the open water. Perhaps when all of this business with Wilder Investments was over, she would be able to take Emily out to dinner on one of the piers. Perhaps . . .

"Come on, Em," she stated with renewed determination. "Let's go."

The Wilder Building was an imposing structure. A concrete and steel skyscraper that towered over the neighboring turn-of-the-century buildings, it proudly boasted smooth modern lines and large, reflective windows. Sheila's stomach began to wind into tight, uncomfortable knots as she and Emily rode the elevator to the thirtieth floor.

The elevator doors parted, and they stepped into a reception area. A plump woman of about sixty greeted Sheila and Emily with a cool but efficient smile.

"Good afternoon. May I help you?"

Sheila gathered in her breath. "I'm looking for Mr. Wilder . . . *Noah* Wilder. Is he in?"

The secretary, whose nameplate indicated that her name was Margaret Trent, shook her perfectly coiffed red tresses. "I'm sorry Miss . . ."

"Lindstrom," Sheila supplied hastily. "I'm Sheila Lindstrom, and this is my daughter, Emily." The daughter smiled frailly.

Maggie showed just the hint of a dimple. So this was the Lindstrom woman all the fuss was about. "I'm Maggie Trent," she said warmly. Then, remembering Sheila's request, continued, "I'm sorry, Miss Lindstrom, but Noah doesn't work here any longer." Her reddish brows drew together behind her glasses. "Didn't you know? Things haven't . . ." Maggie quickly held her tongue. She had been on the verge of divulging some of the secrets of Wilder Investments to this slender young woman with the intense gray eyes, but she quickly thought better of it. She hadn't gotten to be Ben Wilder's personal secretary by idly wagging her tongue at anyone who walked through the door. Quite the opposite. Maggie was a good judge of character and could tell from the looks of the determined woman in the soft blue dress and the well-mannered child that she could trust them, but prudence held her tongue.

The look of disappointment in Sheila's eyes did, however, give her pause. "I think that Noah was planning to go back to Portland," she offered, leaving the rest of the sad story unsaid. It wouldn't do to gossip.

Sheila had to swallow back a dozen questions that were determined to spring to her lips. Intuitively she knew that Maggie was privy to the workings of the Wilder household. The thought that Noah was actually leaving staggered her, and the blood drained from her face. She had to know more. Suddenly it was incredibly important that she see him. "Is it possible to speak with Noah's father?" she asked, tonelessly.

The secretary looked as if Sheila had hit her. "Ben?" she repeated, regaining her composure. "No . . . Mr. Wilder isn't in." The warmth in the woman's eyes faded as she turned back to her typewriter. She looked at Sheila over the top of her glasses. "Was there anything else? Would you like to leave your name and number?"

"No," Sheila said, her voice beginning to quiver. "Thank you."

Together she led Emily to the elevator, and they began the descent. "Mom, are you okay?" Emily asked as they walked back to the car.

"Sure I am."

"You don't look so good."

Sheila forced a smile and gave her daughter a playful pat on the shoulders. "Is that any way to talk to your mother?"

They slid into the car simultaneously, and Sheila turned the key to start the engine. Emily looked out the passenger window, but Sheila saw the trace of a tear in the corner of her daughter's eye. "Emily?" she asked, letting the engine die.

"What?" Emily sniffed.

"What's wrong?"

Emily turned liquid eyes to her mother and her small face crumpled into a mask of despair. "He's gone, really gone, isn't he?"

"Honey . . . what?"

"Noah!" Emily nearly shouted, beginning to lose all control. "I heard that lady at his office. She said he's gone, and I know that he took Sean, too! He left, Mommy, just like Daddy did. He doesn't love me either . . ." Her small voice broke, and her shoulders began to heave with her sobs.

Sheila reached out for her child and wrapped comforting arms around the limp form. "Hey, Em, sshh . . . don't cry.'' Her own voice threatened to break. ''It's not like that, you know. Noah loves you very much.''

''No, he doesn't. He doesn't call. He doesn't come see us. Just like Daddy!''

''Honey, no. Noah's not like Daddy at all.'' Sheila kissed her daughter on the forehead and wiped the tears from the round, dark eyes.

''Then why doesn't he call?''

Sheila closed her eyes and faced the truth, the damning truth. ''Because I asked him not to.''

Emily's body stiffened in Sheila's arms. ''Why, Mommy? I thought you liked him.''

''I did . . . I do.''

''Then *why?*''

''Oh, Em, I wish I knew. . . . We had a fight. A very big fight and . . . I doubt that we'll ever get it straightened out.''

Sheila attempted to comfort Emily as she guided the car out of the heart of the city. Emily's accusations reinforced her own fears, and her mind was swimming by the time that she reached the stone pillars flanking the long driveway of the Wilder estate. She drove without hesitation, knowing that she had to speak to Ben. Surely he would know how to get in touch with his son. Her purpose had shifted. Though her checkbook was still in her purse, its significance diminished and the only thoughts in her mind centered on Noah and the cruel insinuations she had cast upon him the last time they were together. No matter what had happened in the past, Sheila was now face to face with the fact that she still loved him as desperately as ever. She also realized that her love wasn't strong enough to bring them together again—nothing was. Too much mistrust held them away from each other. Too much deceit had blackened their lives.

Sheila pulled on the emergency brake, and Emily eyed

the massive stone house suspiciously. "Who's house is that—it's creepy." Her voice steady, she was once again composed. Her young eyes traveled up the cornerstones of the house and the brick walk that led to the large double doors.

"It's not creepy," Sheila countered, and added, "Ben Wilder lives here."

"Sean's grandpa?" Emily asked, not hiding her enthusiasm.

"That's right."

"Maybe Sean will be here!" Emily was out of the car in a flash, and Sheila had to hurry to catch up with her.

"I don't think so, honey," she said as they both stood on the arched porch. Emily ignored her mother's doubts and pressed the doorbell, which chimed inside the house. Sheila prepared herself to meet George, the butler's, disapproving glare.

Hurried footsteps echoed in the house, and the door was thrust open to expose Sean on the other side. He wore a sneer, but it quickly faded into a brilliant smile of clean, white teeth. He was dressed, as usual, in cut-off jeans and a well-worn football jersey that had once been blue.

"Hi ya, pipsqueak," he greeted Emily. "How're ya?" His grin widened as he pretended to punch her in the arm.

"Good . . . real good," Emily piped back delightedly. An 'I told you so' expression covered her face as she turned to look at Sheila. "See, Mom, Sean *is* here, just like I thought," she declared with a triumphant gleam in her eyes.

Sean's face sobered slightly as he looked at Sheila. She thought he seemed older—more mature—than he had when they were all living at the winery. She couldn't help but notice how similarly featured he was to his father. The sadness and maturity that had entered his gaze reminded her of Noah, and her throat became dry. "Hi, Sheila. You lookin' for Dad?"

Sheila's heart leapt to her throat. "Is he here?"

Sean nodded silently.

"I expected to find your grandfather."

Sean's eyes darted from Sheila to Emily and back again. He bit at his lower lip, scratched his neck and seemed to ponder what he was about to say. It was as if he were hesitant to trust her, and Sheila felt a knife of doubt twist in her heart. What had Noah told his son about their break-up? "Ben isn't here now," Sean explained. "He's . . . at the hospital. I'm not supposed to say anything about it, you know, in case some reporters come nosin' around here, but I suppose it's all right to tell you about it." He didn't seem sure of his last statement.

"Is it serious?" Sheila asked quietly.

Sean shrugged indifferently, but worried lines scarred his flawless forehead. He pushed his hands into the pockets of his ragged shorts. "I think so. Dad doesn't talk about it much."

Sheila felt a deep pang of sadness steal into her heart. "Where is your father, Sean?"

Sean cocked his head toward the back of the house. "He's down at the lake, just walkin' and thinkin', I guess." His blue eyes met the sober expression in Emily's. "Hey, pipsqueak, don't look so down. . . . Maybe you and I can walk down to the park and grab an ice-cream cone. What do ya say?"

Sheila recognized and appreciated Sean's rather obvious way of giving her some time alone with Noah.

"Can I go, Mom, *please?*" The look of expectation on Emily's face couldn't be denied.

"Sure you can, but come back in a couple of hours, okay?"

Sheila doubted if Emily heard her. The child was already racing across the wooded lawn, her dark curls escaping from the neat barrettes over her ears. Sean was loping along beside her, seemingly as excited as Emily.

When the dangerous duo was out of sight, Sheila took in a deep breath of air, hoping to fortify herself against the upcoming confrontation with Noah. As she closed the door behind her and headed through the elegant main hallway of the manor, she wondered if Noah would listen to what she had to say. He had lied to her, it was true, but her reaction had been vicious and cold, entirely without reason. If only she had trusted him a little.

She walked through the den and a pang of remorse touched her heart as she remembered her first night with Noah, the dying fire and the heated love they had shared. Tears burned the back of her eyes as she opened the French doors and stood upon the veranda from which she had attempted to make her escape into the night several months before.

As she leaned against the railing she looked down the rocky cliff on which the veranda was perched. Nearly a hundred feet below her, standing at the edge of the water, was Noah. He stared out at the gray blue water as if entranced by the distant sailboats skimming across the lake. Sheila's throat became dry at the sight of him; her love tore her soul in two.

Without thinking about how she would approach him, she half-ran across the flagstones, her fingers slipping upon the railing, her eyes glued to Noah's unmoving form. The old cable car had seen better years, and it groaned when Sheila pressed the call button. It shuddered and then steadily climbed the cliff to dock at the end of the deck. Sheila climbed inside the cab and pressed against the lever that released the brakes and slowly took the old car back to its original position at the base of the cliff. Noah didn't seem to notice; he didn't glance toward her, but continued to stare out at the cold lapping water.

He seemed to have aged since she last saw him. Deep lines outlined his eyes; his jaw was more defined, his face more sharply angled. Either he hadn't been eating properly or he wasn't able to sleep. Perhaps both. Her heart bled silently for the man she loved and the guilt he bore so proudly. How could she have accused him of everything she had? How could she have been so cruel as to add to his torment? A man who had given up everything to claim his unborn son; a man who had bucked tradition and raised that son alone; a man who had grieved when he thought he had failed with that same precious son.

The wind off the lake blew his hair away from his face, displaying the long lines of anxiety etching his brow. It was cool as it pushed the soft fabric of her dress against her legs and touched her cheeks to chill the unbidden tears that slid from her eyes.

He stood with his feet apart, his hands pressed palms out in the back pockets of his jeans. At the sound of her footsteps in the gravel, he cocked his head in her direction, and when his blue gaze clashed with hers, the expression of mockery froze on his face.

What was there to say to her? Why was she here? And why did she look more beautiful in person than she had in the sleepless nights he had lain awake and imagined her?

Tentatively she reached up and pushed a wayward lock of black hair from his forehead and stood upon her toes to kiss him lightly on the lips. He didn't move.

She lowered herself but continued to rest her fingertips on his shoulders.

"You must have come here because of the money," he said, his voice breaking the thin stillness.

Sheila's voice was firm. "I just found out that you deposited the money in my account, and I decided to come and throw it back in your face."

His smile was still distrustful. "I knew you would."

"You expected me to give it back to you?"

He shook his head at his own folly. "I hoped that you would come and see me face to face. If you hadn't, I had decided to come back to Cascade Valley and try and talk some sense into you. I only waited because I thought we both needed time to cool off."

"You knew we could work things out . . . after all that's happened?"

He looked away from her and out at the lowering sun. "I didn't know anything," he admitted, "except that I couldn't live without you."

"But why didn't you tell me about the fire? Why did you lie?"

"I didn't lie to you, and I just needed more time to look into the cause of the fire. You have to believe that I would never intentionally hurt you, nor would I deceive you."

"Only when you thought it was for my own good."

"Only *until* I had all the answers," he replied quietly.

"And do you?"

He closed his eyes and sighed. "Oh, woman, if only I did!"

When he opened his eyes to look at her again, some of his hostility seemed to have melted. His gaze traveled from her windswept chestnut hair, down the column of her throat, and past the swell of her breasts, draped loosely in a soft blue dress.

"Then why did you want to see me?"

"A few things have changed around here," he responded cryptically.

"Because of Ben's illness?"

Noah nodded and his eyes grew dark. "He's in the hospital again, and the doctors are concerned that he won't get out."

"I'm sorry. . . ."

Noah waved her condolences aside. "Maybe it's better this way." His dark expression didn't falter.

"What do you mean?"

"It's a long story. Basically, the doctor in charge of my father, Dr. Carson, has ordered Ben to give up working. Not only must he step down as president of Wilder Investments, but Ben's got to give up even going into the office."

"And that would kill your father?" she asked, trying to follow Noah's line of reasoning.

"Ben's not the kind of man to sit idle."

"I suppose not."

"He likes to be in the middle of things. Anyway," he continued with an expression of indifference, "the old man asked me to take over as head of the business, sell out my operation in Portland to Betty Averill and move to Seattle. I wasn't too hot for the idea."

Sheila tried to hide her disappointment. "Then you are moving back to Portland," she surmised.

"I thought so, but things have changed." Sheila's heart turned over, and her throat went dry. "Anthony Simmons's report was invalid."

*"What?"*

Sheila didn't know that she was shaking until Noah placed a steadying hand on her shoulder. "What are you saying?" she asked in a hoarse whisper.

"Pac-West Insurance Company continued with its investigation on the fire." Sheila held her breath. "You were right about your father, Sheila; there is no evidence that he started the fire."

"How do you know this?" Tears once again began to slide down her cheeks.

"Because the insurance company found out that Ben hired Simmons to start the fire. Ben's confirmed all this and he's cleared your father's name. Therefore the insurance company is refusing to pay the claim."

"But the money . . . in my account."

"I took it from Wilder Investments to rebuild the winery, as I'd promised. And as far as I'm concerned, the note against the winery has been satisfied. Within a few weeks you should get the legal papers that will acknowledge and guarantee that you are sole owner of the winery."

"Oh, Noah," she whispered hoarsely, her emotions strangling her.

"It's all right, Sheila," he said, wrapping his arms around her and kissing the top of her head. "I'm just sorry that my family had anything to do with your father's death or his financial worries." His voice had lowered. "Ben even admitted that he had been behind the tampered bottles in Montana, in a move to force your father out of business. It looks as if he will be prosecuted for the arson and involuntary manslaughter."

"Oh, God, Noah . . . but he's ill. . . ."

"That's no excuse for the things he's done."

"What are you going to do?" Her tears were running freely.

"I've agreed to run the company since Ben's given me sole authority, and I'm going to try and right my father's mistakes." His mouth twisted into a line of disgust. "I don't know if it's possible. That's why I started with you. Ben tried to cheat you out of the winery rather than just continue to share the profits with you. It's all yours now. Wilder Investments is out of it.''

He watched her reaction, gauged her response. ''You don't understand, do you?'' she whispered. ''Nothing . . . not the winery . . . not my father's reputation . . . none of it means anything unless you're with me.''

''You were the one who left.''

''But only because I didn't understand.'' His arms tightened around her.

His voice caught. ''Dear God, Sheila, if only you knew how much I love you . . . if only you could feel the emptiness I've had to deal with.''

''I do,'' she vowed, ''every night that I'm alone.''

''Never again,'' he promised, ''you'll never be alone again. Promise me that you'll marry me.''

Sobs of joy wracked her body. ''Oh, Noah, I've been such a fool. I love you so dearly and I tried to convince myself that I could forget you. . . . I thought I wanted to.''

''Shhh . . . it's all right. We're together now, and we will be forever. And we're going to have our own family— Sean, Emily and as many more children as you want.''

''Do you mean it?''

''Of course I do, love. More than anything I've ever said. Will you marry me?''

''Do you have to ask?'' she sighed, tipping her head to look at him through the shimmer of unshed tears. A slow, satisfied smile curved his lips, and his eyes caressed hers.

''I love you, Sheila,'' he vowed. ''I promise that I always will.''

''But what about the winery?''

''We'll work that out later. If you want, I'll move the

headquarters of Wilder Investments to Cascade Valley. It doesn't matter where we live, just as long as we're together.''

"Noah . . ."

"Shhh . . . don't worry about anything. Just love me."

"Forever," she vowed against his chest before his lips claimed hers in a kiss filled with the promise of a blissful future they would share.

Silhouette Special Edition. Romances
for the woman who expects a little
more out of love.

# *If you enjoyed this book,*
# *and you're ready*
# *for more great romance*

*…get 4 romance novels FREE when you become*
*a Silhouette Special Edition home subscriber.*

Act now and we'll send you four exciting Silhouette Special
Edition romance novels. They're our gift to introduce you to our
convenient home subscription service. Every month, we'll send
you six new passion-filled Special Edition books. Look them
over for 15 days. If you keep them, pay just $11.70 for all six. Or
return them at no charge.

We'll mail your books to you two full months *before they are*
*available anywhere else.* Plus, with every shipment, you'll receive
the Silhouette Books Newsletter absolutely free. *And with*
*Silhouette Special Edition there are never any shipping or han-*
*dling charges.*

Mail the coupon today to get your four free books—and more
romance than you ever bargained for.

# Silhouette Special Edition

## MORE ROMANCE FOR
## A SPECIAL WAY TO RELAX

### $1.95 each

| | | | |
|---|---|---|---|
| 2 ☐ Hastings | 21 ☐ Hastings | 41 ☐ Halston | 60 ☐ Thorne |
| 3 ☐ Dixon | 22 ☐ Howard | 42 ☐ Drummond | 61 ☐ Beckman |
| 4 ☐ Vitek | 23 ☐ Charles | 43 ☐ Shaw | 62 ☐ Bright |
| 5 ☐ Converse | 24 ☐ Dixon | 44 ☐ Eden | 63 ☐ Wallace |
| 6 ☐ Douglass | 25 ☐ Hardy | 45 ☐ Charles | 64 ☐ Converse |
| 7 ☐ Stanford | 26 ☐ Scott | 46 ☐ Howard | 65 ☐ Cates |
| 8 ☐ Halston | 27 ☐ Wisdom | 47 ☐ Stephens | 66 ☐ Mikels |
| 9 ☐ Baxter | 28 ☐ Ripy | 48 ☐ Ferrell | 67 ☐ Shaw |
| 10 ☐ Thiels | 29 ☐ Bergen | 49 ☐ Hastings | 68 ☐ Sinclair |
| 11 ☐ Thornton | 30 ☐ Stephens | 50 ☐ Browning | 69 ☐ Dalton |
| 12 ☐ Sinclair | 31 ☐ Baxter | 51 ☐ Trent | 70 ☐ Clare |
| 13 ☐ Beckman | 32 ☐ Douglass | 52 ☐ Sinclair | 71 ☐ Skillern |
| 14 ☐ Keene | 33 ☐ Palmer | 53 ☐ Thomas | 72 ☐ Belmont |
| 15 ☐ James | 35 ☐ James | 54 ☐ Hohl | 73 ☐ Taylor |
| 16 ☐ Carr | 36 ☐ Dailey | 55 ☐ Stanford | 74 ☐ Wisdom |
| 17 ☐ John | 37 ☐ Stanford | 56 ☐ Wallace | 75 ☐ John |
| 18 ☐ Hamilton | 38 ☐ John | 57 ☐ Thornton | 76 ☐ Ripy |
| 19 ☐ Shaw | 39 ☐ Milan | 58 ☐ Douglass | 77 ☐ Bergen |
| 20 ☐ Musgrave | 40 ☐ Converse | 59 ☐ Roberts | 78 ☐ Gladstone |

### $2.25 each

| | | | |
|---|---|---|---|
| 79 ☐ Hastings | 87 ☐ Dixon | 95 ☐ Doyle | 103 ☐ Taylor |
| 80 ☐ Douglass | 88 ☐ Saxon | 96 ☐ Baxter | 104 ☐ Wallace |
| 81 ☐ Thornton | 89 ☐ Meriwether | 97 ☐ Shaw | 105 ☐ Sinclair |
| 82 ☐ McKenna | 90 ☐ Justin | 98 ☐ Hurley | 106 ☐ John |
| 83 ☐ Major | 91 ☐ Stanford | 99 ☐ Dixon | 107 ☐ Ross |
| 84 ☐ Stephens | 92 ☐ Hamilton | 100 ☐ Roberts | 108 ☐ Stephens |
| 85 ☐ Beckman | 93 ☐ Lacey | 101 ☐ Bergen | 109 ☐ Beckman |
| 86 ☐ Halston | 94 ☐ Barrie | 102 ☐ Wallace | 110 ☐ Browning |

# Silhouette Special Edition

## $2.25 each

| | | | |
|---|---|---|---|
| 111 ☐ Thorne | 133 ☐ Douglass | 155 ☐ Lacey | 177 ☐ Howard |
| 112 ☐ Belmont | 134 ☐ Ripy | 156 ☐ Hastings | 178 ☐ Bishop |
| 113 ☐ Camp | 135 ☐ Seger | 157 ☐ Taylor | 179 ☐ Meriwether |
| 114 ☐ Ripy | 136 ☐ Scott | 158 ☐ Charles | 180 ☐ Jackson |
| 115 ☐ Halston | 137 ☐ Parker | 159 ☐ Camp | 181 ☐ Browning |
| 116 ☐ Roberts | 138 ☐ Thornton | 160 ☐ Wisdom | 182 ☐ Thornton |
| 117 ☐ Converse | 139 ☐ Halston | 161 ☐ Stanford | 183 ☐ Sinclair |
| 118 ☐ Jackson | 140 ☐ Sinclair | 162 ☐ Roberts | 184 ☐ Daniels |
| 119 ☐ Langan | 141 ☐ Saxon | 163 ☐ Halston | 185 ☐ Gordon |
| 120 ☐ Dixon | 142 ☐ Bergen | 164 ☐ Ripy | 186 ☐ Scott |
| 121 ☐ Shaw | 143 ☐ Bright | 165 ☐ Lee | 187 ☐ Stanford |
| 122 ☐ Walker | 144 ☐ Meriwether | 166 ☐ John | 188 ☐ Lacey |
| 123 ☐ Douglass | 145 ☐ Wallace | 167 ☐ Hurley | 189 ☐ Ripy |
| 124 ☐ Mikels | 146 ☐ Thornton | 168 ☐ Thornton | 190 ☐ Wisdom |
| 125 ☐ Cates | 147 ☐ Dalton | 169 ☐ Beckman | 191 ☐ Hardy |
| 126 ☐ Wildman | 148 ☐ Gordon | 170 ☐ Paige | 192 ☐ Taylor |
| 127 ☐ Taylor | 149 ☐ Claire | 171 ☐ Gray | 193 ☐ John |
| 128 ☐ Macomber | 150 ☐ Dailey | 172 ☐ Hamilton | 194 ☐ Jackson |
| 129 ☐ Rowe | 151 ☐ Shaw | 173 ☐ Belmont | 195 ☐ Griffin |
| 130 ☐ Carr | 152 ☐ Adams | 174 ☐ Dixon | 196 ☐ Cates |
| 131 ☐ Lee | 153 ☐ Sinclair | 175 ☐ Roberts | 197 ☐ Lind |
| 132 ☐ Dailey | 154 ☐ Malek | 176 ☐ Walker | 198 ☐ Bishop |

------------------------------------------

**SILHOUETTE SPECIAL EDITION,** Department SE/2
**1230 Avenue of the Americas**
**New York, NY 10020**

Please send me the books I have checked above. I am enclosing $_____
(please add 75¢ to cover postage and handling. NYS and NYC residents please
add appropriate sales tax). Send check or money order—no cash or C.O.D.'s
please. Allow six weeks for delivery.

NAME _____

ADDRESS _____

CITY _____ STATE/ZIP _____

*Silhouette Special Edition*

┌─ Coming Next Month ─┐

OPPOSITES ATTRACT
by Nora Roberts

•

SEA OF DREAMS
by Angel Milan

•

WILD PASSIONS
by Gena Dalton

•

PROMISES TO KEEP
by Carolyn Thorton

•

DANGEROUS COMPANY
by Laura Parker

•

SOMEDAY SOON
by Kathleen Eagle